"Quest narratives haven't been the fashion in American fiction for quite some time, but Scott Spencer's new novel *The Rich Man's Table* could give the genre a surge of new life . . . Rarely do five pages go by without the appearance of a legitimately startling image or turn of phrase."

—*New York Times Book Review*

"Enjoyable . . . some of the scenes in which Billy wrestles with his demons evoke the power of Spencer's best novels."

—*Time Out New York*

"This story strikes universal notes about longing and self-knowledge . . . the desire to connect with and be accepted by a parent is an urge so primal . . . and Spencer handles it with wit and grace."

—*San Francisco Chronicle*

"Luke Fairchild is startlingly Dylanesque . . . Spencer's bold prose captures the grotesque world in which rock and roll deities reside."

—*St. Louis Post-Dispatch*

"Deft dialogue."

—*Vogue*

"In *The Rich Man's Table,* Scott Spencer revisits some of his favorite themes—the search for connections in times totally out of joint, the absurdities of fame and fortune—with the kind of boomer-effacing humor that makes you laugh until it hurts."

—*Minneapolis Star-Tribune*

"Rendered with vigor and clarity."

—*Kirkus Reviews*

"An intriguing, satirical take on the meaning of fame."

—*Playboy*

"Scott Spencer has written another wonderful book in *The Rich Man's Table* . . . Spencer is one of our great writers, able to stop your heart with his phrasing."

—*Dayton Daily News*

"A brilliant exploration of the 1960s . . . Spencer gives us a story of family and commitment that is stronger than any one moment in history—that is, in fact, ageless."

—*Madison Capital Times*

(continued on next page)

. . . and the previous novels of Scott Spencer:

Waking the Dead

"A terrific novel . . . It's powerful, complex, fascinating, passionate . . . and occasionally a scene comes across as so elegantly rounded and complete I admit to gasping from sheer pleasure."

—Fay Weldon, *New York Times Book Review*

Secret Anniversaries

"It has a vivid, continual force . . . It bears the hallmark of his previous work yet breaks additional ground . . . His characters are passionate, committed . . . There is wit here and real rage. The historical dimensions ring absolutely true."

—Nicholas Delbanco, *Chicago Tribune*

Endless Love

"Scott Spencer is a magnificent writer, and *Endless Love* is his finest novel."
—Anne Tyler, *The New Republic*

"In a literary age marked by cool, cerebral fiction, Spencer writes from the heart."
—*New York* magazine

The
Rich Man's
Table

Scott Spencer

BERKLEY BOOKS, NEW YORK

THE RICH MAN'S TABLE

A Berkley Book / published by arrangement with
Alfred A. Knopf, Inc.

PRINTING HISTORY
Alfred A. Knopf edition published 1998
Berkley trade paperback edition / August 1999

The Penguin Putnam Inc. World Wide Web site address is
http://www.penguinputnam.com

ISBN: 0-425-16945-6

BERKLEY®
Berkley Books are published by
The Berkley Publishing Group, a member of Penguin Putnam Inc.,
375 Hudson Street, New York, New York 10014.
BERKLEY and the "B" design are trademarks
belonging to Berkley Publishing Corporation.

PRINTED IN THE UNITED STATES OF AMERICA

10 9 8 7 6 5 4 3 2 1

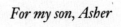

For my son, Asher

Once there was a rich man who dressed in purple and fine linen and who feasted splendidly every day. At his gate lay a poor beggar named Lazarus, who was covered with sores. Lazarus longed to eat the scraps that fell from the rich man's table.

—*Luke 16:19–21*

The Rich Man's Table

Prologue

WHEN I was a child I joked as a child, but now I am older and have put aside childish things. Then I knew only the half of things. Now I see a little more, and there are times when I can scarcely bear to remember that sallow little runt running around MacDougal, Thompson, and Sullivan Streets in New York City with my fatherless friend Charlie O'Mara, playing "Is That Your Dad?" I want to say it was our favorite game, but there was nothing really with which to compare it. The game was our bond, our curse, the secret we kept between us and which radiated at the core of our buddyhood.

"Is That Your Dad?" was not something we set time aside for, or proposed, or prepared for in any way. We played it all of the sudden. Half of its entertainment value was its unexpectedness, or, to be more precise, the unverbalized, ad hoc quality that allowed us to pretend it was unexpected. We played the game the way some young girls end up having sex, with a kind of delusionary self-kidding, so we could tell ourselves that it was something that "just happened." In the couple of years Charlie and I were best friends we played "Is That Your Dad?" more and more frequently, until it was the undeclared entirety of our time together. We played it on weekends, we played it after school; we begged our mothers not to send us to camp so we could play it all summer.

"Is That Your Dad?" was based on the fact that not only were both Charlie and I fatherless, but neither of us had ever had contact with our dads. Charlie went to a public school in the neighborhood, P.S. 41, and in his grade there were, by his count, nine out of thirty kids who lived with their mother. Of the nine, five spent weekends with their father, and half a handful of the holidays—usually the unsentimental ones, like Columbus Day or Veterans Day. One of the kids in Charlie's grade spent a full fifty percent of his time with his father; one flew to Atlanta every summer to spend three months with his father; and the final two had dead fathers. All of them were thus disqualified from playing our sad little game. I went to a private school in the neighborhood, the Little Red School-house. There were only seventeen kids in my class. Little Red was a sweet, open-hearted bastion of progressive education and drew students from all over the city who came from left-wing, artistic, bohemian households. Nevertheless, the only possible participant from my class was a girl named Merle Klein, a heavy, sullen girl with a face as blunt and expression-less as a knee, whose mother, an anthropologist, returned pregnant from Labrador and carried Merle to term. But Merle wouldn't have wanted to play with Charlie and me; she never had anything to do with anyone except for a few of the teachers and she never laughed, and I was certain she'd fail to find the humor in her own fatherlessness.

The game went like this. Either Charlie or I would sud-denly pick someone out of a crowd, or it could be someone waiting to cross the street, or even sleeping on a bench. We'd stop in our tracks, feign amazement, and, pointing, say, "Is that your dad?? There! Over there!" The other person was then obligated to also stop in his tracks and approach whoever had been pointed to. Then he would have to accost the "dad" and thrust himself upon the stranger's paternal mercy. Often, the joke within the joke would be the man's absurd unsuitability. He might be a snoozing drunk, or a man so fat he had to walk with two canes, he might be a priest, or a flamboyantly swish homosexual. He might be a loony shouting through a bullhorn about Armageddon on the corner of Bleecker and Tenth, or a junkie jiggling his change on a tenement porch stoop waiting for his connection. At other times, the phantom father might be a much more plausible candidate: a guy working in a bookstore, a cabbie sipping coffee at a red light, an artist with paint-spattered shoes and brushes in his shirt pocket, chomping on a cannoli as he strolled down Sullivan Street.

One day in the summer of 1973, when I was nine years old and Charlie was ten, we were coming out of the Waverly Theater, on Sixth Avenue. It was a soon-to-be-stormy afternoon: the sky seethed like an ocean; the headlights of the cars were as yellow as egg yolks in the watery, purplish light. We'd just seen a movie about two people who met in a singles bar, went back to the man's apartment, made love, woke up, started quarreling, made up, and then, at the very end of the movie, told each other their first names. It was completely meaningless to both of us, like seeing a film about the occupational hazards of boot making. I'd wolfed down a huge box of buttered popcorn and felt like I'd eaten the inside of a mattress. It might not have been August, but it certainly felt like it; the city was an old cook stove leaking gas. We crossed Sixth Avenue; we were going to go either to my apartment on Sullivan or to Charlie's on West Third. We were bored with the day, bored with each other— but in that way children have, which is to say we would have howled in agony if anyone had tried to separate us.

As soon as we were on the east side of Sixth Avenue, Charlie stopped. He rarely failed to give his all to "Is That Your Dad?" and today was no exception. His heavily hooded eyes snapped open, his lips moved soundlessly, his finger trembled as he pointed to a man in his thirties. Today's father was tall but stooped, with a skim-milk pallor that suggested he rarely saw the daylight. He had wavy black hair, muttonchop sideburns, and he dressed in jeans and a blue work shirt. He looked high-strung, opinionated, and sad. He was the kind of downtown New York Jew that, even as a child, I knew and liked.

"Is that your father?" Charlie said. "There. Over there."

I usually laughed or groaned at Charlie's choices, but this time it was different. The guy he picked out actually seemed possible, desirable. I remember the pang that went through me, I remembered it all through growing up, and I remember it now, with the stinging, humbling clarity with which you remember a slap in the face. I had not gone through my nine years on earth without longing for a father, but until now the longing had always had a utilitarian dimension. Which is to say, I was not one to sob silently in my bed, but I was not above invoking my fatherlessness in front of my mother or my grand-parents if it served my purposes—if it made them feel sorry for me and perhaps induced them to give me privileges I otherwise would not have received. But now, suddenly, the wanting of a father opened within me like an umbrella, sticking me with its rods, lifting my heart and shoving it up into my throat.

The very plausibility of Charlie's choice made me realize how reasonable it was to want a father. I was not asking for the world, after all. I was not asking for X-ray vision or a magic lamp. All I wanted was a father. And the sight of that man, who was now stepping into the street to look north at the clock on top of what once was the Women's House of Detention, and then stepping back to safety, with his expression betraying nei-ther satisfaction nor alarm with the time of day—the very ordi-nary mystery of him made him appear not just possible as a father—he seemed ideal. He had dark circles beneath his eyes.

He was surely not the sort of man to make a fuss about bed-time. He looked unhealthy and would surely understand why there were some days you couldn't get out of bed for school, and some days it was all you could do to hold down a bowl of vanilla ice cream.

I was taking too long to play my part of the game. Charlie looked at me with something near alarm, and then he leaned into me with his shoulder, the way animals petition your attention by rubbing against you.

"Dad?" I called, cupping my hands on the sides of my mouth. The lights were green all the way up to Fourteenth Street and the cars and trucks moved with a quick steady hiss. Thunder rolled like ball bearings around the stone bowl of sky clamped over the city. There was a death-defying, and maybe even a death-wishing, aspect to the game, which called for your making your way toward the fictive father no matter what the obstacles, and so I wound my way across the four lanes of traffic, dodging taxis, feinting left and right, stepping back and then racing forward, until I was at Muttonchops's side. Like most young boys, I was fearless to the point of insanity, a zealot in the true religion of childhood, the indestructible self.

"Dad?" I said, looking up at the stranger. Now that I was close to him, I smelled the stale tobacco on his wrinkled shirt, saw the broken veins in his eyes, scrawled like red EKG lines. "Dad? Dad? Is that you?"

There was nothing improvised in this bit of psychotic patter; it was all carefully encoded in the rules of the game. What you could say afterward, *that* could be improvised. You could beg for money, or bring news of far-fetched family developments (inheritances, kidnappings). If the targeted male seemed harmless enough, you could even get physical, fall to your knees and wrap your arms around his legs, or climb into his lap if he was sitting on a bench; you could follow him for blocks, humiliating him with your entreaties, and depending on the neighborhood and the time of day, you'd have up to five thousand witnesses, ten percent of whom could be counted on to glare at the paternal patsy: How could you deny this child? What kind of deadbeat dad are you?

Today's "Dad" looked at me now without horror, without nervousness, or annoyance, or even much surprise: his gaze held mostly concern, and I think I knew right there that I had crossed a line—not the line between good and bad behavior, but that other, more fateful line between good and bad luck.

"Billy?" the stranger, who evidently was not a total stranger, said.

I let go of him. I backed away. But that was not the end of it.

"Billy Rothschild?" he said, and though his voice still had that interrogative lilt with which we expose our uncertainty, his eyes were calm and sure of themselves.

I turned and hurried away. "He knew me, man!" I said to Charlie, as we began blindly running. "He fucking knew me!" We ran west on Bleecker Street, past Zito's bakery and Ottomanelli's meat store, with its savage displays of pheasants and rabbits in the window, and on and on, until the familiar food stores gave way to antique stores with their otherworldly displays of leather-clad mannequins curled up on Queen Anne sofas and little satin Satans riding American Flyer sleds in a windowful of artificial snow.

An hour later, I returned home. Home, then, was five bright rooms on the second floor of an old blue brick walkup building on Sullivan Street, and as I made my way up that woozy stairway, which seemed to me as unstable as a gangplank, there was only one thing on my mind, and that was the hope, both passive and fervent, that my mother was home, for, despite my closing in on the age when boys are meant to begin putting a little distance between themselves and their mothers, she was still the world to me.

I was not disappointed. I let myself in—the door, with its trinity of locks (Yale, Medeco, and Fox), opened to our wooden-plank-floor kitchen. A crystal hung by a length of fishing line in the window, where, on better days, it captured the sinking sun and squeezed it out in the form of a half-dozen rainbows that shimmered on the walls, the ceiling, the edge of the sink. The smell of curry was in the air. Music from the radio played—dignified, pessimistic, probably Gustav Mahler. And sitting at the kitchen table was my mother, Esther, with Neil Schwartz, the man who an hour earlier I had called Dad. I felt naked and ashamed, caught, and my face burned with shame.

"Oh, there you are," my mother said. "We were just talking about you." Her voice was musical, slightly deep for a woman—only her laughter and crying went toward the soprano range—and in its combination of Brooklyn, Greenwich Village, and WQXR (our local classical music station) it represented to me all that was humane and reassuring: fairness, forgiveness, nonviolence, poetry, freedom, pleasure, and pleasure's limits.

I didn't say anything. I closed the door behind me, flipped the Medeco, and prepared myself to face the music. Though she wasn't a pushover, my mother wasn't wired for punishing, and I was not one of those kids with a quaking sense of consequence. Nevertheless, I felt I had disgraced myself and, worse, that I had humiliated her. The aloneness that being without a father caused me to feel was something I tried to keep secret from her, and now my terrible secret was out. This man had somehow found out where I lived and had told her that I, her son, her weak and ungrateful son, was accosting strangers on the street and asking them if they might be my father. I would have rather been caught smoking or stealing. I would have rather fallen down the stairs and broken my arm.

Neil Schwartz rose from his chair and announced that he had someplace else he must be, and my mother rose, too, took his hands in hers, and offered her Indian-princess cheek for him to kiss.

"I'd like to take you up on that dinner invitation some-time," Neil said.

"I'd like that," she said. "Call me."

"I will. But do you really mean it?"

"Of course I do."

Neil didn't exactly look glad—his morose features showing happiness would have been as difficult as an egg timer measuring the wind—but there was some hint of relief on his face. He seemed to contemplate giving her a final goodbye smooch, but he thought better of it and turned to me.

"Take it easy, Billy," he said. Before letting himself out, Neil winked and pointed his finger at me as if it were a gun, cocking the thumb, and I had all the sour, slightly contemptuous thoughts about him common in fatherless boys who pine for a man's love.

I sat down at the kitchen table and Esther relocked the door and then dragged her chair next to mine, sat, and took my hands. Her touch was tender, and I blurted out: "It was just a game!"

"Billy," she said, "I think it's time I told you who your father is."

"Okay," I said.

"I know this is something that's been on your mind," she said, her voice suddenly pleading. Is there anything more upsetting than hearing a parent ask for mercy and understanding? "And I've wanted to tell you. I've gotten bad advice—but it was my fault for taking it. You deserve to know, Billy. I mean, the truth, this time."

The truth? The moment she said those words, the fictitious father she had given me clutched his chest, keeled over, and died of heart failure. I realize now that she had to this moment in my little life told me very little, next to nothing, but I had somehow pieced together the little scraps, evasions, and non sequiturs she had dolorously doled out to me and had constructed a straw man of a father, a camera-shy goofball who lived far away, not much more than a boy himself, whom she did not know how to contact. I even gave this man a name: Zero, after Zero Mostel, a hero of my grandfather's, but also after the number, the absence, the void.

"I want to tell you who your father is, Billy. I think you're old enough to know."

And then, in a feverish flash, it struck me that she was about to say it was Neil Schwartz. But I was wrong—though Neil was, in fact, in our life, already by that time scraping out a living writing about my father, with two books already published and another half-dozen to come.

But I didn't get to dwell on the possibility that my father was Neil for very long. Now that she had set the stage to finally tell me the truth, my mother wanted to get on with it.

"Now, Billy," she said, drawing and brushing my hair off my forehead. "It's kind of a big deal, and I think maybe it would be best if you didn't tell people. It's why I didn't want to tell you until you were older."

"I *am* older."

"I know that. You've really grown up."

She smiled and let out a long sigh. She knew we were crossing a bridge and that life would never be the same.

"It's Luke."

"Luke?"

She looked a little disappointed, faintly amazed. How could I not know? To her, Luke needed no explanation, no second name; he was like Elvis, Jesus, Marilyn. But then she remembered: I was only nine years old. He was not the bard of *my* generation.

"Luke Fairchild, sweetie—that's who your father is. He was my boyfriend for a couple of years. More like three, I guess."

I nodded. Luke Fairchild. I knew he was famous. I knew we had his records and that people who came to visit us were continually talking about him. His picture was in shop windows all over our neighborhood. Often, I had overheard my mother listening to his records on the stereo set, softly as I went to sleep. More than a few times I had found her on the sofa, asleep, while an empty wine bottle dozed next to her on the carpet, and the phonograph needle clicked and hissed in the grooveless circle around the red label on one of his records.

"So then where is he?" I asked.

"I'm not sure. He moves around. A lot. He's got a lot of houses."

"So he's rich."

"Yes, he is, in terms of money."

I winced with filial impatience. My mother was so very, very moral. Yet who was she to say something like "in terms of money" when she didn't even know where the father of her son was?

"So how come he doesn't ever come to see you?"

"Sometimes when people are very close and then they aren't anymore it's too hard to see each other."

I nodded, but I think I might have had a sour expression. My mother's eyes filled with tears, but I wasn't able to care about that, just then.

"Is he mad at me, too?"

"Oh no, Billy. Of course not."

"So how come he doesn't come over and see me? He doesn't even buy me anything or go anywhere with me."

"I know. I really hate him for that, Billy."

"Well, maybe if you stopped hating him he'd come over."

"I have stopped hating him, honey."

"But you just said—"

"It's complicated."

Just then, I remembered something. I went into the living room, with its gated windows that looked out onto the fire escape, and the high, peeling plaster ceiling. One entire wall was covered with shelves, where Mother kept her hundreds of books and framed pictures of me, and of her, and of her family—old sepia photos of Grandma and Grandpa's wedding in a huge Flatbush synagogue, and of Esther's graduation from Hunter College, and of four-year-old, spindly-legged, fringe-shirted, chaps-wearing me on a Shetland pony whose expression was filled with abjectness, catatonia, and disgust, taken at a petting zoo in Pennsylvania, and pictures of aunts and uncles and great-grandparents and third cousins, ranging from devout Eastern European Jews, gloomy, dressed in black, with beards and babushkas and humorless eyes, who reminded me of the Amish we saw not far from the petting zoo, to a child-psychologist cousin in Miami, and a real-estate-swindler second cousin in San Diego. A hundred times over, perhaps a thousand, Esther had looked at these pictures with me, identifying each of them, trying, I suppose, to stanch the bleeding of my wounded heart with a tourniquet of relatives.

The bottom two shelves of the case were filled with Esther's records, and I crouched before them, knowing exactly what I wished to find. She had nine of Luke's records, all neatly shelved together. I pulled out the one called *Village Idiot*. The cover showed my sudden father, a substantial man to my young eyes, but really just an arrogant, possessed, rowdy, aging boy, twenty-two years old, with sunken cheeks, zonked blue eyes, and a wild meringue of auburn curls, with his arm around a bony woman a half-inch taller than he, a woman with black hair, luxuriant eyebrows, photographed with her head tilted down and to the side, so that her face was mostly obscure, but who I was now realizing was my mother. Luke and Esther were hurrying along Bleecker Street, with the wind at their back, lifting the collars of their matching buckskin jackets, whipping their hair around. They seemed entirely happy and in love. They wore boots, jeans; their bodies exuded confidence and satisfaction. Luke had a guitar case slung over his left shoulder; Esther carried a string bag filled with oranges and a skinny loaf of Italian bread from Zito's, a bit of product placement that Luke engineered in exchange for five hundred dollars' worth of credit at the bakery.

My mother had followed me into the living room, and I held the album up for her to see. She had poured herself a very large glass of red wine and she walked carefully so as not to spill it.

"Is this you?" I asked.

She drank her wine and then patted her lips with the back of her hand.

"This is exactly what I was afraid of," she said.

1

I HAVE been trying to tell this story for more than twenty years. Often, I thought of stopping everything and doing a kind of Huck Finn and taking off for the territory of my father. There was always something to stop me. The hurdle jump of my daily life. Exhaustion. Fear. Lack of money. An illusion that it was no longer necessary and that I could do very well without a father, especially a father who had abandoned my mother. I did not have a particularly good life and I was not a particularly good man, but, as we say in our ambivalent culture, *on the other hand*, I wasn't leading a *bad* life and I wasn't a bad man, so there were always reasons—persistent if not persuasive—to leave well enough alone.

I don't know that there was a vivid, defining moment that launched me in pursuit of Luke. I had always kept an eye on him. I read the adoring biographies, bought the albums, followed the gossip, and made it my business to attend whatever concerts I could—staring now at his spotlit figure on the stage and now at the enraptured faces of the fans in the rows around me. Over the years, I was not exactly secret about Luke being my father. I mentioned it whenever it suited my purposes—it was obviously a great sexual aid, a kind of celebrity-mad Spanish fly. And then, about three years ago, using my job as a substitute teacher to finance my research, I began to devote myself to the study of my father in earnest, thinking and dreaming of little else, writing letters, having long phone conversations, and crisscrossing the country to gather the testimony of anyone who knew him.

There were things I wanted to know: how did a shapeless Jewish kid from the Midwest become so famous, so beloved, so despised, so lonely, so pious, so drug-addicted, so vicious, so misunderstood, so overanalyzed? How did he break so many hearts, crash so many cars, how did all that money rush in and out like water through the gills of a fish? The history of my father, it's been said, is the history of the second half of twentieth-century America. I mention this not only to impress (you), but to excuse (me)—for pursuing him, even though I am past the age when it can be considered in any way seemly.

I think I look like him (high forehead; less-than-granite chin; graceful, girlish hands). And my mother, upon repeated questionings, made it clear there is no possibility, logical or biological, that any other man could have planted the seed in her in the winter of 1964. Nevertheless, Luke has never admitted I was his son. By the time she told me that Luke was my father, my mother had given up trying to get him to accept his responsibility. She had made her peace with the situation and with him—though there was a slightly nauseating implication of payoff when he gave her shared composing credit in three songs off his fifth album. But that wasn't much of a bribe, it was just uncharacteristically decent behavior on Luke's part, since my mother in fact did help write "Early to Bed," "Sweet Freedom," and "Lorca in New York," the publishing rights to which largely financed my private-school education and which, even as they sputtered into antiquity—they were not exactly Luke's Greatest Hits—still shed enough capital for Mother to buy an antique little house near the Hudson River in Leyden, New York.

It was there that I saw her on what turned out to be my last field trip in search of new bits of Lukology. I'd taken a couple of days off from work; there were some people I couldn't get to on weekends. It was the last week in May, and I was primarily concentrating on the priest who had been so central to Dad's Christian conversion, Father Richard Parker, who had been oddly neglected in all of the many, many books about Luke. I spent all day Monday and the beginning of Tuesday with my Aiwa, filling those dollhouse tapes with testimony.

On my way back to New York from Father Parker in Albany, and a couple of other upstate stops while I was at it (Gig Kurowsky, Luke's old bassist, and Terrence St. James, Dad's driver and drug courier in the early seventies), I stopped to see my mother. I came to her isolated cabin (steep snow-resistant roof, red shutters) on Snake Mountain Road in Leyden, which is exactly one hundred miles, to the last click of the odometer, from my apartment on West 105th Street.

As I drove toward her house, the spring sky was streaked with sunset colors—light charcoal clouds strewn like rubble in a field of flame red—but around her house the night had already settled in. I smelled the flowering trees—the crab apples, the peach—but I couldn't see them.

There wasn't another house within a mile of Mother's. The sound of my car's engine brought her onto the porch, and as my headlights turned this way and that on her winding drive-way, illuminating here a flowering mountain laurel, and there a copper-eyed cat perched on a capped well, Esther shielded her eyes against the glare of my brights. She wore a long flowered dress, a crocheted shawl, Chinese slippers. Her long dark hair was well past her shoulders and showed a fair amount of gray.

I parked next to her maroon van and stretched the monotonous thruway miles out of my aching back—these bottom-of-the-line rental cars are murder on the spine. As glad as she was to see me, Esther stayed on the porch, waiting for me to approach her. The most beautiful girl in Greenwich Village doesn't run toward anyone, not even her own son. She waited for me, the golden light of the windows behind her, giant moths orbiting frantically around her yellow porch light.

"Billy," she said, holding her hands out to me.

We embraced, kissed, embraced again. She smelled faintly of camphor; she was forever storing and unpacking her clothes. She had of late become careful about material things, even a little compulsive. She wanted to extend the life of every possession. Her house was paid for, but she worried about the property taxes. That sort of thing. Her share of the royalties from the songs she wrote with Luke couldn't keep up with inflation. To stretch her funds, Mother had gotten into the stock market and was, in fact, weirdly successful with her investments, which she chose on wild but somehow useful hunches, bringing in astrology and her own personal assessment of the company's products.

"You look tired," she said, breaking our embrace, stepping back to look at me more closely.

"Can I spend the night? I can't drive another inch."

"Since when do you have to ask?" She narrowed her eyes. "Your color's not good."

"I have to be at school by eight-fifteen. That means getting up by five."

"Fine by me. I'm up before dawn anyhow. I'll go out and get fresh bagels."

It was code, her way of telling me she wasn't drinking. When there was alcohol in her life, she woke at noon, sometimes slept straight through until dinner, with the curtains drawn, the phone unplugged.

She linked her arm through mine, pulled me indoors.

Her house was neat, but it showed evidence of someone living alone with her own thoughts. There were tidy little piles of things in the corners and on the tables, books to be read, books to be loaned or returned, clothes she planned to repair or restyle. There were flats of geraniums in the windows and a half-completed jigsaw puzzle (nuns, balloons) on the thread-bare Persian rug. The fireplace was swept clean of its long winter of silvery ash and was filled now with dried flowers—pale purple, rust orange, and white. Mother had no TV, nor did she own a radio. Like a one-woman jury in a trial without end, she lived sequestered from the media.

I stood with her in the kitchen while she took our dinner out of the oven—lasagna. I found a couple of clean plates and she served it up.

"So what's going on with you and Joan?" she asked me. "I was hoping you'd have her with you."

Joan Odiack. My girlfriend. A well-packaged bundle of nerves. Raised in Detroit by elderly Slav immigrants, she'd been on her own since running away from their not terribly tender mercies at the age of fifteen. Self-taught and self-justifying, she had chopped fish in canneries, slept in parks, stolen. I'd met her at a bookstore reading by Grace Paley, bit deeply into the hook of her pathologically passionate nature, and had been either with her or waiting for her to come back to me for nearly two years. Now, just past her quarter-century mark, she was finally getting tired of being poor; and the fact that I was Luke's son, which had impressed her far less than most of my girlfriends, had now begun to gall her. Where was the money?

"Get a more luxurious house and she'll visit. Maybe something with an indoor swimming pool. She could do laps while we talked."

"You are with her, aren't you?"

"She moved back in with me. I guess her great romantic adventure fell flat. She expected me to take her back." I shrugged. I thought that was going to sound rather more jaunty than it had.

"You took her back because you missed her."

"She was with someone from Louisiana. A businessman, fat as a pig. And she's brought his little habits home with her. She's got me drinking all this New Orleans coffee and eating Cajun food and listening to Professor Longhair."

"You shouldn't be drinking coffee. And I'm not so sure about that Cajun food, either. Anyhow, you must be glad to have her back."

"If I was well, I probably wouldn't even know her. We went to bed three hours after we met. Things like that never work out."

"You said she loved you. You were sitting in this very room and you said that."

"I was deluded. She wasn't into Luke—I mistook that for love. I don't seem to know the difference."

"She's very beautiful, in that wild way. A runaway horse."

"She sees ghosts and she's in a bad mood at least forty hours a week. She's got a mood that ought to be paying her a salary."

We ate in the kitchen; the night and its tiny flying things ticked against the windows, hungry for the pale orange candlelight. Esther's sink was full of pots and pans, but in the candlelight it wasn't very noticeable. We talked about the job Esther had taken, a two-day-a-week gig reading Thackeray to a rich old woman who lived in a spooky old Leyden estate on a bluff overlooking the Hudson.

"She wants me to read as slowly as possible," my mother said. "She's convinced she'll die when it's over."

"Maybe she'll leave you all her money," I say.

"Yes. I'm sure she will. Like in a fairy tale."

She breathed deeply and exhaled slowly. I had a sudden, frightening sense of her, a body running down, slowly but surely. Time was catching up with her, its bony hands plucking at her skirt as she tried to outdistance it. And there was something else, a more specific heaviness on her spirit: she could not abide my continuing to look for clues about my father. Each time she thought I'd finally come to the end of it, I disappointed her by beginning the search again. I was not and could not be cured of it, and she watched at the bedside of my life as the fever took me again and again.

"Why don't you just say it," I said.

"Say what?"

"Whatever's bothering you. I know what it is anyhow."

"Do you now."

"Yes. I do."

"Then there's no real reason to converse, is there?"

"Just say it, Mom. You don't like it when I rummage through the past, talking to people who knew Dad."

"Dad," she says, shaking her head. "Dad. Daddy. Da-da."

"Well, he is my father. Whatever else he may or may not be."

"Do you really think you're going to get the goods on him?" she said, resting her fork a little too carefully against the edge of her plate. She folded her hands, moved her face closer to mine. "And then what? Write a book about it? Do you think you're going to blow him out of the water with a torpedo made of words?"

"Sounds good to me."

"But is that what you want?"

"I don't know. It might be. I won't know until . . . until I know."

I closed my eyes but I felt the room move a little and I quickly opened them again.

"Then what, Billy? Are you trying to settle a score?"

"That can never be done. Not after what he's done to us."

"Us? Speak for yourself, Billy. Please don't delude yourself into thinking you're doing this for me. I don't want it. And all you're going to succeed in doing is racking up a ton of bad karma."

"Spare me. Bad karma. There's too many goddamned Buddhist retreats up here. Where's your anger?"

"Gone. What do I need with it? I have my son, my house, my friends, my plants."

"Your *plants?*"

"Stop it, Billy. I don't appreciate that kind of rough kidding. What I'm trying to tell you is, I feel no anger toward him. Luke and I had a relationship and then we broke up. That's not exactly a capital offense. I should be grateful."

"Grateful?"

"Yes. For the time I had with him. The places he goes, in his mind, with his music, the things he understands, the things he feels—a normal person can hang on for just so long."

"You can't believe this. You're just trying to—"

"Even when he was wrong, or mean, or too stoned to make sense, there was always something there. Even when he blew out his voice, or couldn't hold a tune—he's a genius, Billy. A real live genius. And he was mine, for a while. He loved me, deeply. Why shouldn't I be grateful?"

"He wrote songs about you. He invaded your privacy. He wrote songs about your vagina, for Christ's sake."

"We have no idea whose vagina that song was about. And why do you dwell on that one, anyhow? He wrote so many songs. His songs got people out of jail—"

"Yeah, and some of them were murderers, like Sergei Karpanov."

She drew back a little. We did not speak lightly of Sergei; we barely spoke of him at all. Was what Luke did for Sergei worse than what he didn't do for us? Perhaps; perhaps not. But

since Esther seemed willing now to forget, or at least mini-
mize, the wrongs Luke committed against her and her son,
Sergei seemed to stand in for everything that might be rotted
at the core of her old lover.

"Luke made people brave," said Esther, recovered, and
even stronger than she was the moment before. "When some
of us thought we could change the world, it was partly because
of him. He wrote our songs. Genius is its own defense, Billy. I
don't need to protect him. But I certainly don't need to take
pot shots at him, and neither do you."

"He betrayed you. He left you with a child."

"I loved being your mother. I was fine."

"But what about me?"

"I hate that phrase."

"I know you do. But I wanted a father. Even now, when I
see kids, little kids with their father, it makes me ache. I see
them holding hands. I see them kissing. Little boys and their
fathers in the sunshine, kissing on the lips. Not handshakes, or
hugs, or little pecks on the cheek. Lips! The whole world is like
one big Father's Day picnic." I tepeed my fingers and tapped
the tips together.

"That's new. You wouldn't have had that, anyhow. Look at
you. My goodness."

"Exactly. Look at me. I'm stuck. I'm spinning my wheels. I
want to know him. I don't even know why anymore. Maybe
just to blow past him, and get my life started."

"I meant the way you're holding your fingers—it's just like
Luke used to."

"So you've said. Look, Mom, he won't even return my calls.
He won't say he's related to me, or that he even knows me."

"Feel sorry for him, then, for what he's missed."

"I can't. And I don't even want to. I want him to tell me he's
my father and then I want to tell him to go fuck himself."

"He was the love of my life, Billy. The kind of love that only happens once."

Her eyes misted over. Lately, she had been drifting into sentimentality. Age. She seemed to enjoy it. Poignant memories, a good cry, it all appealed to her. The previous winter, staying in her house, I discovered her sitting in the living room at the window, watching the day break. The red glow of the rising sun moved across the frozen landscape like blood through icy veins. When she heard my footsteps, she turned. And I saw her face streaked with tears. Mom? I said, frightened for a moment. What's wrong? And she shook her head, smiled. It's all so beautiful, is what she said. Our little planet. All alone in space. And what I thought was: Oh my God, she's losing her mind. Yet I envied her the voluptuousness of her feelings. A few months before that she had visited me in New York and when we walked through the Village—MacDougal Street, West Third Street, her old haunts—she was so overcome by feelings that she was breathless, we had to stop a dozen times and finally fled in a taxi. Yet even as we rattled up Sixth Avenue, I thought: There are no streets that mean as much to me as these streets mean to her; I have no memories to match hers. What am I doing with my life? I remember clutching at my heart.

ABOUT my heart. Despite the lurid distractions of a bohemian boyhood, in which years wafted by, borne on clouds of incense and, of course, on the wings of song, my mother and, nominally, I were ceaselessly visited by those beatniks and hippies who seemed so annoying then but whom I view with a certain misty nostalgia now, musicians, painters, political exiles, mind readers, suitors in buckskin, suitors in silk, even suitors in suits, hotshot politicos, schizophrenics, filmmakers, and sleazy journalists, despite all the commotion, the noise, the hope, the gossip, the overdoses, and the sense that history was a tidal wave on its way to our shores, despite all of that, my getting sick remains the humid, terrifying center of my mother's accounts of my middle childhood years: the time I ran a fever of 107 and I screamed weakly each night as my fevered brain was visited by hundreds of hallucinations; her fear that I would die, her tears, her prayers, her nightly negotiations with God.

I remember very little about the rheumatic fever itself. I recall the leaden weight of the bedclothes, the astonishing distance between my head and my feet—my toes looked like pedestrians viewed from the twentieth floor, when I gathered the strength to prop myself up on my elbows and look at them. I remember the flavor of the medicines, especially the unpalatable sulfa carelessly hidden in the gruesome grape syrup. I remember the wet soupy stink of my piss-soaked pajamas as my mother led me on my tardy journey from bed to bathroom. Faces, muffled voices, the somber, almost scary dust on the Venetian blinds. A low drone. An animal sound. A feeling of having fallen off a mountaintop. The feeling of drowning in my own sweat. The icy stethoscope. Grandpa's friend Dr. Greenwald's kindly eye suddenly covered by an iron mask through which a blinding beam of white light shined directly into me.

The sensitive, practically infected issue of Luke's not once coming to visit me in the hospital, of his never helping my mother, and his not paying so much as a dime of the massive medical expenses, obsessed Esther, and continued to after I was released from St. Vincent's, on and on, season after season, until, shortly before my twelfth birthday, just when two years without my heart popping like a balloon had finally convinced my mother that I might just possibly survive, if not a game of baseball, then at least a game of stoop ball or a swim in the public pool on Varick Street, Esther pulled me out of my class at the Little Red Schoolhouse, and the two of us left for Morocco.

On the advice of friends, she had stopped expressing her loneliness and contempt for Luke, but these feelings did not disappear—if you think matter cannot be created or destroyed, try your hand with passions. Instead, they burrowed parasitically within her and nibbled night and day on her senses of equilibrium, humor, perspective, and self-worth, until she was sure she would never take a deep, clear breath until she was away from Luke, away from the city, the state, the time zone, the country. And so when my mother and I boarded the Yugolinia freighter bound for Tangier, all she had by way of sanity was her love for me and her determination to somehow survive. Everything else had been blown to smithereens or scorched beyond easy recognition by her million-megaton realization that nothing—neither the king nor the king's horses and men—could put her and Luke back together again.

The freighter left New York on a hazy, warm October afternoon, carrying a cargo of red and white ambulances and a dozen or so hippie travelers. Back then there was such a thing as countercultural travelers, and they circled the globe, forging a well-worn path to high times and enlightenment that went from Marrakesh and Amsterdam to Beirut, Bombay, and Katmandu. And there was such a thing as Yugoslavia, and Yugoslavians themselves were known for their good humor and fairness. Yugolinia was a hip way of beginning the journey, a way of saving money—and what could be more romantic than leaving by sea? What could put you in closer spiritual touch with the expats of the past—the John Reeds, the Chester Himeses—than to bid a long goodbye to your native shore as it slowly, heartbreakingly floats farther and farther away, until finally it is sucked like a strand of spaghetti into the maw of the horizon and all that remains is the sea?

And what more fitting for my mother's melancholy sailing than to spend those last few minutes with her elbows on the deck's rail, scouring the waterfront for Luke. Even if Luke had known we were leaving, he would not have "come to his senses" and tried to stop or join us. Even I could have told my mother that. But I was bound to remain at her side for the entire, morbid fantasy of her final watch, and then I turned away from the vanished shore and the screeching gulls that flew in formation over the V of our wake, and saw that we were not alone. Standing at a reasonably respectful distance from Esther were seven of our fellow passengers, fans of Luke who had quickly recognized my mother as Esther, the Esther, the Esther of the love songs.

The acolytes were our constant companions through the six-day journey, their questioning voices as steady as the tuneless song of the ship's old engines. In that way, Luke remained with us on our long sail, knot by knot, and by the time we reached port in Tangier—despite Mother saying "Look, Billy! Africa!" and despite my seeing a group of Moroccan stevedores dressed in djellabas—it seemed to me that we had come a long, long distance only to arrive at the same Fairchild-haunted place Esther had forced us to leave.

At first, I pined for America. I missed hamburgers, peanut butter, neon, baseball, my few friends. I even missed school. I could not bear to blame Esther for my misfortune, and so I heaped more hate upon my father than I'd ever heaped before. Now he was not so much an unattainable god who had turned his back on me, but a creature full of vengeance who had pushed me away—away from him, away from my country, my friends, my life.

But Mother seemed to thrive in our expatriation. After a kif-drenched month in Marrakesh, where we lived in a small, brightly tiled house in the medina, with a double-decker balcony over a shady, aromatic courtyard, and where Esther became a kind of opium den mother to the resident hippies, we boarded another boat—this time the ultra-posh *Da Vinci*, which we picked up in Gibraltar—and headed for Italy.

They say you went to Italy
Where you spend the coin of my desire for you
With your summer dresses, sparkling wine
You're feeding Christians to the lions
Do you tell the Roman senator how you held yourself above me?
Do you tell the blind child that you never really loved me?

—"Good Riddance Farewell," recorded 1979

After shaking Luke's songs by their heels and studying all the spare change and pocket litter that poured out, I have come to be wary of the autobiographical presumption—too many of the lyrics are free associations, or panicky lunges at rhyme—and I have also come to accept (and adopt) Luke's own bitter assessment of the hagiographers' obsessive scannings of his work and the presumptuous, pathetic interpretations these devout hacks have devised as they create a kind of alternative universe in which a word like "crosstown" must refer to Galilee, and a phrase like "my steely sleeping beauty lies naked in her chamber" must make reference to Luke's father's suicide by gunshot. Nevertheless, I am fairly sure that the "blind child" in "Good Riddance Farewell" is me. But what was my blindness? An insinuation of my weakened heart? Or an allusion to how many times I had already gazed into his, Luke's, face and failed to know that here without question was my father? Or was the blindness meant to suggest a kind of delusion, an insistence upon the patent absurdity that this sperm-less demigod was father? Whatever afflicted the lyric's blind child, however, the notion that Esther would tell me or anyone that she never really loved Luke is just pure paranoia.

In Italy, Esther rented an old farmhouse near the town of Todi. The house had not been occupied for five years, but the land around it was still cultivated by a neighboring farmer, a young, bare-chested Adonis who drove his noisy red tractor through the rows of gigantic sunflowers, their immense, oily yellow heads too heavy for their thick green stalks. Unlike Marrakesh, where the steady stream of stoned travelers included many Fairchild fans and even a budding Lukologist or two, and where, within days, Mother was widely known, even by some of the Moroccans, as Esther of the Album Cover, Todi was almost completely free of expatriates, and we were known simply as the beautiful American woman and her sickly son.

We were used to being around people all the time—in that way, the medina had been an extension of Sullivan Street—and it was blissful, at least for me, to suddenly plunge into this bottomless Umbrian sea of tranquility. Privacy. Silence. My mother, I suddenly realized, had been raising me in the midst of some perpetual party, a mad binge that had been the background noise of my entire life. But now we were alone and I saw her as never before—curled in a chair reading aloud in a studious murmur from a beginner's Italian grammar, humming to herself while she washed out her pantyhose in the bathroom sink, walking slowly through the winding, sun-blind streets of Todi with her string bag filled with cheeses and blood oranges, a jar of Nivea for her, and a jar of Nutella for me, and wishing me good night while perched at the edge of my stern little cot, with the soft indigo remains of the persistent Italian daylight boring through the shutters, and taking her time for once because there was no pot of communal pasta steaming on the stove, no waiting tearful, possibly suicidal friend who had come for Esther's advice to the lovelorn, no suede-booted folk singers who would raid the refrigerator, chug-a-lug the wine, and maybe even curl up like dogs on the carpet if she didn't get back to them soon. Now, in that old tilted farmhouse, which we soon called Todi Hall, with its almost purely decorative lamps with their twenty-watt bulbs, its inexplicable drafts, its carved oak doors, its oxblood beams, and its ancient kitchen in which even toasted bread seemed like a feast, there, at last, I had her to myself, and if this was somehow the culmination of my Oedipal drive, it was also its termination. Italy had done for me what I might have all along been hoping Luke would do— it had driven out the hordes, and now that Esther was available to me I could more or less stop longing for her.

But it was all destined to change a few weeks later, when, with the sadly predictable return of a malarial fever, Mother acquired a new suitor. He was a German named Gerald, a former medical student who had come to Italy to study in Bologna and had fainted during his first surgery. He was tall, sturdy, blond, but nonetheless far from Teutonic: his psychological frailty, his trembling hands, his dark, sad eyes made him appear more a potential victim than a perpetrator of Master Race theories. He and Mother met while she was sitting in a café on Todi's central square. Esther was drinking from her late-morning carafe of white wine; I was in the steep side streets behind the square, stalking the gray doves that hopped and flitted from awning to arbor. By the time I got back Gerald had already ordered a second carafe of wine and a shocking bowl of dirt-black spaghetti in truffle sauce, and though Esther pushed her steel-legged chair out from the table and patted her thighs, beckoning me to sit upon her lap, I was nonetheless excluded from their conversation, except when I occasionally and acidly corrected the minuscule malapropisms Gerald would commit—the shoe has fallen off the other foot, saving up rainy days, that sort of thing.

Gerald had ended up in Todi because the brother of an Italian friend owned the very café at which my mother had been sitting with her Pinot Grigio; Gerald helped manage the place, and it had been his idea to rename it Caffè di Todi, and to expand the menu. Gerald might have been a depressive, but he knew dozens of people in Todi, and soon my mother was in a social circle that included chefs, waiters, vintners, lawyers, a priest, a jeweler, and Todi's mayor. It made Mother happy to be a part of things in the town, and I imagine that when Gerald began spending the night at our house, that made her happy, too. She was a vital woman, passionate, expressive, and despite having a son who was a jealous pain in the ass, she was only thirty-three, far too young to live the life of a grass widow.

Looking back at it now, Esther and Gerald were not half-bad as a pair; comparing the relationship with others my mother had, and, surely, comparing it with my own tattered history of fraught flings and nerve-wracking stalemates, my dark brooding mom and her anguished Aryan lover were actually, in hindsight, very appealing. They laughed; they slow-danced to the radio; they played chess; they chased after and netted bright Umbrian butterflies and then set them free; they read poetry aloud; they drank, probably to considerable excess.

And then, somewhere in early July—those Todi days were nicely numberless—I had a more or less complete physical breakdown. I went to bed one night with aching legs, but we put that off to a day's touring on foot through the nearby town of Perugia. I was also feeling nauseated, but Gerald pointed out that those free samples at the Perugia chocolate factory were probably the cause. However, the next morning everything was worse. My body was so wracked with fever I couldn't muster the strength to get out of my little Catholic cot and so was obliged to spew the clotted contents of my stomach onto the bedroom's stone floor. I called weakly for my mother. She somehow heard me through two closed doors and a haunted hallway, but by the time she reached me I had fallen unconscious.

Mother and Gerald tended me through the day, but when I got no better Gerald proposed they put me in his car and drive me all the way to Bologna, where he knew at least one doctor whose competence he trusted. Though Bologna was at least a day's hard drive, it was actually a compromise solution. Gerald had really wanted to take me to Germany, or at the least to Switzerland; his true opinion was that every doctor in Italy was backward.

The days went slowly, the nights stood still
Checked the hour on a clock without hands
All I wanted was to be myself
Me and my traveling band
The city so quiet, not a soul around
Except for fools who quote me chapter and verse
I thought I would get over you soon
But things just went from bad to worse.

I looked for you in San Antone
Called your name in old Tangier
I had to find you or at least die trying
That much was coming clear
Loving you was all I knew
Though love was like a curse
Had to find you before the next daylight
Things were going bad to worse.

Followed your trail to Italy
To a little brown town in the hills
Heard you were there with a son and a lover
Living on wine and pills
By the time I was there you were gone
The Harlequin said you'd split with your nurse

So I went to the church and damned my fate
Things had gone from bad to worse . . .

—"From Bad to Worse," recorded 1980

Not only is "From Bad to Worse" one of Dad's most successful songs, finding its way onto the first *Best of Luke Fairchild*
compilation, as well as all the subsequent anthologies (*Golden
Luke, Acoustic Luke, Luke Revisited,* and, during the semisilence
of the post-Karpanov years, *Remembering Luke*), but it is also
one of his most remunerative, having been covered by the
Byrds, Judy Collins, Emmylou Harris, Foghat, Eddie Vedder,
Arlo Guthrie, Sting, and the Neville Brothers, and by more
unlikely performers such as Julio Iglesias, Frank Sinatra, the
Gypsy Kings, Mel Tormé, ABBA, Liza Minnelli, and Andy
Williams. Its merits aside, the song functions as a kind of
diary—or "dia-reeya," as Luke put it, in a particularly candid
(i.e., drunken) interview given live on WNEW, while he and
Sergei were rocketing around Manhattan. Fact: he did miss
Esther horribly once she and I were gone. Fact: he worked
hard to garner information about where we had gone. Fact: he
flew to Casablanca, hired a car to speed him through the souks
and camel-tilled farms on the road to Marrakesh. (The "old
Tangier" was allowed through that special poetic license issued
to people too lazy to find a rhyme for "Marrakesh.") The
brown town in Italy was, of course, Todi, and Gerald, in Luke's
homophobic lexicon, was the nurse. I, of course, was the son,
though the lyric might have proven more poignant if he had
written "*my* son." But there's no arguing with success. What's
my famished ego compared to a half-dozen gold records?

Meanwhile, our trip to Bologna proved pointless, a fool's
errand that began the rapid demise of Mother and Gerald's
love affair, though they remained friendly and we continued to

take an occasional meal at the Caffè di Todi. I was treated for an intestinal parasite that I probably picked up from the archaeologic plumbing at our ancient hovel, or perhaps from the runoff from the chemicals so blithely spread over the sunflower fields by the bare-chested farmhand. From then on it was strictly bottled water, even for tooth brushing, and no more showers, only baths. I was confined to a hospital, but I was better in a few days, after which Mother, who was now on her own again, and I headed back to Todi, via rail.

Todi, of course, had not changed in our absence, but our place in the little town was certainly transformed. Luke had spent two entire days there, at first searching for Esther, and then just waiting for her to appear. Though people readily directed him to our house, no one knew where we had gone. By the time we returned, Luke was already back in the U.S.A. ("*I like to see that Statue called Liberty / She carries a torch, just like me*"), but he was hurt and angry enough to strip all the beds in the house and throw the yellowed, well-worn linens into the dusty shrubbery on the house's southern downward slope, where the distant Tiber shimmered two hundred meters below. My mother and I walked slowly, fearfully, and silently through the house, looking for any other sign of his furious visit. My mother's hands were shaking. She touched her lower lip with the tip of her tongue and moistened that same little spot over and over. Luke had even stripped the stern little single bed in my room. The ancient horsehair mattress with its faded peach-and-gray-striped ticking looked forlorn, funereal, the bed in which some child had died, and it was not much of a leap at all for me to imagine that in his fury he had wished me grievous harm. When my mother left the room, I lifted the mattress to make sure the monster had not discovered the small spiral notebook in which I had written the words to fifty of his songs.

THAT night in Leyden, Esther retired to her room early, a generally reliable sign that she was not drinking. During dinner I had noted the absence of beer or wine, but I wasn't entirely convinced that she rode in the Wagon with any comfort. I suspected her, not out of any meanness of spirit, nor from any desire to belittle her by trying to control her actions. But I worried about her, deeply at times, almost convulsively. (And not without cause, as it happened.) She kissed me sweetly on the cheek, tousled my hair, and fairly floated toward her bedroom. A few minutes later, the thread of light disappeared from the bottom of her bedroom door and I snooped through her kitchen cabinets. There was a huge supply of ramen noodles, there were herbs and tinctures she used to treat her one tiny patch of psoriasis (elbow, winter) and vitamins of all descriptions, cans of low-fat vegetarian chile, hearts of palm, fava beans, but not a thing as spirited as even a bottle of cooking sherry.

I was, naturally, relieved. Unhappiness had, in the past, caused my mother to drink, and to make foolish calls in the middle of the night: to her mother, while she lived; to her father; to her brother, until he started screening his calls; to Luke, when she could find him; and to me. The unhappiness caused drinking and the drinking, in turn, caused unhappiness, its own unhappiness—remorse, hangovers, embarrassment, bloating. I worried about her. I worried about what she might do. There were crummy bars ten minutes downhill from her cabin. I could imagine her walking into one of them, wearing jeans, a tight shirt, I could see her sidling up to some computer repairman, dipping her finger into his beer and flicking the suds into his face, ripple dissolve, a half-hour later, in a motel, or a camper, the two of them tearing off their clothes. It's not that I begrudged her her sexuality. I just dreaded her unhappiness and embarrassment upon awakening. She would have to imbue her man of the night with so many qualities he did not possess—she'd have to pretend he was a naturalist when he was only a hunter, or that he was a socialist when he was only on welfare. Her drinking terrified me.

Satisfied that the house was dry—and somehow not having the wit to even consider that her stash was safely locked behind her bedroom door and that she was at this very moment drinking Wild Turkey right from the bottle—I settled down onto the sofa and went over my notes from today's interview.

Richard Parker—priest for past twenty-five years—nearing fifty—fat—swollen feet—white hair, red, veiny nose—Friar Tuck—Catholic church in crumbling, postindustrial slum Troy, New York—announcements of bingo, baseball card swap-a-thons—stained glass window showing Mary with dead Jesus in her lap, metal grill protecting it from vandals—Father Parker in his study behind desk—distractible—fidgety as child—smelling of lilac water, garlic—a palpable weakness for the finer things in life, exiled now—so glad to talk to someone about the old days, his brief ride on the Tail of the Tiger—

I took off my shoes, settled myself beneath one of Mother's handmade afghans, and fished my micro-tape recorder out of my bag. I switched off the lamp behind my head as I plugged the Aiwa into my ear. I pressed Play. The red droplet of light appeared, and then a few moments of magnetic hiss, and then Father Parker's rich plummy voice.

"Is it on?"

"Try to ignore the tape. You were going to tell me

how you happened to go on the road with Luke and his band."

"Yes. Well. Luke was on the Tail of the Tiger tour, playing as many as five concerts a week. It was a grueling schedule and everyone on the tour was exhausted. I was your basic young-at-heart parish priest [*laughter*] in San Francisco. This was 1983, and believe me we had our work cut out for us. [*laughter*] Well, the archbishop was up in arms because rumors about the Tiger tour were flying fast and furious—it was a big drug party, a kind of wandering circus capturing the hearts and minds of young people, and all the rumors about young girls being abducted and defiled. Very exaggerated, of course. And personally embarrassing to me, since it was well known in the Church that I was a huge Luke Fairchild fan and had been since the early folk music days. They actually wanted me to speak out against Luke and the whole rock subculture. It was strictly a reactionary stance. I understood where they were coming from, but my point was, What could be more self-defeating? We were having a difficult enough time reaching young people with Jesus's message of universal love. Why shoot ourselves in the foot, you know?

"Then, who should contact me but Alice Burns."

I clicked off the machine. Alice Burns. I'd seen her myself, a few months before, in a noisy little Italian restaurant on East Fifty-fifth Street. She was living in New York, teaching music at a Catholic girls' school on the Upper East Side. She had strong, rather masculine features—a solid jaw, large hands— and she dressed with some formality. Pearls, a silk scarf. Her black hair was expensively cut. She was married to a pediatrician; they had two children and lived on Sutton Place. We talked about teaching; we talked about a recent outbreak of measles in some of the city's poorest neighborhoods. Her piercing blue eyes drank in all of the ways I resembled Luke, whom she hadn't seen in fifteen years.

I pressed Play.

"She was a San Francisco girl, a regular at the Church of the Ascension, and had gotten to know me when I was a novice. Then she went east to Manhattanville College of the Sacred Heart. She wrote me from time to time, about spiritual matters. She had a fine mind. She was also a fine musician. She played violin, keyboards, and she had the voice of an angel. She was on the Tail of the Tiger tour and she wanted to talk to me about Luke.

"The first thing she did was assure me that the stories about the debauchery that had been running in the press were completely exaggerated. I tried to put her at her ease. I wasn't interested in judging her, or Luke, or anyone else. But there was obviously something else she wished to communicate. I mean, she didn't come to my parish at nine in the morning after a concert in Los Angeles and a plane trip just to tell me that the stories about Luke were distorted.

"What she wanted to tell me was that over the past several weeks she had been talking to Luke about Jesus Christ and they had been reading the Bible together.

"I was somewhat surprised to hear this. I remembered hearing somewhere or other that Luke came from a Jewish background. And of course he had been so closely associated with the contemporary movements of sexual liberty and antiestablishment this and that. But to tell you the truth, I wasn't shocked. I had always heard the righteousness in Luke's poetry. And every good Catholic believes in the correctness of the Church's

teachings, and since we believe men are rational crea-
tures it stands to reason that reasonable people will
eventually come to accept the Catholic faith.

"She told me that Luke had been suffering a great
deal. Fame and money and his travels had not healed his
spiritual wounds. In fact, the more he gained in the
world, the more he longed for God. He was having
heart problems. His hands were cold. He was having
bowel problems. He was frightened. He worried about
death, and he was extremely worried about going to
Hell.

"It's not so unusual. She said that Luke wasn't really
ready to commit to the conversion process, but he was
interested, and she wondered if I would agree to meet
with him. It was all I could do to keep from leaping in
the air and shouting with happiness. I was a big fan, a
very great admirer. In fact, I had used a few of Luke's
songs in my sermons. My 'Talkin' Hell on Earth' raised
a few eyebrows in the archdiocese, I can tell you. Anyhow, I kept a solemn face and told Alice I would be
happy to meet with Luke, and then she told me he was
right outside the church, sitting in a limo and waiting
for the okay to come in."

Alice's large hands made me wonder about her last meeting
with Luke. She had slapped his face—very hard, by all
reports—and I imagined, sitting there over our pasta on the
East Side, that it must have really stung. Yet I found it extraordinarily difficult to bring up that final meeting outside of the
church in St. Louis, when the Tail of the Tiger tour had
degenerated into utter sexual and biochemical chaos. She was
so dignified and remote, it made me wonder why she had
agreed to see me. I could talk about Luke and her in a general

way, but once I crossed the threshold of her reserve and asked her about her love affair with him, she took her starched white napkin off her lap and dropped it over her linguine and left me there.

Father Parker's voice was going on.

"You want to know my first impression? Here was a man who had spent his entire life looking for his match. He was always looking for that moment when a hand—heavenly or otherwise—would be laid on his shoulder and a voice would say: No! Now you listen to me! He had thrown himself into so many things—communistic thinking, Hinduism, drugs, patriotism, materialism, you name it. Whatever he could find. But he always burned right through it—it was never enough, it could never hold his attention, or his heart. He always found the fault. There's an arrogance in that, to be sure. He always ended up thinking he was too smart for any of the systems of belief that people presented him. And perhaps he was right in that. Perhaps he was right.

"But my second impression is the one that has stayed more powerfully with me. I saw in Luke . . . a man haunted by God. There was an immensity to him, for all his physical slightness. A great goodness in a pitched struggle with, oh, I don't know, baser elements. I have met only a very few people like him in my life. His Holiness, the Pope, has something in common with Luke. A sense of being possessed by spirit, a kindness offset by wariness—too many people have asked too much of Luke. But in Luke, there was also a struggle. He struggled for his serenity. He longed to be good. Sometimes I think there are people, just a few of them, and they are really at the center of the struggle between God and the

Devil. Whoever wins this soul wins the world. Not that one, and not that one there. But this one. You. Can you imagine how terrifying that must be? God must worry, and even the Devil. But for that one soul? How terrifying every day must be! I looked at this man, not much more than a boy, really, with all his money and houses and cars and celebrity, and all his fears and doubts, and, Billy, I felt so sorry for him. So deeply, deeply sorry. It has never ceased to haunt me.

"Oh, did I tell you? I saw him in concert two years ago. . . ."

2

I WAS THERE, too. Luke was making his performance comeback on an outdoor stage on Martha's Vineyard, beneath a thick starry blur of eternity, with meteorites table-hopping around the universe, and a salty sea smell in the night wind. By my father's standards it was to be an intimate recital—nothing like the years playing festivals from Cape Town to Helsinki, in soccer stadiums, all-weather domes, always the largest venues available. This Vineyard gig was meant to be somehow reminiscent of Dad's early days in smoky folk clubs in Greenwich Village, before it became big business, where he once played for drinks and worked the crowd afterwards for a place to stay. Luke must have thought that the nature of the island would automatically limit the turnout. Martha's Vineyard normally restricts the size of the visiting population by controlling the number of ferries that make the forty-five-minute sail from Woods Hole on Cape Cod to Vineyard Haven on the island—people who want to summer on the Vineyard often buy their ferry tickets a year in advance.

Only a fraction of the people who came to see and hear Luke Fairchild were able to snag ferry tickets—although I did; I booked passage even before word of the concert leaked out into the subculture of hard-core Luke fanatics. The rest of the fans—and here we're talking about more than twenty thousand—made their way to the island on a flotilla of schooners and trimarans and tugboats and fishing boats, sailed by a crew of enterprising islanders, who saw in the emergent Lukemania a chance to make thousands of dollars, more than enough to tide them over a long winter.

Woods Hole, the taking-off spot for the sail to the Vineyard, and normally a staid little village, reigned over by the aquatic academics of the Woods Hole Oceanographic Institution, the only spot on earth where the typical Ph.D. has shapely, nicely tanned legs, was at an absolute standstill. Father's worshippers clogged the narrow streets, cleaned out the stores like an invading army, and struck their deals with the boatsmen. The bay was clogged with boats, so greedily and perilously overloaded that the slightest wave came sloshing onto the decks, eliciting shrieks that drowned out the imploring calls of the hovering gulls.

It was an event. The media people were beside themselves, scratching at each other like a pack of Siamese cats. They were interviewing everyone they could shove a microphone at. Why are you here? When was the last time you saw Luke? What does Luke's music mean to you? (If they had gotten wind that I was around, Luke's bastard son, and a person not utterly unknown to hard-core Lukologists, they would have cannibalized me.) Those seven years without public appearance had ending up doing Luke more good than harm. It may as well have been a publicity stunt. But it had not been a publicity stunt. It had taken him that long to recover from the public debacle of having defended Sergei Karpanov.

Strange now, to be talking at last about my father, and having to circle back to Sergei. Even with what I partially know, I can say that the Karpanov incident has never been reported truthfully in the press or in any of the books about Luke.

Luke met Sergei at a party at Ken Steinberg's house in Bucks County, Pennsylvania—just one of the many houses Steinberg had paid for with the money he'd made since signing on as Luke's manager in 1965. (The Fairchild-Steinberg deal was the end of the dream for the naive and idealistic core of Luke's early followers. Steinberg was a tough, Bronx-raised, put-the-money-on-the-fucking-table sort of guy, with a keen eye for the main chance and a kind of weird visionary quality when it came to business, unlike Luke's first manager, the late Big Tom Pierpont, who, with his barrel chest and blood-red shirts, his pirate eyepatch and whiskey breath, was basically a sentimentalist, always more than willing to send Luke to a mineworkers' benefit in Utah or a regional ACLU meeting in L.A., and who saw in Luke not the beginning of a new world but the survival of the old.)

It was a Sunday summer party, with middle-aging music-business executives and their rapier-thin young wives, their high-strung children and gloomy, homesick nannies. Tacos and cocaine around the swimming pool. Steinberg expressly forbade any talk of business at these Sunday parties; if he caught you whispering about publishing rights or about signing up a new act, you'd be asked to leave. A pickup softball game was going in the former cow pasture behind Steinberg's postmodernist farmhouse. A game of horseshoes—nice country touch. Parties were art-directed, now that everyone was so ridiculously rich: great-looking food; photogenic, unattached women to keep the young wives on their toes; the ungrazed meadows cut just so. Hard to believe that funky chaotic angry pimply rock and roll had brought them to all this.

Luke was with the kids—he had a real affinity for children. (It was child support that gave him trouble.) He loved them and they were crazy about him. They liked his wild hair, his conspiratorial winks, his leftover feline grace, the constant threat of spilled secrets and sudden hilarity in his voice, his way of leveling with them, speaking to them as if they had a real stake in the world.

"Come here, Luke," Ken said. Steinberg was by now balding and bearded, his once fidgety, fuzzy body now conquered by utter obesity, bloated to bursting with Burgundy, smoked salmon, and Mallomars. Pop a pin in him and he'd zoom around the room like a balloon. "Luke! Leave the kids alone for a minute, will you, for crying out loud! Jeremy! Uncle Luke's going to talk to Daddy now, okay? You can go fly your airplane over there, away from the house. By the slave quarters." This was Steinberg's fun name for the tenant house where the property's farmer used to live. Ken had spent time being poor himself and he thought it gave him the right.

Sergei Karpanov had won a silver medal at the Montreal Olympics and he wore it over his raucous Hawaiian shirt. His chest hair was straight and silky like the hair on a newborn's head. His legs were mighty oaks. He carried a fistful of canapés in a napkin upon which had been printed a picture of Ken's house.

Ken made the introductions; if Sergei was a Fairchild fan, he gave no initial indication. "Ken wants me to get you back in shape, because you look terrible," was all he said.

"Oh, thank you, Sergei," said Ken, "that's so fucking diplomatic. And it just makes my job so much easier."

Sergei grabbed Luke, felt his spongy upper arms, poked the clouds along the horizon of his waist.

"This is rock and roll?" said Sergei, frowning dramatically, shaking his anvil-shaped head. "Rock and roll is very simple business. You play your music and the youth want you to sex them up. If they are girls they want you to lick their pussies or stick your fingers inside them or take them in a car to the seaside with the top down and the moon up high and pull down their panties and spread their legs—"

Luke started to laugh.

"—and then hammer yourself into them, maybe to split them in half. You smile. Yes? But you know, you know. And even the boys in the auditorium—"

"Oh my God, Ken," said Luke, still laughing, "you didn't tell him about the boys!"

"*Da!* Even the boys must want you to fuck them, or to bring them to girls who they can sex in, or to teach them the best way. I have studied this. It's the same in weightlifting." Sergei lifted his shirt and showed his corrugated stomach, and thumped his hand on it as if sounding out the ripeness of a melon. "They don't want to hear from some fat peasant with tits like a woman. They want a man of steel."

"Like Superman," said Luke, trying for a straight face. "Superman in a porn flick."

Three days after the party, Sergei began working for Luke as a part-time security specialist, but primarily as a coach: Luke wanted to increase his endurance, in preparation for another world tour. He wanted to go back to the beginning, wherever that was—he couldn't quite remember. His sense of his own origins was obscured by a thousand faces, a thousand beds, truckloads of money, shouts, spotlights; his ass had been kissed so passionately he sometimes forgot its function. More had happened than he could retain. The biochemical structure that enables us to hold on to our own experiences had been altered by the deluge of incident and information, and he was staggering around inside his own life like a man lost in a blizzard.

After three months with Sergei, Luke was hard and lean. The veins and tendons of his neck were ropey, powerful; the rate of his heartbeat had decreased twenty-five percent. He was sleeping only four or five hours a night, living on seltzer, raw vegetables, unsalted cashews, and after a relatively flaccid few months at the conclusion of his Christian period, he was now sleeping with a bushy-browed waitress who worked in a nearby health food restaurant, a Nordic, neurotic marketing

VP at Epoch, and a breathtaking six-foot Tanzanian model calling herself Orchid.

> *I left the chapel*
> *Got hard as a rock*
> *See you later Saint Augustine*
> *That's all folks. What's up, Doc?*
> *Go Johnny go to the back of the class*
> *Taking Russian history and practical math . . .*

—"Back of the Class," recorded 1987

Luke and Sergei were practically in love, though there was nothing overtly sexual between them. They jogged, played paddleball, pumped iron. They went to plays, movies, and even braved a downtown dance club, where Luke was slipped in through a back entrance wearing denim overalls and a straw hat, and Sergei danced for an hour with Brooke Shields, until he ended up tearing the sleeve of her linen shirt when she tried to escape him. Luke cavorted so wildly that he wrenched his back and had to go with Sergei the next day down to the Lower East Side, for physical therapy in a turn-of-the-century Russian-style steam bath.

Luke hadn't realized there were so many Russians in New York. Sergei seemed to know them all—priests, shop girls, bus-boys, big punched-up-looking guys with broken noses and scarred eyebrows who were running scams in contraband furs, cheap watches, escort services. It was years before the disbanding of the Soviet Union, but suddenly it seemed the Russians were everywhere. Jewish organizations in New York sponsored quite a few of them. Some bought their way over; others seemed to have shadowy connections to domestic intelligence and law enforcement agencies. They were a lively bunch, to say the least. They didn't waste any time, and they didn't relax, or nap. In fact they barely slept. Their faces were as white as yogurt, their eyes were radioactive blackberries, their gestures were wild. They loved to party. No matter how hard their day's work was, there was energy left for the night. They were mad about intercourse. Sex—the act of it, the search for it—was a constant topic among both the Russian men and the women. Relationships began and ended, often in a matter of weeks, or even a night. Women were slapped in front of dance clubs; husbands were crudely denounced by their wives with such pitiless accuracy that the dinner guests banged their fists on the table and cheered.

It was into this atmosphere of expatriate acquisitiveness, caffeine, vodka, sex, and hilarity that Sergei's beautiful wife, Katarina Gorky (a great-grandniece of the writer), arrived from Moscow that winter. Katarina was beautiful, petite. She had jet hair; pale, sun-starved skin; a few touching birthmarks; large, secretive eyes; nicotine-stained fingers. She was a physician, on tour with other Soviet doctors, meeting sympathetic doctors in New York, inspecting ghetto emergency rooms, spending her meager savings on presents for relatives and friends back home.

A week into her tour she was found dead, bludgeoned to death in her room at the Hotel Iroquois in midtown Manhattan. Her roommate, not strictly a doctor herself, but a professor of chemistry who had finagled her way onto the junket, had just come back from a visit to the New York Stock Exchange. She found Katarina, unclothed, raped, drenched in her own blood. It was in all the newspapers, the national TV news, it was worldwide; and a day later Sergei, who had been identified by several hotel employees who said they saw him leaving Katarina's room, was arrested and charged with murder.

He was dragged out of Luke's house on Washington Square with his sneakers untied, a Yankees jacket pulled over his head, like a mobster. Someone had tipped off the press. Cameras were everywhere. Strobe lights flashed in the townhouse windows, the grillwork of the parked cars. "Sergei! Sergei!" the reporters howled, as if Sergei knew them, as if he might hear their voices and uncover his face. They crowded close to him as the cops hurried him into the squad car. They were shoving cameras and microphones into his face. They were lucky he was cuffed; he could have broken any of them in half. The cops pushed his head down, ostensibly to keep him from cracking his skull as he got into the car. He was sobbing without restraint. The reporters could hear his cries from beneath the jacket. The streetlights came on, illuminating little swirling squalls of snow.

The police, the courts, and the press were seeing eye to eye. Bail was denied because Sergei was liable to flee—not only the state, but the country. The *Times* ran a two-part profile of Sergei and Katarina: she the hard-line Brezhnev-style Communist, content in her cramped, cold-water life in a Moscow suburb; he the musclebound, skirt-chasing playboy, half-Ukrainian, his father shown in a grainy old photo waving a Nazi flag from a belfry of a village church as the Germans rolled through.

Luke visited Sergei in Rikers Island, where he was being held while the DA prepared his case for the grand jury. Luke slipped in a side entrance and was allowed to meet with Sergei at an off-hour.

> *Not even the bars could stop the slant of the sun*
> *Not the searches or seizures or hassles*
> *The fear in the air, the wasted lives*
> *Where justice is a whore dressed in tassels . . .*

—"Rikers Island," recorded 1985

Sergei was dazed, frightened, his spirit doused like a cigar dropped into a toilet. He could barely look Luke in the eyes. He kept glancing at the grim, mustachioed Puerto Rican guard, as if to ask if the time was up.

"I need a lawyer, a very good lawyer," said Sergei. His eyes were like those of a dying animal, full of uncomprehending fear.

"Tell me what happened."

"They want to send me back to Moscow. Do you know what will happen to me then? There is no fair trial for me in Moscow."

"Tell me. Tell me what happened."

Sadly, Sergei shook his head, his eyes filled with tears. "Somebody killed my wife, they killed my Katarina."

"Who?"

"I don't know."

"Was it you, Sergei?" By now, Luke was whispering so low, the guard leaned forward.

"No! I swear to the most holy God in Heaven and to all the saints, no. I would never do such a thing. Never." He bowed his head against the Plexiglas divider; a tuft of his hair poked through the airholes.

"Then who?" asked Luke.

Sergei looked up, his eyes suddenly furious. "The Soviets, that's who. The KGB. What do you think? Don't you see the nose on your face?" Sergei's spittle flecked the Plexiglas. "I am a diplomatic embarrassment to them. The most famous athlete in all of the Soviet empire and now I choose to defect. So?" He held his hands out, as if the rest were self-evident, an open-and-shut case. "They have no choice. They must discredit me. And spilling the blood of the innocent Katarina—what do they care?"

And soon after that came *American Shakedown*. Six out of eight songs about Sergei. It was rushed through production and shipped into the stores—fifteen weeks in all. It was the first time Luke had tried to enter history with a song since the late sixties and, naturally, interest was keen. Lukologists who had fallen by the wayside during his twists and turns through psychedelia, irony, cynicism, bitterness, wealth, country music, Christianity, and silence were once again churning out articles, spewing out appreciation—he was back! the real Luke! (Which meant that their own youth might boomerang back as well.) Critics and acolytes were so impressed that once again Luke was trying to move mountains with his small, pleading voice, no one spent quite enough time questioning whether the object of Luke's rekindled passions was someone who really ought to go free.

He could move the weight of the world
With his hands and his back
A samovar Samson
Whoa mama, that's a natural fact
Like Samson he tore down the unholy temple
And the kings of the empire wanted to make him an example.

Sergei, oh Sergei they've accused you of a murderous crime.
But the blood's not on your hands and I won't have it on mine . . .

—"Sergei," recorded 1985

Venerable Philip Adams, who had produced Luke's first albums, and who had been locked out of the Luke business since the Steinberg era, was with Luke in the studio on West Fifty-fourth Street. Here's what he told a writer for the little quarterly calling itself *FIG* (Fairchild Is God):

I was there to keep track of costs for the Epoch brass, but everything else was in Luke's control. It was Luke's idea having me there. Maybe he was sending a message to Steinberg, maybe he just wanted someone he trusted. I was glad to do it, glad to work with the kid again.

It was really his show, though. I can't take credit for what I did not do. Lukey hired the musicians, chose the order of the songs, he just ran everything. He wanted some violins, he'd be on the phone. I had no idea where he was getting these names, but he seemed to know every musician in New York. He needed six cellos, six cellists were there within the hour.

I must say, it brought a tear to an old man's eye. No kidding. I couldn't stop thinking what it was like being with Luke when we made that first album, when he was the darling of all the folk music people down in the Village. You know, don't you, I was the one who discovered him when he was hanging out in Chicago with an old soul artist named Little Joe Washington?

Yeah, well I guess that story's been told enough.

Anyhow, just in case you haven't heard it, there was Luke, twenty years old, or some ridiculous age like that, and we're in the old Epoch studios on West 43rd Street—the place is a shelter for runaway teens now, by the way, which is fitting—and, anyhow, none of the Epoch brass wanted me to sign him, so when they finally gave in—and oh how I begged—they only gave us one measly little day to make a record. Quite a difference from what it is now, when these kids can take over a year to get ten songs down on tape. One day, and if it goes over that then it comes out of my pocket. Ouch! I may have a wealthy father but once I got into the music business Dad never gave me fifteen cents. Well, Luke was as nervous as a one-eyed cat peeking in the seafood store. And he didn't know shit from Shinola when it came to making a record, back then. He didn't know where to stand, he didn't know what a microphone did to your voice, he didn't know how to put his personality into a song without any audience there—let's face it, he was used to playing for meals, a place to crash, and for the heart of whatever comely young thing happened to be in the room. But he had a will to succeed. A will to survive. That's what the kids did back then, they sang to save their own lives.

But what I'm trying to say here is on *American Shakedown* it was all Luke. He was running the musicians, he was running the engineers. At one point, I realized I was reading the same newspaper for the third time through and I said to Luke, Luke I could always split you know, there's really nothing for me to do here. And he looks at me and says Do you think Sergei is innocent. Bam. Just like that, out of nowhere. And I said, Sure, I think he's innocent, though really I had no idea. Then stay, says Luke, and puts his hand on my shoulder and I realized it was the first time he touched me in over twenty years.

So I stayed and Luke produced the album. This whole Sergei thing didn't mean a thing to me, but the record was a beauty—as time will eventually confirm. Mazurkas, Russian folk songs, klezmer music, a little Rimsky-Korsakov. Would it be all right if I mentioned here how when these guys want to record efficiently they seem to have no trouble at all getting the job done? No? Fine. Sorry. Then let's just say that by the time the record was made, Luke had wound his way back through two centuries of Russian music, East European music, sonatas, Slavic dances, rondos, rhapsodies, you name it. He burrowed his way into the heart of a whole musical culture and even back into his own Jewishness—those fiddles, and Andy Goldfarb's brilliant clarinet. It's all there. Eat your big fat cancerous heart out Ken Steinberg, I was thinking. I sat up in the control booth, next to Keith Gladstone, who was the engineer Luke wanted, and every now and then we'd just look at each other and shake our heads, we were so blown away at what Luke was putting down. Finally, Gladdy asked me, Are you okay? And I said Sure, why do you ask? And he touched his face and I touched mine and I noticed my cheeks were soaked. I was bawling like a goddamn baby, is what I was doing. That's how much I loved the music. After all these years. You see, I still had the spark! Not bad for an old man, right? Is that what you're thinking?

BY THE TIME Luke took the stage in his comeback concert under the stars, the distant smell of salt and seaweed and beach roses had been replaced by the more urgent aromas of pot, body heat, fast food, and shit. I feared for my life; my weakened heart, in its long convalescence, had developed its own means of communication, a language entirely composed of warnings—I need air, I need blood, I need silence, peace, love. No, the irony of actually dropping dead the moment my father took the stage did not escape me, but it was an irony without consolation, assuming ironies ever can console.

The sunset was a bright orange crack in the dark blue bowl of sky. I'd been there for twenty hours, so I was close to the stage—in fact, I'd watched the squadron of hirsute hammerjockeys putting the thing together, and I'd been there as well for the sound checks, the lighting checks, all of the techy tedium that precedes a concert. Luckily for me, I'd inherited some errant height gene—from my mother's maternal great-uncle, a veritable water tower in a family of rain barrels, though perhaps I'd been given a bit of extra altitude by some tall Kramer, which was Dad's name before he changed it to Fairchild. Kramer. Stuart Kramer—Stuart Melvin Kramer, to be exact. And so I had a good view of Luke when he came ambling onto the stage, looking completely engrossed in tuning his guitar, giving the impression of having forgotten he was about to perform. He was dressed in black jeans, no shirt, a black leather vest. The Sergei-induced muscles had gone slack. There was a hitch in his stride, tension in his shoulders. He turned away from us and checked on his musicians—once twenty years ago his backup guitarist didn't show up for a concert, and since then Luke always took attendance.

Danny Manning was on drums. Danny courted my mother after Luke was (officially) out of the picture, yet even then he had to endure the fabled Fairchildian wrath. But that was now all forgotten, and as Luke leaned back toward Danny and said something under the noise of the ecstatic crowd, the two of them seemed to share a laugh. Mike Silverman was on lap guitar, fiddle, accordion, and marimba. Dutch Conners, Ken Yoshiba, and Graham Ross rounded out the group, and all of them stood like statues of sidemen in some rock and roll wax museum while the crowd went wild. Everyone around me was screaming, shouting, yelling, ululating, whistling, whooping, weeping. This was more than show business; this was religion. Luke had come back to teach us how to live, how to talk and gesture, how to see through the game, how to face down death; he had come to anoint us. History coursed through him like an electric current, and when he grabbed you the power passed from his hand into yours, and it made your hair rise, too. Every now and then, Luke made a gesture as if to begin playing, but like a swimmer pushed back to shore by a tumult of waves, he gave up each time. Every now and then, I softly said to myself, That's my father up there, but the thought made my heart race in a way that felt absolutely dangerous. What a way to die! Slumped onto the slimy ground, trampled to death by my father's fans.

He looked surprisingly well, though no longer young. There was no longer even a trace of his faintly girlish beauty. He was a man, gray-bearded now (though the beard would be gone in weeks); there was gray in his once juvenile Jewfro. The mockery was gone from his eyes, replaced by caution, unhappiness. Growing older wasn't a mess he could leave for the others to clean up.

Finally, we in the front noticed he was starting to sing. It took another couple of minutes for the silence to spread all the way to the rear, to the trampled-down fences, and the sway-backed tops of the vans, and the hills and the treetops where the last of the pilgrims had gathered, and by then Luke was halfway through his first song.

> *When I tell you the truth babe*
> *You only get mad*
> *You want me to help you find something*
> *You never had*
> *Shut the window*
> *Slam the door*
> *I'm not so sure*
> *No no*
> *I'm not so sure*
> *I*
> *Ever*
> *Loved you.*

I was stunned. His first song in public in seven years and he'd chosen a hate song! By the time he had come to the final verse, he was no longer even singing. He just stood there playing his guitar and let the audience carry the song, and when it was done, he smiled and indulged in the night's sole line of stage patter: "Where you guys been?" Another five minutes of worshipful cheers followed. And as I looked around, it stirred me and frightened me, too, to see how many in the crowd were openly weeping. They sobbed, they buried their faces in their hands and rubbed their eyes and then looked up at the stage again, humbled, worshipful. It was as if my father were an apparition, the Virgin Mary on the summit of a war-torn mountain, Christ in concrete.

Luke in concert sometimes scoldingly steered clear of the hits, the archetypal Luke songs, and as the evening wore on, and some of the crowd began to worry that they might never get to hear, say, "Rivers of Steel" or "Lullaby of the Apocalypse"—which would mean that they weren't going to get the ultimate Luke experience, the one they could tell their friends about, their grandchildren—a few in the audience grew restive, and began to shout out the titles, at first in a loud, reminding sort of way, and eventually with a kind of frantic fury, a howl of cultural panic. But Luke gave not the slightest indication of even hearing them, much less being interested in altering his play list to suit their tastes. His choice of material had a vein of petulance going through it; he concentrated on songs from albums that had tanked. He even tempted the large contingent of journalists present by singing a song from *American Shakedown*, a touching little mazurka called "Romance in Odessa," which was at the time of its composition meant to be a poetic re-creation of Sergei and Katarina's courtship, but which managed to survive as a meditation on young love in general, and made me think about Luke's love affair with my mother, a liaison which remained far more emblematic of romantic excess than anything that had ever happened to me.

I had known about this concert for months—that was how I was able to get a ferry ticket to the island, whereas most of the fans had to become Boat People. My source of information was

Wendy Crabtree, the distaff side of one of my father's longest-lasting relationships. There had been a long antipathy between Wendy and my mother, and we steered clear of each other until I began to compile facts about Luke, traveling the country as widely as my moth-eaten wallet would permit, in order to interview people once associated with Luke. I caught up with Wendy in Dorset, Vermont, where she was visiting her adopted daughters Sophie and Marlene, strapping strawberry-blond twins with none of Wendy's darkness and delicacy, who were living then in a lesbian commune, where thirty or so women supported themselves in the most agrarian, regressive ways imaginable, hours of stoop labor, raising sheep and weaving sweaters from the wool, growing fruits and selling little Mason jars of jam—just the sort of thing women did before they were allowed to go to school and vote and smoke in public. Wendy had been doing me a favor, letting me talk to her there—normally she lived in Carmel, California, and she wanted to save me the journey. We met in town; men were forbidden from entering the women's collective, and there was no point pushing it. I was sitting in the designated café when Wendy walked in. She wore a cobalt parka; the hood was lined with silver fur. Her face looked like a carving. I raised a finger: It's me. She sat down in the chair opposite mine, pulled off her moon-walk gloves. The skin around her eyes was multicolored and looked as delicate as the wings of a butterfly.

"My God, you're Luke all over again."

"And you didn't even believe I was his son."

"You're right. I didn't. But I must have believed something. Otherwise, why would the conspiracy of starlight have led me here?"

By the end of our afternoon together, not only was Wendy convinced of the veracity of my claims to be Luke's son, but, piecing together a few dates and dim memories, she also figured out that when my mother came to Chicago to tell Luke that she was pregnant (with me), Wendy and Luke were just beginning their own love affair. "That was you inside your mother's tummy then, that was you," she said, almost as if I would be pleased.

Wendy tipped me off about Luke's concert, and a few weeks later she sent me a laminated (limited access) backstage pass. "Sorry," the note had said, "it's not All Access, but there are NO all access passes for this show. When LF is involved, paranoia runs deep."

Tonight, Wendy was dressed Gypsy-style, phyllo pastry layers of sheer skirts, orange and blue and brown. Her breadstick arms each impaled fifty silver bracelets. She dragged a shawl behind her like a matador's cape. With her free arm, she waved at the audience, which greeted her appearance with a roar of what seemed as much like lust as it did welcome. It was good timing all around, since after two hours of Luke, and calling out for songs he refused to sing, and listening as his voice tired and lost its edge, its pitch, and started sounding like a swarm of bees, the crowd was ready for some fresh blood.

The band began playing "Shiva the Destroyer" and Wendy grabbed the microphone and said, "Hi, everyone. I'm Wendy Crabtree!"

> *Down by the Ganges*
> *A workingman in shirtsleeves*
> *Back by the station*
> *Talking incarnation*
> *The sun drips blood*
> *After the flood*
> *Shiva says to the kid*
> *I'm afraid your name is mud!*

I figured them for three songs and then two encores—Luke never did more than two—and so I wound my way closer to the left side of the stage. I wanted to be there with my backstage pass the moment the music stopped. It was hell getting through. Despite giving every outward sign of being blissfully transported by the concert, every pilgrim seemed acutely aware of their spot in the mass and viewed my coming forward as a kind of encroachment, an imperialistic gesture, a land grab. This was worse than emptying a full cart of groceries onto the conveyor belt at the express register, while the fellow with a bottle of seltzer and a box of Cascade glares murderously at you. This was a high crime; this was war. People were actually grabbing at me, trying to pull me back. People were blocking my way, saying Fuck you, man, where you going? I am Luke Fairchild's son, I might have said, not that any of them would have believed me, and not that it would have made a difference. Getting as close to Luke as possible was a kind of wild and irrational emergency. They wanted to touch the hem of his garment, and they scrambled and scratched for a place close to him as if it could save their lives, like those poor panic-struck people leaping for the bottom of the helicopter as the last chopper out of Saigon took off from the embassy roof:

Whirly-birds turning in the yellow heat of day
Open the doors, take me away?
Let me inside your mighty machine
Make me an American, awww I want to come clean . . .

—"The Citizen Ship," recorded 1974

But I was not to be deterred. Fatherless boys are used to going where we are not wanted. I endured, I pushed back, I wedged, edged, and waited, I slid between, I was as valiant as the one sperm fighting its way through a condom, past a diaphragm and its dab of deadly goo, through a seething rain forest of endometrium to its final, fateful rendezvous with the egg. And my timing—which is, after all, everything—was perfect. By the time I made it to the front row and was face to face with the security guards, who stood with their arms folded over their implacable chests, Luke and Wendy and half the crowd were singing "Stacked Deck," one of Dad's existential cowboy songs:

> *He never knew violence*
> *He specialized in a different kind of pain*
> *Black hat or white hat*
> *to Earl it was really all the same*
> *She said how it hurts me*
> *to see you looking such a wreck*
> *He could barely meet her eyes*
> *He was dealing from a stacked deck . . .*

It was the concert's final encore, and I had already taken the laminated backstage pass from my pocket, peeled off the back of it, and stuck it to the center of my T-shirt, where it glowed like an oblong orange heart.

I was suddenly in a knot of the chosen, all of them bearing passes. As usual, Luke had attracted a lot of celebrities—more tonight than usual, because of the long layoff. On one side of me was Teddy Kennedy, an Easter ham in lime-green shorts and a pink Lacoste shirt, and on the other stood Bob Rafelson, who directed Luke's stupendously failed movie debut, the comic-epic western *Chile Con Carne*, a production that saw a rape, several arrests for cocaine use and cocaine smuggling, and a middle-aged male studio executive stealing into Dad's trailer with romance on his mind and a subsequent outburst of violence that put the studio executive in the hospital and Dad behind bars, though each for only twenty-four hours. Also among the backstagers was the director of Dad's second movie, which fared even more poorly than *Chile*. This director—nameless here, for legal reasons—was one of those Europeans who wear their jackets draped over their shoulders, and he tried to keep Luke happy on the most unhappy set by sharing his own tastes for heroin and elaborate, theatrical sex—charades of desire that would have perplexed the Marquis de Sade.

There were a few whom I recognized—Carly Simon, Mike Wallace—and a few whose identity I only figured out later—Alan Dershowitz, Quincy Jones, John Mellencamp. In all, there were perhaps fifty of us, the chosen, and the security guards broke us off from the pack and herded us quickly behind the stage. We stepped through a morass of thick electric cables that looked like the roots of live oaks, and pasture grass shiny and slick with spilled drinks.

"Backstage" really meant behind the stage, where there was a modest wooden platform the performers mounted before heading onto the stage proper. Beyond the platform was a huge trailer, which had surely functioned as Luke's dressing room, and which now sat idling in the night, sending its silvery exhaust up into an open window of moonlight. And beyond that were at least twenty massive trucks, a few of them bearing the logo of MO BILL SOUNDZ. Off to the side, a striped green-and-white tent had been pitched, and that was where we were herded, winding our way through teamsters and roadies and sound men and electricians, like a busload of tourists who've been brought by guides to gawk at the workers in a native factory.

Inside the tent, a table had been set up, with seltzer, beers, Cokes, and huge plastic bowls of potato chips. So this was the Good Life! We milled around. The seltzer went fast; a few beers were opened. Luke, of course, was nowhere to be seen, nor was Wendy. That would happen later, if at all. They were in the dressing room / van, peeling off sweaty shirts, coming down from the nerve-shattering high of performing. As a kind of sacrificial lamb thrown to the celebrities, Danny Manning was sent into the visitors' tent, still holding his drumsticks, his gaunt face pale with exhaustion, his black suit soaked through in back, his eyes throbbing like little blue hearts. He was a sweet guy, but he looked a little shifty, like a card cheat. A diamond stickpin winked in the center of his hula-girl tie; his pocket-watch chain swung back and forth like a strand of drool.

Danny hadn't seen me since I was twelve or thirteen; I'd grown eleven inches, put on eighty pounds. When he saw me, I registered to him as someone he somehow knew.

"Hey, Danny," I said. "Billy Rothschild."

"Billy! You're here!" he said, breathing his remarkable garlicky breath—he ate several cloves a day to ward off colds. He clutched my shoulders and shook me back and forth while he grinned wildly.

"Good show, Danny," I said.

"How's your mom, Billy? How's the lovely Esther?"

"Still lovely. Is Luke coming out soon?"

"Who knows, man. He doesn't tell me shit. Never has and never will. Some things never change, huh?"

"I'm hoping to see him."

"The thing is? You just did. You saw the very best of him. He was so fucking on tonight. Some of those songs—they never sounded better. I was beating my drums and crying. On 'Trust Fund Mama'? and 'Mushroom Cloud'? So where's your mom? Still in the same old place?"

I was about to say yes, but then I remembered that Danny hadn't seen my mother in nearly ten years, and to him the same old place was our walkup on Sullivan Street, with the catfight air shaft, the jade plants the size of armchairs, the onion-skin Oriental runners, the stained-glass panes in the French doors.

"No, she's in the country now."

"No shit?"

"No shit, Danny. She gardens, she sews. . . ."

"Ah, that's beautiful, man. My old lady does all that shit. Very life affirming. She just lays out that steady four-four time and I can go as crazy as I want. That's what you need in an old lady—someone to put down that steady beat, just like laying brick."

Just then, his eyes left me to scan the room, and when they returned, for a moment's farewell, the light had already vanished from them. I was used to the seduction of show-business types, that way they have of overwhelming you with their undivided attention one minute and blowing you off the next. Depending on these people was like trying to garden in a place where the sun shines brilliantly fifteen minutes a day. I knew how to not take it personally, for the most part.

"You gonna be around?" he asked, backing off.

"Sure. I'm right here."

"Great to see you, Billy. Tell your mother to stay in touch."

"Where do you live?" I asked, but Danny had already turned and was heading toward Martin Sheen, and he didn't hear me.

I lingered in the VIP tent for more than an hour, without a sign or even a rumor of Luke. The rest of the band came in, and so did Wendy—she waved briefly at me but was engrossed with Carly Simon and someone who I suddenly recognized was David Byrne. I stepped out, telling myself I wanted to take a look at the concert area, to see if the crowd was still lingering, the way they do in St. Peter's long after the Pope has gone inside.

I could tell they were still there as soon as I was under the dome of stars. I could hear the voices. I walked to the edge of the stage and peeked out. Hundreds of tents had been pitched and others were going up. Fires burned. Someone threw a log on a nearby flame and it shot up an explosion of dark orange sparks. The smell of food cooking. No one wanted to leave, and besides, there was nowhere to go—the next ferry sailed at daybreak, and even the most enterprising of the islanders probably wouldn't be shuttling passengers in the middle of the night. It was a tent city for Luke, just like the old days.

I hadn't bothered to try and get into Dad's trailer. Two security guards languished in front of it, wearing black T-shirts, the oil in their Afros glistening in the moonlight. They eyed me when I first walked past them—these guys get bored, of course, and many of them would appreciate it if you tried to get away with something—and now as I returned to the tent they looked me over again. Over the years hanging around the carefully patrolled outskirts of my father's life, I had perfected a kind of nod that seemed somehow to convey the following information: I have a right to be here; No you may not help me, I know exactly where I am going; We have already been through this and there's no need to do so again; and I just might have enough pull to get you fired. I gave them this nod and they rocked back on their heels.

Just then, however, the door to the trailer opened. A V of bright light poured out, whitening the grass, the tops of the guards' paratrooper boots. And then: Luke. He had changed into a Harvard sweatshirt (honorary degree ten years before) and a pair of jeans. He held a dark red apple in one hand, and with the other hand he stroked his chin, as if wondering whether or not he needed to shave. Now that he was visible, the guards became extra-vigilant. They immediately stood between Luke and me.

"Luke!" I called, knowing I had but a moment.

Did he know me at all? Luke had seen me often when I was a baby, he had even held me, fed me, without ever admitting he was my father, but still wanting to be near Esther. But finally my mother could tolerate his trying to worm out of paternity no longer. She cut off all contact, while he remembered her in songs, got richer off his harrowing, lovesick memories of her, and blasted off into the stratosphere, propelled further and further from anything resembling the terra firma of normal life by the booster rockets of fame and fame and fame, and by then whatever residual temptation she might have felt to see and to love him again was made moot by his inaccessibility. When I began to insist to her that she help me know my father, she had no better idea of how to reach him than the average fan.

Yet the curiosity I felt was more than idle wondering. It was subject to that sorrowful alchemy of the emotions: the more it was denied, the stronger it grew. Once I knew who my father was, I burned to see him. I began dreaming of him sometime shortly after Esther told me his name, and by the time I had a little Benedictine fringe of hair around my dick I was in a rapture of my own fatherlessness. Everything broken or unsatisfactory in my life was explained by Luke's abandonment of me. Tears on my pillow, as the song goes. Over the years, I had written to him, sent him pictures of myself, hunted down his ever-changing private phone number, nabbed him once backstage at Madison Square Garden, once at the Nassau Coliseum, and once again, most recently, at Antoine's restaurant in New Orleans, where I caught him eating crayfish with Allen Toussaint, and where two elderly but athletic waiters blocked my path to the table and whisked me out into the humid, dank night before I could say a word.

And now, here he was again. To be this close to him exceeded my hopes for what the night would bring—though anything less would have sent me into a fit of depression. He stopped in his tracks to look me over. His face was half-lit by the luminous echoes of lights that were elsewhere—lights from the stage that bounced off the ground and settled into the crowns of the trees, lights from the windows of his trailer, lights from the VIP tent.

"Hi, kid," he said, his voice pounded and shredded and raw from the concert. "How'd I do?"

"Fine," I managed to say. I'd had no idea I was going to get this close to him, and had prepared no words, no attitude. He looked bad—terrible, in fact. His skin was gray, the skin beneath his eyes grayer still. He looked like, and probably was, a junkie. But with Luke, you never knew; he had access to limitless drugs and an equal number of cures—he burned through disease and health like he burned through love and hate, loyalty and betrayal, belief and contempt, and everything, everything, everything else.

"This is the loneliest time," he said. "Right now. After."

We walked together, toward the tent.

"Been in there yet?" he asked.

"Yes," I said, and then waited for the next question.

But there was no next question. We walked into the VIP party. Without anyone actually moving, you could feel the balance and weight of the room shift, as the crowd ached with wanting to gather around him, and tried to respect that piece of high-priced real estate called His Personal Space. I wondered if Luke had any idea who I was. Did he see for that moment I was his son? Or at least did he recognize me as Esther's boy? Or was I simply one of those ten thousand souls whom he faintly recognized? Was I just someone who happened to be standing there beneath the Cape Cod constellations when he came out of his trailer?

Luke was no longer at my side. I stood there for what seemed a very long time. I didn't even get a beer. I just watched Luke from afar and I tried to maintain a relaxed demeanor, in case he might glance in my direction and consider coming back to collect me. But Luke was never one for glancing in anyone's direction, unless you were a young woman and he wanted to fuck you, and sometimes not even then. I could feel my time running out. And I noted the following curious emotion: I felt strangely *more* like his son now that he was adrift in the room, accepting a Heineken from Danny, and putting his other hand over his face while a black-haired, knobby-kneed child in Ted Kennedy's care tried to take a picture of Luke with her brightly flashing Instamatic. Standing alone, I was back in familiar territory.

At least a half-hour had passed, and I knew Luke would not stay in this tent or with these people for many more minutes. He would leave in a mysterious rush; he would take a step backward and disappear. What were the chances of his coming back for me before he left? I stayed put, with the sweaty palms and queasy belly of an unsuccessful suitor.

Until I could bear it no longer. It was clear he was not about to resume his conversation with me, a conversation that had, after all, consisted of just a handful of words, none of them having anything to do with acknowledging who I really was, or even remembering my name. A fire of humiliation burned within me, filling my head with smoke, blinding and choking me. This was something I would never get used to, though, in a sense, my entire life had been spent in modes of banishment: calling numbers that had been disconnected, waiting for limos that had already left the underground garage, sending letters to beachfront "cottages" that were already shuttered and locked, put on hold by assistants and left out there in the fiber-optic ether until the rage made me slam the phone down, and then pick it up again to slam it down harder.

At last, I turned away from Luke, momentarily forgot how to get out of the tent, and then walked quickly through the flap, away from the slightly noxious smell of the huge gas heaters that burned at the tent's periphery, and out into the cool Atlantic night.

I walked away from the white light and diamond-hard laughter of the VIP tent, past the security guards who smoked and talked around Luke's trailer, past the stage filled with roadies wrapping up long coils of electric cables and carrying away keyboards and drums, and made my half-dazed way into the passless multitude.

Tents were scattered over the dewy, star-struck field; Coleman stoves and kerosene lamps glowed behind the raised flaps. All that was missing was the muttering of horses and the soft moans of the wounded, and Mathew Brady setting up his tripod.

There were no more taxis waiting to take people to town, and no room for me in town even if I were to get there. The temperature was falling, and I really wanted to get inside one of those tents. I had a feeling I would have to end up convincing someone I was Luke's son before I'd be given shelter, but I did try for straight charity a few times before resorting to using Luke's name—though, in fairness to me, I'm not convinced that simply telling the truth about yourself qualifies as name dropping.

I ended up in a tent with a college student named Amy and we ended up making love. My position as the king's bastard son had not granted me the license of the king himself, but it did allow me to leave far behind the normal rhythms of romantic life, with its timid approaches and its stunning sexual setbacks. Announcing that I was Luke's son opened doors, and God knows it spread legs. I don't want to complain about it, because I enjoyed the sex and I needed the company. But there was a price, and the price was an after-burn of anger—at Luke, at myself, and at the women who fucked me for all the wrong reasons. I sometimes longed for a woman to love me who knew nothing of Luke, but where was I going to find this creature? The Japanese exchange student with the cashmere sweater and the tiny crucifix resting in the fragile hollow of her long neck?

Forget it; Luke was bigger in Kyoto than he was in Cleveland—bootlegs of his early stuff sold there for more than the stereo that played it. Then how about that exchange student from Sierra Leone? Well, Luke had played Freetown, she'd been there, the police had come because the president's wife had had her purse snatched. Every now and then, I did meet someone who had never heard of Dad, or who had, but only vaguely, and to whom Dad meant absolutely nothing; but, unfortunately, this gap was just part of a yawning mouthful of cultural cavities—she would have never seen *The Mary Tyler Moore Show*, never heard of Andy Warhol, had no idea who Hank Aaron was, didn't care who killed the Kennedys.

Next morning, I was up with the sun. I made my way through the field, which now, in the silver foggy mystical light of daybreak, looked like the aftermath of the battle at Gettysburg, with bodies strewn as far as the eye could see, and fires smoldering everywhere.

There were quite a few people leaving the concert site, and we walked in a mass to the ferry, a hundred of us at least, like marchers in a demonstration, but without placards or chants.

Those ferries are prompt, down to the second. Loaded up with Luke's fans, some in cars, most of us in the first leg of a journey home that would entail buses, trains, and hitched rides, it plowed through the steely waters. As it was when I arrived, the water was full of smaller craft in which local sailors were still carrying the concertgoers with whom they had cut private deals. I stood on the deck, pretending that the cool air was a shower. The benches were filled with dozing Luke fans. Near the bow, a tall kid in overalls and matted hair played guitar and sang Luke songs while a few adoring girls sat Indian-style on the floor listening to him.

Standing next to me was a boy about eight years old. He wore a plain white T-shirt, khaki pants. He had the slightly cross look of a curious, independent child, the kind of boy who is lonely a lot because other children bore him. If he'd been up half the night, he didn't seem any the worse for wear. The top rail was exactly as tall as he was, and he leaned against it with his hand raised. Between his thumb and forefinger he held a piece of bread.

Suddenly, a gull—half the size of the kid, with a fierce dab of paint for an eye—swooped down and snatched the bread out of his fingers with its scimitar beak.

I was so startled that I jumped back. The kid took another piece of bread out of his pocket and held it over the railing. This time at least ten gulls appeared. Their massive wings made minute adjustments as they tried to float next to the boy. All of them trained their left eye on the kid, who stood absolutely still, with the half-inch of bread held out to lure the birds even closer. At last, one of the flock pointed its left wing down toward the foaming wake of the ferry and in a moment's grace and greed snatched the bread away.

Over and over, the kid performed his feat of self-control. Once, one of the gulls clearly got a bite of finger along with the bread, but all the kid did was to check if he was bleeding. He knew I was watching him; now and then he acknowledged me with a quick sideways glance. He offered me a small piece of bread, but I shook my head. I knew I'd drop it into the ocean as soon as the gulls were close to me, or would try to toss it up in the hope that one of the gulls would grab it midair. He shrugged and finished feeding the birds the last of the bread.

When he was done, he sat on one of the seats on deck, next to his father, a portly, sweet-faced guy about forty, whose sneakered feet rested on a hastily baled-up mess of camping equipment.

"I'm done," the kid said, showing his father his empty hands.

"Okay," the father said. "I saw that one gull nail you."

"It didn't hurt," the kid said. He held his hand away from his father.

"You sure?" The father stroked his son's auburn cap of recently cut hair.

The boy closed his eyes. Fatigue. Pleasure. Safety. He sat straight and still for another moment and then succumbed and rested his head against his father's meaty shoulder. His father drew him closer, put his arm around him, and kissed the top of his son's head. The kid was absolutely made.

I turned away and looked at the sky, the sea, the hundreds of sailboats, motor boats, and yachts that were making the crossing with us. I could feel the color rising in my face. I felt my soul welling up inside me like a kind of nausea, the illness of being the self we can neither bear nor escape.

3

Now, two years later, after a long, difficult night on my mother's sofa, my wristwatch's electronic mosquito alarm got me up the next morning at five. The house was still in darkness, save the pale fan of lamplight that swept out of Esther's bedroom. I looked out of the window; her van was gone. I sank back into the motherly softness and warmth of the sofa, but then forced myself up again. The batteries in my tape recorder were dead. I pressed the Eject button and the little tape popped out. I labeled it, put it in my briefcase. I tried to hurry. Though my substitute teaching job was marginal, I was in no position to lose it.

By the time I got my shoes on, the phone was ringing.

"Is this the home of Esther Rothschild?" a woman's voice asked. She sounded young and very nervous.

"Yes, it is." I had no advance degrees in life's tragedies, but I knew I wasn't getting this call before daybreak because anything less than mayhem was loose in my life.

"To whom am I speaking, please?"

"This is her son. What's going on?"

"Ummm. Your mother?"

"Yes?"

"She's had a car accident. She's in Leyden Hospital, in the emergency room."

"Oh my God! My God . . . Is she all right?"

"I don't know, sir."

And so forth. By the time the day had broken, I was already there—I sped down the mountain, past the spot, not a mile away, where the road crew were towing the twisted remains of Mother's car away from the spot where she'd lost control of it. She was already out of the emergency room and into surgery before I arrived.

Hours passed.

I sat there.

Mother didn't have her own doctor, didn't quite subscribe to Western medicine, though I don't think even she would have chosen herbs and kitchen wisdom and acupuncture for burns, a shattered leg, uncountable lacerations, broken teeth, and crushed ribs. According to the attending physician, a somewhat high concentration of alcohol was found in her blood. The doctor's name was Robert Heilborn. Only a year or two older than me, he nevertheless called me Billy and didn't tell me his first name. He had carefully combed brown hair, as neat as paint on a puppet. Someone must have stressed the importance of eye contact to him, because he stared as if to hypnotize me. It was hard to believe my mother's life was in his small, scrubbed hands.

"You did a blood test on her?" I said, my voice rising.

"Routine," he said. "It's the law. I have to do it, it's my job."

"You have only one job," I said, "and that is to save her life."

"We're doing everything we can, Billy. All of us. When she stabilizes a little, I've arranged a medevac to Albany, where they can deal with her burns more effectively than we can."

"You can't deal with her burns?"

"It's a matter of equipment."

"And we can't get her up to Albany now?"

He shook his head. A fist closed on my heart and squeezed, like trying to get the last drop of juice out of a lemon.

Was it all that talk of Luke that rattled her enough to send her car out of control? Did I somehow help her get drunk the night before? What was going on in that hour before dawn? She was on her way to get bagels for our breakfast—granted, known, check. But what then? Was it a hallucination, or perhaps a seizure, that led her into that huge granite boulder on the side of the road—a damp gray monolith upon which someone had painted a grinning shark with a mouthful of ravenous red teeth? Shattered glass, twisted metal, and, finally, fire. By the time rescue workers got her out, she was unconscious, great mercy of the nervous system.

No one from the press had gotten wind of this yet, though eventually I knew that would happen. Luke had written dozens of songs about her, and she had figured prominently in most of the Luke biographies. Some enterprising little shit would put it together—I could count on it.

THOUGH my mother's name is Rothschild, she bears no relation to the rich and powerful Rothschilds. There are no bankers, no vintners perched in Mother's family tree. Hers was not even the sort of family that had a family tree. The origins of her family were somehow lost in the European mists, their roots buried beneath the mulch of pogroms, panicky migrations; and until prosperity struck some of the American Rothschilds after World War II, no one had paid much attention to who'd begot whom. In the World According to Grandpa, the fixation on ancestors was the folly of the goyim, and fancy-shmancy Jews. For Esther's Rothschilds, my Rothschilds, there was a prevailing sense that if you looked deep enough into our origins, then you'd only find struggle, poverty, failure, shadiness, and shame.

The second thing about my mother was she was beautiful: raven-haired, fine-boned, bottle-green-eyed, porcelain-skinned, full-lipped, high-breasted, Jewish-American, soulful, outrageously beautiful.

> *You were my conscience, you were my guide*
> *I felt like a king just to walk by your side*
> *Your loveliness lit the sky like the dawn*
> *So pink, so bright, I could go on and on.*
>
> *Obsidian hair, black as coal*
> *Green eyes that could look right into my soul*
> *Beauty so vast, as deep as the sea*
> *What were you doing with a clown like me?*

—"Open Sesame," recorded 1964

She was from Brooklyn, the only child of leftist, denunciatory parents, who filled her with Marxist orthodoxy and made her not only serious but heartbroken over the injustices of the world. It wasn't what they intended, but Esther's parents bequeathed to her the kind of geopolitical heebie-jeebies that made her sexually restless, a little less than careful, dressed her in black, put circles under her eyes, made her chew her cuticles so they looked like thatched roofs. She was, nonetheless, by the time she graduated Erasmus Hall High and entered Hunter College, a catch. Rich kids (relatively speaking), the best students, the handsomest and most popular boys, all flocked around Esther. At first, she accepted this incomprehensible rush of attention, because it seemed inhospitable not to, and then, soon, she began to crave it, and, finally, she expected it. She wore black jeans, black cotton pullovers, dangling silver earrings from Mexico, a little eyeliner, lily-of-the-valley cologne. Professors fell all over themselves; the guys in the cafeteria heaped extra helpings of waxed beans, beets, and meat loaf onto her plate. Sid Holtzman, who went on to win the Pulitzer Prize for drama and who was then in the Hunter College Dramatic Society, wrote several plays expressly for her, but she never agreed to act in any of them, preferring to paint scenery, make suggestions, and offer that special, knowledgeable, sympathetic encouragement which soon would be nearly as heralded as her beauty.

> *Hey hey everybody did you hear the news?*
> *I just got lucky and slept with The Muse.*

—"Talking MacDougal Street Blues,"
   recorded 1963

After college, she got a job waitressing at the Zen Cafe, working from seven in the evening until three in the morning. By day, she picketed the Woolworth's in Greenwich Village in support of the Negroes who were trying to get served a little pie and ice cream, a cup of coffee for crying out loud, in various Woolworth's south of the Mason-Dixon line, and were getting kicked, clubbed, and spit on for their efforts. When the news crew from NBC came down to photograph them picketing on Sixth Avenue, they made Esther the center of the story. Her picture ended up in *Life* and in *Collier's;* for a while, she was the poster girl of the northern civil rights movement: a gorgeous Jewish college girl in a very becoming sweater.

She was still at Hunter when she met Luke. Though she kept her own place, Esther was living with the folk singer Loren Nelson, who was a relation to President Taft. Loren was a large man who made no secret of the fact that his American roots ran deep. Singing Communist songs in Italian or talking about the dharma wasn't his style, and he basically believed that anyone who could change cultures probably didn't have a culture to begin with. Loren believed in prairie rectitude, hard work, handshake deals, and music that quenched your thirst like a dipper full of icy spring water. Esther and Loren lived in an apartment on West Tenth Street, above a bar whose pounding juke box kept them up until dawn but whose owner gave them credit. They lived on Guinness stout and hamburgers, and they lived for folk music.

In the early sixties, Greenwich Village was full of folk singers. They came to MacDougal Street like the lame went to Lourdes. There were rich ones, poor ones, fat ones, short ones; they had beards, long hair, dirty feet, and sandals; their eyes were radiant with ambition or dulled over by hunger. The girls had voices so high and plaintive that when they sang the angels flew from the tops of Christmas trees and turned to snow. The boys dreamed of riding the rails, splitting wood, kicking the shit out of their fathers, screwing girls, and maybe one day settling down and writing that novel. From Austin, from Queens, from Bangor, Seattle, Tampa, Scarsdale, and Muncie, the folkies arrived in Greenwich Village, toting their instruments, sharing their songs, falling in and out of love, cheering each other on.

There were plenty of places to sing, but none more central to the intersection of desire and opportunity than Golden's Folklore Village. It was on Sixth Avenue, one rickety flight above Golden's Guitar Village, where stringed instruments were sold and young singers could buy a guitar for fifty dollars, then bring it upstairs and accompany themselves on it in front of the regulars at the Folklore Village, aka the Winter Palace, aka People's Parque.

Beer-bellied, bald, bombastic Sandy Golden, in his sixties, ran the place as if it were a union hall. There was nothing on the peeling brick walls except announcements of upcoming events. A couple of ceiling fans pushed the stale air around.

Bare wooden floors, a stage covered in stained, colorless carpet. Folding chairs, folding tables, coffee, sparkling water, apple juice with cinnamon sticks. It cost a dollar and a half to get in, two dollars if you wanted to perform, except on Thursdays, Fridays, and Saturdays, when Sandy booked performers who had already made something of a name for themselves, and then he charged three dollars admission. Sandy was effusive, forgetful; the real brains of the operation was his wife, Flora, gaunt and pure, fiercely ideological, and phobic about money—she washed in sudsy hot water every piece of change the club took in and wore Playtex rubber gloves when she counted the dollar bills.

The first time Luke played the Folklore Village he sang a set of straight folk songs, the kind of ballads you could find on any folk music record, or from the stage at Pie in the Oven, or the Pegged Leg, or Harmony, or Mr. Dinky's, or any of the other fourscore folk music dives in the Village. Luke sang as if he were English, as if he were Irish, as if he was a hardworking man from Oklahoma. He sang about moonlight, silver daggers, hungry foxes, and the high seas. None of this was in the least natural to him. He sang folk songs because they were a going thing, not because he particularly liked them. His taste ran toward blues. He grew up on the blues and he had apprenticed with the great soul singer Little Joe Washington. He would have liked to try a Chuck Jackson song. But he saw no opportunity to make a dollar or a name for himself as a reverse minstrel. The audience wanted folk songs, so he gave them folk songs.

Did he bring down the house, that first time? Absolutely not—not even the legend mongers try to sell that story any longer. But he survived, he did not embarrass himself, he got a slightly better-than-polite round of applause, a few adoring glances—adoring glances grew on trees, back then—and, most importantly, he pleased Sandy Golden, who was not only Folklore's owner but its self-described Commissar of Culture.

"Luke Fairchild!" Golden bellowed to the audience, raising up Luke's arm, as if declaring the new bantamweight champion of the world.

"I don't have any place to stay," Luke whispered to Golden—he'd heard Sandy was a soft touch, figured he'd try his luck.

Sandy smiled, as if that was great news. "People?" he said. "We need someone to give our friend a place to sleep tonight. Any volunteers?" For Sandy, it was like the thirties again, a rough-and-tumble time, comradeship.

To hear Luke tell it (and the hagiographers repeat it), every woman in the place wanted to take Luke home. But in fact, he left with Judy Whitimore because she was the only one who came forward. Granted, she was quick about it, and maybe there were others who were considering offering Luke a place to stay and who were discouraged by the rapidity and vehemence of Judy's response—"I've got a perfect spot for him!" she cried out. She was dressed in a sailor suit; she smoked a tiny cigar. She came full-blown, an eccentric, vain, and aimless woman out of a Luke Fairchild song that had yet to be written (but which would be, at least ten times over: "Trust Fund Mama," "Another Charm on Your Bracelet," "Payment on Demand," among others).

Judy Whitimore has already weighed in with her own version of her months with Luke, *Come to Mama*, which was published in 1990 by FIN (an acronym for Fairchild International News), a Frankfurt, Kentucky, house wholly devoted to (fairly specious) Lukology. According to Whitimore, she and Luke lived together in her penthouse on lower Fifth Avenue, where he played, sang, and plotted out his career for six months. He learned from her how to eat lobster, Brie, and croissants; he read widely in her library of twentieth-century American poetry. He slept curled next to her—Chapter 1 of *Come to Mama* is called "Fetal Attraction"—and where, according to Whitimore, his greatest sexual pleasure was to have her gently kiss the side of his face and whisper into his ear while he masturbated.

"Gentle boy," Whitimore writes,

> manchild, man-cub, oh Pan with your Magik pipe. How I loved thee. I loved thee but, yea, I knew we were doomed. I taught you to make love. I held your Pan pipe and guided it into me and when you asked me if it was all right I said Yes yes, yes I said yes.
>
> When I introduced you to Allen Ginsberg, he fell in love with you and came with us when we shopped for your clothes on 8th Street. He held my hand while we waited for you to come out of the changing room and he said, "Judy, the whole world is a changing room to Luke. Don't try too hard to hold onto him." Because *you* want him, Allen? I said, because he was a poet and a mystic and you could say absolutely anything to him. He looked a little surprised by—my bluntness? And then he patted my hand and said, "Luke is a killer who has not yet found his thing to kill."

By the time my mother and Loren Nelson went to Golden's to see Luke, he was writing and singing his own songs, though most of his performances concentrated on the folk music classics, which he sang with less and less purity. Boredom was pushing him toward style. He was writing songs that were mostly about his life as a young man on the prowl in New York, throwing in brand names, radio call letters, politicians, and current events. And: he was getting handsome. His cheeks were sunken; his eyes were large, pleading—they backed you up and slammed you against the wall. He wore a billowing purple pirate shirt, faded jeans, boots, compliments of Judy. Though his hair was long, he wore it slicked back and it gave him a kind of buccaneer sleekness. The only piece of paper he owned that bore his original name, Stuart Kramer, was his Social Security card, and soon he would get rid of that.

Judy Whitimore claims she was in Golden's Folklore Village the night my mother and Loren came to hear Luke and she even claims to have noticed the expression on Esther's face when Luke finished singing "Riding the Rails," the first song he composed that really caught on. Again from *Come to Mama:*

> Sitting at the next table was Esther Rothschild, who had made somewhat of a name for herself around the Village as a cock-tease and a Communist. It was she who would get Luke into the whole Politically Correct school of folk singing, but that night at Golden's she sure as hell wasn't thinking about integration, world peace, or the goddamned Indians. She was staring at Luke with pure and undisguised lust. I heard her say to her friend of the moment—Loren Nelson, who himself was on The Scene, but always on the fringes—"Can you imagine what someone who plays the harmonica like that could do with a woman?"

This story is apocryphal, though it has shown up in those oral histories into which Whitimore has been able to insert herself. There are not forests enough to grow trees enough to make paper enough to correct every misstatement about Luke, and I don't intend to, or need to, or even care to. But statements concerning my mother must be dealt with forthrightly. She would be incapable of saying something so crude and unkind to a man whom she was, after all, living with—and I might add she would under any circumstances think too highly of herself to openly lust after a stranger. And that comparison between Luke's agility on the harmonica with his supposed talents between a woman's legs is (im)pure Whitimore, perhaps the product of some unfinished business between her and Luke.

> *Get your hands off my head*
> *Don't push me down*
> *Do it yourself*
> *It's scary down there.*

> —"Trust Fund Mama,"
> recorded 1965

Neil Schwartz writes (in *Fairchild in the Promised Land*) rather more convincingly about the night my parents met. Before Luke denounced him in interviews as a "parasite" and a "bucket of snot," Schwartz had a favored position among the Lukologists. Luke trusted and enjoyed him, and spoke freely— though not always honestly—to him. Beginning in the early sixties and continuing through 1971, Schwartz traveled with Luke on various tours; went on fishing trips with Luke during the infamous "ultra-right phase," when Luke played the Grand Ole Opry and reveled in the company of steel guitarists, fiddlers, and paunchy, xenophobic country singers; and was the recipient of countless late-night phone calls from Luke, who tried out lyrics on him, attacked imitators and competitors, and, quite frequently, mourned angrily and self-pityingly over his separation from my mother.

"To most of the Luke-niks and groupies who soon turned Golden's Folklore Village into Mecca," wrote Schwartz,

the club was where Fairchild got his first real attention, the spot where Richard Berle of *The New York Times* saw him and wrote, "If you want to see the future of folk music then you better do-si-do down to Gulden's [sic]." But to Fairchild, Golden's was and always will be connected to a much more personal memory. It was the place where he met Esther Rothschild.

Fairchild was still living in the penthouse with Judy Whitimore, but relations between them had soured. Now, when Luke made his gigs he insisted that Judy either stay home or go someplace else. Anything but show up in the club. Part of the reason for this was Luke had written, without Judy's knowledge, a few songs to which she would certainly object, songs that put their relationship in a less than flattering light—most notably "Trust Fund Mama" and the never-recorded and even more wounding "I Thought You Should Know," in which the singer describes his lover as an orangutan, a Hydra, peeling paint, Hitler, Rockefeller, Johnny Mathis, and the atomic bomb. And the other main reason was that Judy might get in the way when Luke indulged in his favorite after-gig activity, namely cruising the club and coming on to girls.

While playing his opening set on June 20th, Luke was in fine form. He played a selection of the standard folk songs he had been performing since coming to New York, mixed in with an ever-increasing number of his own compositions. There was, of course, no spotlight at Golden's and so Luke had a good view of the packed house. Somewhere during "Trouble in Mind" Luke first laid eyes on the woman who was to change his life— Esther Rothschild.

Esther was a typical Village beauty, by way of Brooklyn. She combined Old Left morality with a decidedly new breed of Sexual Freedom. Dressed in a billowing home-made skirt and peasant blouse, her loveliness and the enthusiasm of her applause were not lost on Luke, and he kept his eyes fixed on her as he went through all the remaining numbers of his first set. Somewhere in the middle of "Talking Sit-in Blues," Esther stopped making any attempt to look away from Luke's piercing gaze. The two of them simply stared at each other, as if Luke was performing for her and her only, and all the other chairs and tables were empty.

And so my father sat at my mother's table, despite the fact that Loren was five inches taller and fifty pounds heavier than Luke.

"Your songs were good," said Loren, feeling for one deluded moment that he could control the situation. "Really beautiful."

My father, ruthless in courtship, turned his chair so all Loren could see was his back.

"I've been looking for you," Luke said to my mother.

"That sounds like a line," she said.

"It is. Take it and hold it, I'm drifting out to sea." Luke smiled; his teeth showed years of neglect, Coke, coffee, cigarettes; he didn't actually own a tooth brush.

> *Brush my teeth,*
> *Blow my nose*
> *Get me out of these cowboy clothes*
> *You want me Red?*
> *Hell, I been blue*
> *One way or the other*
> *I belong to you.*

> —"One Way or the Other,"
> recorded 1964

Luke had an hour before he had to be onstage again. It's a little unclear how he managed to get Esther and Loren to take him back to their apartment, but that's where they ended up. Loren's remarks about Luke's behavior in their apartment, printed as a letter to the editor in *Rolling Stone*, are worth quoting:

He grabbed my best guitar but showed almost no talent in playing it. In all modesty, I myself was something of a virtuoso, though lacking, obviously, the talent for novelty that Luke possessed. When it came to the simple mechanics of playing the instrument, Luke was clumsy. When he saw me staring at him with disbelief, he became angry and started strumming my precious Martin furiously, knocking it out of tune. All the while, I was thinking: This is the guy everyone in the Village is talking about? I thought he was a bit of a joke. He couldn't play, his voice was weak. What he did have was a canny sense of timing. He had a way of phrasing things that was unique. When he finally left to go back to Golden's Folklore Village, my girlfriend Esther Rothschild, much to my surprise, decided to accompany him. A week later, Esther and Luke were living together and were the talk of MacDougal Street.

It's frankly difficult for me to imagine my mother acting so precipitously. In my view of her, she was forever encumbered by excesses of loyalty—loyalty to ideas, ideals, people. She lived in a trance of loyalty, a miasma; she staggered through her life beneath a spell of sentiment. She was gentle with children, old people, beggars, the birds in Washington Square Park. She walked so softly, she seemed to glide. There was safety in her smile, solace in her touch; her voice was soothing, like a warm towel on the back of your neck. That she could simply walk out on Loren Nelson was inconceivable to me. Even Whitimore's *Come to Mama* strongly implies otherwise:

> Luke stayed with me and in some ways our sex life was more explosive than ever, but I knew he was beginning to stray. His lifetime as an alley cat made all the sudden fame just so totally irresistible. I knew he was seeing other women. Antonia Rivera, a.k.a. Groucho, because of her eyebrows, that horny little speed freak who called herself Crystal, Esther Rothschild (Our Lady of the Bleeding Heart), and, most hurtful of all, my manipulative, torpedo-titted little sister Roxanne, who was unsuccessful in luring Luke into her perverted sexual fantasies and took her revenge on him by spreading rumors that Luke was queer.

Wading through Whitimore's river of venom, at least one thing becomes clear: Luke continued to live with Judy Whitimore after he met my mother, and he went out with my mother for a time before they became deeply involved. In my view, this goes a long way toward contradicting Nelson's suggestion that my mother took one look at Luke and packed her bags the next day.

I DON'T mean to suggest that Nelson was lying. In fact, of the many people upon whom I called in my attempt to gain some clarity about what happened between my mother and Luke, Loren Nelson was one of the very kindest. When I wrote to him (*Rolling Stone* is also to be thanked for their efficiency in forwarding my letter to Loren), he replied immediately, saying, in effect, that if I wanted to talk about my mother, he was more than happy to be my host, and I was welcome to come stay with him in Southampton for a day, or for however long I needed to answer my questions.

It was summer, and I was just beginning my first bout of living with Joan Odiack, my difficult but involving girlfriend from Detroit. Joan was not rich, but she thought rich, and it was hot in the city and she was feeling stuck with me in our small, smoldering apartment. She was eager to accompany me out to Long Island—in Joan's view, it was an injustice that we didn't have a beach house of our own to repair to in the summer months. Joan herself worked for a tyrannical toy importer in the Flatiron Building, and I was living on a schoolteacher's salary—but that made little difference to her.

Loren met us at the train station in Southampton. He was driving an old MG; the top was down in the brilliant sunlight, the flowery, tingly heat. He drove us through town, gesturing expansively, pointing out the sights—which were mainly the walls, gates, and high hedges behind which lived either Famous People or Good Families. Joan liked Loren immediately; she responded to the romance of his faded wealth, his delicate, wounded good looks. For my part, perched in the back of the car, I was very grateful he had agreed to see me and had invited us to the beach, but I was having to cope with the sight of what he had become. I could not imagine him living with my mother, nor could I reconcile this man with the pictures of him as a virtuous Woody Guthrie clone I'd seen in *Hootenanny Heaven* or in Mark Halifax's spotty but useful *A Musical History of the Sixties*. He was still handsome, trim; he was even tan. But there was an air of degeneracy about him. The love of easy money and leisure of every sort was all over him—in his strange little smile, his cloudy eyes, his perfectly cut silver hair. He smelled as if he'd just splashed on a generous amount of cologne before coming to get us. There was a kind of hysteria in his devotion to living well.

"You know who would hate it here?" Loren said, turning back to me. We were on a narrow beach road now and he drove it without looking.

"My mother?"

"Exactly. It would really offend her."

"I think it's beautiful," said Joan. She breathed deeply. "The air. The light. The architecture. Everything."

"Oh, I do, too, I absolutely do," said Loren. He smiled expensively at Joan. "But Esther is another matter altogether. She hates wealth, luxury, the whole nine yards. She's terribly pure; her judgment is your basic swift sword."

"God," said Joan, shaking her head, as if the scandal of my mother's high principles had been kept secret from her.

"You know that phrase," said Loren, " 'the whole nine yards'? Do you know what it means?"

"Something about football, I guess," said Joan. "A first down."

"Well, actually, you need ten yards for a first down," said Loren. "I just read this, so I'm very, very excited. The old machine guns? The belts with the bullets on them, that you'd feed through the machine gun? They were nine yards long."

"Ah," said Joan.

"Isn't that great?" said Loren. "Isn't that instantly one of your favorite things of life?"

He turned the car into a sandy driveway, the gate to which was open wide. We drove past sweet-smelling honeysuckle hedges, on our way toward his house, a salt-stained, vaguely Gothic old house, on a rise of reinforced dune. I was cramped; he was flirting with my girlfriend. But I kept it to myself. Soon, we were in the house, seated in wicker chairs on his back porch, with its glimpse of roiling gray ocean, and the famished, hysterical gulls wheeling overhead. The housekeeper gave us gin-and-tonics and Loren directed his attention toward me.

"You look just like your mother," he said. "You have her eyes. And her hair, of course. You should let it grow."

"I don't see where he looks that much like Luke Fairchild," said Joan.

Loren squinted at me, as if I were some ship on the distant horizon. Then he shrugged, let it go at that. He took a long swallow of his gin, coughed softly into the back of his hand.

"How long did you live with my mother?" I asked.

"Not very long. That's the weird thing. What did she say? Does she even remember me?" He laughed, pasting a brittle hearty veneer over a bit of sentimentality. "Oh, maybe we were together four months. Five? But she was so central. I've never forgotten her, even now, after all these years. She was the most remarkable woman I've ever known. Say, Joan. The word 'together'? Take it apart and you—"

"In your letter to the editor—" I said, interrupting him.

"Oh, I know, I know. I made it seem as if she just walked out on me. I shouldn't have written that. Fact is, no one's walked out on me. I . . . I have a way with women."

Yeah, right. I glanced at Joan, to see if she was taking this in. She fished the lime out of her drink with her baby finger-nail.

"How long after meeting Luke did my mother move in with him?" I asked.

"How long?" Loren asked, quizzically, almost peevishly, as if by asking this I had completely changed the subject of conversation. "I don't really know. A while." And then, softly, rather sadly, he added, "Things were ending with us anyhow."

My heart had somehow sneaked away from me and attached itself to Loren's; I don't know why it would do such a thing, but it sank as his did. I felt the kinship of ruined lives.

A bright red Saab pulled alongside the house. A dark-haired woman in a linen dress and sleeveless blouse got out of the car and waved up at Loren. If you had just arrived from Sri Lanka you would have still easily guessed she was a real estate agent.

"Yoohoo, Loren," she called. "I've got the Persigs to see the house."

"Bring them right in and sell them the fucking place, and then take your six percent and shove it up your twat," Loren said softly, all the time waving and smiling and making the OK sign with his fingers. A moment later, a couple in their twenties, somehow rich enough to buy the Nelson house, emerged from the Saab.

Joan stared at them with undisguised envy. "They're going to buy your house?"

"God willing."

"That's awful," she said. "It must feel terrible to have strangers looking over something so personal and full of family feeling."

"Yeah, well nothing that four and a half million dollars won't cure."

The real estate agent led the Persigs in, gesturing toward the Atlantic, the sky, the cedar plank walkways, the empty, vine-choked swimming pool. The Persigs nodded, poker-faced—they were already used to having dough, knew that it put them in charge over every transaction this side of a mugging.

"You know, Billy," Loren said, finishing his drink, "your mother was one of the most important people in the Village those days. I mean, people tell the story as if she was so lucky to win Luke, but the truth is, he was the lucky one."

"Important how?" I asked.

"Well, in order to answer that we'd have to go back. The fifties were over, thank God."

Loren's housekeeper, a stout, vigorous, middle-aged Hispanic woman in jeans and a San Diego Padres T-shirt, came in with fresh gin-and-tonics. She placed them down and went back into the house.

"Mercedes loves to see me smashed," said Loren, picking up the new glass. "It makes her day."

"I hope she'll like seeing me loaded, too," said Joan.

"Oh, she will, she will," said Loren. "Anyhow. Your mother." He sighed, leaned back in his chair, and closed his eyes. "Your mother was, above and beyond any other thing, a political person."

"Would you say she was a Communist?" I asked.

"She was a big Communist. Sandy Golden was a Communist, and half the people around the Folklore Village were Reds, too," said Loren. "Those people Esther worked for at *Lift Ev'ry Voice*, Pete Seeger, the Weavers, the whole lot of them. Woody Guthrie, of course. Do these names mean anything at all to you?"

"Of course they do."

"Not that you had to be a Communist to be a folk singer. I wasn't a Communist. I really liked the old English ballads—I liked Richard Dyer-Bennet, people like that. To me, folk music was about purity, and prettiness, and the old-fashioned life. To Esther, it was protest music, but we got along. Everyone in the Village folk scene got along, basically. There was always a party, always a new club opening. On weekends, the Village was mobbed. People came from all over. Squares who wanted to rub shoulders with the harmless beatniks, and kids who wanted to break out and be free. They had to close the streets in the summer. Cars couldn't even get through. It was astonishing. Folk music. It was a craze, a goddamned fad. Folk singing was huge back then, it was everywhere. There were folk music hits on the radio, for crying out loud. There was plenty of work for everybody. I knew early on that I wasn't very special, but I loved performing. I played the basket clubs."

"What are those?" I asked.

"Clubs where you wouldn't get paid, but they passed around a little wicker basket and people gave what they pleased. Usually you wouldn't make more than three or four bucks, but it was enough for a couple of beers for you and a girl."

Loren went silent. He drank his gin and then put it down and rubbed his eyes.

"I can still see the light in those places," Loren said. "And the coffee—oh man, the coffee! Thick as mud. And bitter?" He laughed. "As bitter as I sometimes feel."

"Esther still remembers you very fondly," I said, softly. I guess I was trying to cheer him up, for by now he was starting to slump in his chair. He had taken off his loafers; his feet were bare, sunburned; each bony toe had a tuft of hair on top of it.

"Really?" he said, hopefully.

"It's hard to get her to talk about these things. But a while ago, at Thanksgiving, your name came up."

"My name came up?"

"She was talking about you. Very fondly."

"You said that already, Billy," said Joan. I gave her a "later for you" look.

"I'd sort of like to know what she was saying," Loren said.

"That you had a beautiful voice."

"I had a serviceable voice. What else did she say?"

"I remember her saying she was crazy about you," I said, though I remembered no such thing. What was I doing? Pimping my mom to make the interview go smoothly?

"Crazy about me?" said Loren. He smiled, shook his head. I wondered when I would come to that time of life, when I would believe anything if it made me feel better. But then I realized I had always more or less been at that time of life.

"She was something," said Loren. "She was a trip."

"Do you think Loren would recognize her now?" Joan asked.

"Of course he would," I answered, making no attempt to disguise my annoyance. Joan was trying to imply that the years, as they say, had not been kind to Esther—when, in fact, she was still quite beautiful.

Loren was visibly disturbed by the sudden tension between Joan and me. Living alone, as he did, he no longer had any tolerance for discord. He drank the rest of his G&T and then quickly stood up.

"Let's take a walk on the beach and soak up some negative ions," he said.

We walked for miles, for the most part silently, letting the hypnotic seething of the ocean and the ever-changing light stand in for conversation. Joan picked up shells, carrying a handful in one hand and her shoes in the other. She seemed truly content. She scampered away from the tide, like a long and lovely child. As we got further and further away from Loren's house, a realignment of our walking order took place. In the beginning, we were walking three abreast; then it was Joan in front, followed by me and then Loren. But soon it was Loren and Joan, more or less side by side, with me falling increasingly in the rear. By the time the afternoon shadows began to lengthen and the tide had gone out, leaving a litter of broken scallop shells and the prehistoric husks of skate fish, they were walking a full ten paces in front of me. I deliberately slowed down, to see if they'd notice, or be embarrassed enough to wait for me to catch up. At one point, Joan even pulled Loren's shirt collar and dropped a couple of shells down his back; the sound of the ocean rolled over their laughter.

Back at the house, the housekeeper served us supper on the deck. The green canvas awning flapped mightily in the wind; down below, in the sand, several white paper napkins were entwined in the beach grass. You could picture them blowing off the deck and the "oh, well" look on Loren's face. We ate pork chops, which I don't normally give a second thought to, but somehow this time I wondered if the depths of my Jewishness might be being plumbed, if Loren, in his ever-mounting inebriation and the sense of recklessness and moral exhaustion it engendered, wasn't sticking the oar of his Waspiness into my genetic pool. It wasn't just the pork chops—which were, incidentally, delicious, and sparked a mini-orgy of pig meat that lasted six months—but a sudden flurry of Old Boy references, to his prep school (St. Andrew's), the funny thing that Fuddy Van Fart said at the New York Athletic Club, the shocking state of disrepair of his uncle's Newport cottage, that made me suspect that in Loren's desultory desperation he had settled into a kind of low-grade anti-Semitism.

Indeed, after dinner, as we drank brandy out of smudgy snifters, and the candles guttered in their pewter sticks, casting their last frantic flickerings on our faces, and the sound of the ocean out there in the darkness was like some strange mixture of Eternity and a pack of vicious dogs, Loren held forth on Luke.

"The thing I could never get over," he said, "was Luke didn't even like folk music. He cared as much about tradition, for God's sake, as he did about—oh, I don't know—Shaker furniture. Oh, he knew a great many songs, and, really, he sang them creditably. Considering. You know, his voice, and all. But he had no real . . . connection to the songs. Take me." Loren paused, smiled, and gestured for our indulgence. "I sang English ballads, Welsh mining songs. But my family, for God's sake, is English. You see what I mean?"

"Well, the Jews of St. Louis didn't write that many folk songs," I said.

"Exactly my point! He didn't necessarily have that tradition to draw on. It's no one's fault, obviously. The Clancy Brothers can sing Irish songs, but they're Irish. And Doc Watson can sing Appalachian music, but that's who he is. All I'm saying is, if you don't have a tradition, then don't pretend you do, and don't, whatever you do, just willy-nilly adopt someone else's tradition and tell the world it's your own. It's not very nice, and in the end no one's going to believe you. You'll be exposed as a goddamned liar."

He finished his brandy, poured some more. It was from California, Christian Brothers; I was sure he'd rather be drinking cognac.

"Then how did he make such a name for himself?" I asked. I leaned back in my chair. For a moment, I imagined slipping back, toppling over, landing on my back. I quickly came forward, rested my hands on the table. Loren poured some more brandy into Joan's snifter. "No one ever accused him of having a good voice. He didn't like folk music. He had no tradition. What put him over?"

"Who was the audience?" said Loren, pouncing on it. "That's what you have to ask yourself. The audience wasn't a jury of folk music purists from the Smithsonian. No. The audience didn't really like folk music, either. They thought they did, because folk music was a thing. But they didn't really like folk music any more than Luke did. And the audience was just a bunch of mutts, too—college kids, leftists, and a whole lot of bridge-and-tunnel traffic. They weren't people with traditions, or people who even cared that much about tradition. And you know what? They weren't particularly musical, either. What they were interested in, it turned out, was self-expression, of all things. And who would be a more fitting avatar for the Age of Self-Expression than our very own Luke?" Loren stopped himself, if only for a moment. He watched as I wrote down everything I could in the red spiral notebook I had brought along.

"You know, Billy," he said, "maybe not being raised by Luke Fairchild was the luckiest thing that ever happened to you."

I shrugged. It wasn't as if it had never occurred to me. Even as a young boy with a child's tender heart, even as I lay those long and nervous New York nights in my bed and literally prayed for him, prayed for him to find me, to claim me, to come down from the clouds like an angel out of Blake, even then it crossed and double-crossed my mind that I might be better off without him. My mother told me as much, gently; my grandparents told me, too, and not so gently, not so gently at all.

It was late, and Loren was too drunk to carry the conversation any further. He showed Joan and me to an unkempt and musty little guest room, with two metal-framed single beds on either side of it. "Not exactly the Carlyle," he said, retreating with a smile.

Joan and I lay in our beds, like ornery siblings, sick of each other. The light switch was under her control, on the wall next to her bed, and as soon as I started to make conversation she flicked the switch. I was certain it was me she wanted to turn off, as well as the bare light bulb overhead. The sheets were clammy and the white nubby cotton bedspread wasn't nearly warm enough for the suddenly chilly night. I really wanted to be next to Joan. I didn't even care about making love with her, I just wanted to spoon next to her, to feel her warmth, and maybe take a little comfort in the simple fact of her. These trips in search of Luke always left me feeling a little bruised, as if my soul, far heavier than I realized, had lunged at a shadow and fallen flat.

"Joan?" I whispered, but she was silent. I heard her breathing and then the ocean and then her breathing again. I closed my eyes, feeling abandoned and a little wild with insomniac longings. But soon I dropped off to sleep, and when I awoke— was accidentally awakened—the moon had traveled the sky to the point where it shone in the room's only window, leaving a reflection of window frame on the wall and part of the ceiling.

Loren had crept back into the room, dressed in his robe, holding a bottle of something. He was leaning over Joan's bed.

The ocean seemed to have disappeared. All I could hear was Loren's sodden breath.

"Joan?" he whispered, in a voice humbled, urgent, a little ashamed of itself.

I pretended to sleep, wondering what she would do.

She made a sleeper's noise and turned over. Loren crouched down, unstably, stuck the bottle down on the floor for extra balance, and, with his other hand, patted Joan's long, wavy brown hair.

I was no longer even blinking; my eyes were drier than the moon. But the instinct to do something finally overcame me and I propped myself up on one elbow and said, "What in the fuck are you doing?"

He scuttled out of the room like a land crab, closing the door so hard behind him that Joan awakened.

"What?" she said, sitting up. She touched her hair; she must have sensed on some helpless level what was going on. But before I could answer, she fell flat on her back and was asleep.

I lay there all night, my heart thumping with righteous indignation. How I regretted making up those nice things my mother said about Loren. And then, finally, to calm myself, I tried to blot out the Loren that had just been revealed with the Loren who first appeared—a cooperative, friendly, rather sad man, who had invited us out to help me learn more about Luke, and to allow himself a chance to relive what were, in all likelihood, the best days of his life. I managed to fall asleep and catch a couple hours of rest before the room was completely light.

When I awoke, Joan was getting into bed with me, hung over, miserable, and freezing cold. "Hold me," she said, her teeth chattering. I was glad to, but then I told her what had happened last night and we both realized that we needed to get out of there as soon as possible. We dressed, crept downstairs, and called a taxi to take us to the Long Island Railroad station. When we went to the refrigerator, we saw that Loren had written a note to us and stuck it under a magnetized little banana.

Dear Billy and Joan,

Sorry about any misunderstanding. And Billy, if you insist upon judging me, remember that thing we call "The Sixties," and the behavior implied, was started by your goddamned parents!

L.

I STOOD at her bedside while my mummified mother, bandaged, comatose, played her vast and silent game with Death, pushing him back with one breath, bringing him closer with the next. White light poured through the streaked window. The wheels of a gurney whinnied in the hall. I smelled her scorched flesh, the burned meat of her. My mother, my beautiful, kind, opinionated, resourceful, forgiving mother. The nurses who had bandaged her left an opening at the mouth so they could put a glass tube in.

It should have been me.

Nurses came in and out; they fussed with her bandages, checked if she was still unconscious, still breathing; I tried to get what they were seeing, what their assessment was. No one answered any of my questions; they had learned to simplify things by ignoring people like me. It is like a dream, in that way. I was here, but not here.

I sat in silence. I would have given her my blood. I would have given her my skin, if someone could figure a way to sew it onto her.

Every now and then I said "Mom?" or "I'm here, Mom," just in case.

4

AFTER the concert on Martha's Vineyard, I had a run of failures in my attempt to cross paths with Luke again. I even stepped back from the Quest, tried to devote myself to other pursuits, including making some sort of reasonable life for myself. And then, through no efforts of my own, I was presented with an opportunity to see him again.

This was just a year ago. I was on summer break from substitute teaching. Before the end of the semester, a principal at a school on West 100th Street had tried to encourage me to move on to teaching full-time. I could have my own class, a stable schedule, but the commitment was too much for me. It would be like having a real life, and I didn't want a real life until I got that nameless but essential thing I was looking for from Luke.

I was questioning, as well, my commitment to Joan Odiack. No matter how much time I put in with her, I could not get used to her emotional style, that dizzying shuffle of devotion, withdrawal, and explosion, a sucker's game in which her love was as mysteriously hidden as the red queen in a game of three-card monte. I can see now, I provoked her and, though I wanted her to be more constant, I offered her very little security. But even so, she was a terrifying person when she was angry. When I told her I had turned down a full-time teaching job, she seemed to take it symbolically, as if it proved I would always be tangential to everything—and if I hovered above my own life as if it were something not quite real, what did that make her? Soon after, Joan announced she was returning to Michigan for the summer, offering, at first, no explanation, and then, when pushed, screaming at me that she wasn't my property and that the day was over when a woman had to ask a man for permission to leave the house.

In a quick and not entirely wise countermove, I ended up spending the summer with another teacher, a reading specialist named Natalie Abernathy, a woman a few years my senior, with a pale, haunted face and a mountain of Pre-Raphaelite curls the color of Celestial Seasonings Red Zinger tea. Natalie's summer place was in the boring, bucolic little town of Ghent, New York, a little speed trap near the Massachusetts border. It was while staying with Natalie that I learned there was a rumor that Luke was in the area. According to reports, he was checked into a spa under an assumed name. Bernie Lefkowitz. He must have been tired of passing.

The *Ghent Gazette* reported that Luke had been spotted on a blanket on the great lawn at the Tanglewood Music Festival, listening to Stravinsky, all alone, with a bottle of mineral water balanced on his little pot belly. "Rumor has it that Mr. Fairchild is in our area for July, getting back into shape at the newly renovated 'New Age' spa, Wellspring, in Lenox, Mass."

"You should see him," said Natalie.

"I don't want to. And I promise you he doesn't want to see me."

"But he's your father."

"He won't take any blood tests."

"Billy," she said, taking my hand, gazing into my eyes in a way that, in the beginning of the summer, I had found sort of irresistible, but which was now starting to make me want to howl like a wolf. "Go see him. It's what you want." It was what she wanted, too, though not necessarily through any fault of her own. My courtship inevitably contained a number of references to my provenance, and it just so happened that Natalie had every record Luke had ever made. Natalie stood on the porch of her cabin as I pulled away in her Mustang. Her son stayed inside, probably glad to get rid of me, if memory serves, glad to have his mother to himself for the day. "Invite him back, if you want to," she called after. "It'd be wild to meet him."

I waved, trying to tell her with my expression that the last thing I needed in my life was knowing another person longing to meet Luke Fairchild.

It was only a half-hour ride to Lenox, and once in Lenox I had no trouble finding Wellspring; but getting into the spa itself was another matter. They were catering to media celebrities, and not only was the place surrounded by a fence, but there were only two gates in and out, and both of them were guarded by tight-T-shirted, curly-headed bruisers, who looked as if they might have done a little wet work for Israeli intelligence.

"I'm here to see Luke Fairchild," I said to the guard at the East Gate. (The guard at the West Gate had already waved me away, before I could say a word to him.)

I got out of my car, stood right next to the striped umbrella beneath which he lounged in a beach chair, eating cherries and reading a fitness magazine. He glanced up. His eyes were the green of sea foam and had that insane cast people get after a long time in the desert. He rose from his chair. He seemed exceptionally glad for the opportunity to explain a few of the Wellspring rules.

"You see, here in this community," he said, in a mad, overly patient voice, "we have no visitors, nothing from the outside world. That is why people come here. It is a place but not a place. You understand? A time where there is no time."

"I'm his son," I said. I wasn't sure if the guard even knew who Luke was. He had some kind of accent, or a blend of accents—Syrian-Spanish-English?

"It doesn't matter if you are his two sons. You understand me? I cannot even tell you if the person who you wish to see is here."

"But he is."

"Or he isn't." The guard grinned. He was in no hurry.

After a few more attempts to make him see things my way, I finally convinced the guard to accept a note from me and to give it or not give it to Luke if he was or was not there. "I bring greetings from my mother, Esther Rothschild," the note said. "Interested in taking a little time off and talking about the old days?" I said I would be waiting for him at Cafe Organique, a little health-food joint I noticed on my way through town.

I sat there for an hour, nursing a bowl of hand-harvested-Portuguese-lentil soup—the menu described the life and death of every item—and a salad of sliced tomatoes that had been hydroponically grown in pure spring water by a company called San Remo.

I couldn't resist the tomatoes, because the San Remo Company was the labor-intensive hobby of Luke's former wife, Annabelle Stevenson. Annabelle Stevenson was a quiet, earnest, I would say clinically depressed heiress. She was, and is, beautiful, with dark, minky hair and rich, creamy skin. After a ten-day courtship, she and Luke were married in Vera Cruz. She gave birth to twins, Felix and Tess, in the second of her three years with Luke. I had once seen a picture of Annabelle, Felix, and Tess Stevenson on the Sunday *Times Magazine* food page. The twins, fifteen at the time of the picture, eighteen now, held wicker baskets full of tomatoes and were posed on either side of Annabelle on the terrace of their apartment in the San Remo, on Central Park West. I clipped the picture and stared at it often, marveling at their sheer, unencumbered joy. I saw, or read, so much in their faces: beauty, health, wit, intelligence, optimism, confidence, and even compassion. At first, Luke had made no denials that the twins were his, but after the marriage ended he began dropping hints that they were the product of one of Annabelle's many affairs, and then he stopped mentioning them altogether. Yet even so, it was painfully clear to me that Felix and Tess were coping with the possibility of being Luke's children with far more ease than I was. Maybe the fact that he had once allowed that he was their father was all they needed. Maybe they were just better at life than I was. Or maybe, in their own way, they were as restless and miserable as could be. When I contacted them, introducing myself in a letter as their half-brother, my request for a meeting went unanswered—Annabelle's doing, I learned later.

Just then, I happened to look out the window and saw Luke. He had pulled up to the curb in an old Volvo. (He seemed to have the right car for every environment: Jeeps for Santa Fe, a BMW for Manhattan, a little red Porsche for L.A.) He had both hands on the wheel and he was staring in at me and when I finally looked at him he opened his eyes a little wider, as if to say: Well?

I dropped a few bucks on the table and hurried out to the street, before Luke could change his mind. I went around to the passenger side, wondering as I passed in front of him if Luke might suddenly gun the motor and be rid of me once and for all. The door was unlocked. I got in. I was shaking from head to foot.

He shifted the car into first gear and popped the clutch. It was a surviving midwesternism: let your transmission do the talking. He was wearing a Wellspring T-shirt, a pair of Levi's, snakeskin cowboy boots. The hair on his arms had turned blond from the sunlight. A nascent bald spot showed through the graying copper corkscrews on top of his head. I tried not to stare at him, tried to behave in a way that would suggest that what was happening here was a normal, everyday occurrence.

"Where we going?" I finally asked, after we had driven in silence through Lenox and were on a blacktop winding our way up the side of a lush mountainside of giant ferns and towering hemlock.

"So?" he said. "How's Esther?"

"Where are we going?"

"Is she married, or living with someone? You don't have a picture with you, do you?"

"I don't want to talk about her right now," I said.

"Yeah? Well, then, what do you want?"

I was silent. I didn't know where to begin. Over the years, the things I wanted from Luke had changed. I once wanted a father, a manly voice to say good night to me. I wanted someone to take me to Yankee Stadium, someone to carry me on his shoulders, tousle my hair, teach me to fish—what the fuck did I know? My mother's few boyfriends were always guarded around me, as if I were a spy Luke had left behind, a surveillance camera that would photograph their clumsiness, their second-rateness. They were all doomed to compare themselves to Luke—or, rather, to Luke's legend—and my presence made their lives impossible. They were taking as a lover the woman who had once lived with the man who had written a hundred songs celebrating his own sexual prowess and had even had a hit about the length of his penis ("Rescue Rope," recorded 1982).

Those who were drawn to my mother precisely because she had once lived with Luke Fairchild ultimately wilted from the terror of his legacy. And as for me: I was his representative here on earth. If Luke was God, then I was his first, and for quite a while his only, Son. Even if my claim to be Luke's son was, to say the least, controversial, even if many Lukologists routinely discounted my claims—working out some ridiculous rigma-role having to do with the time his relationship with my mother ended and when I was born (as if there were no such thing as an attempt at reconciliation, or a little roll in the hay for old times' sake), or citing medical reports of Luke's sperm's moribund state, its low motility, and Luke's song "Firing Blanks"—I knew it to be true, and so, of course, did my mother, and anyone who was drawn into the orbit of our family life in those sunny rooms on Sullivan Street could either choose to believe it or to leave.

But did I still, after all these years, want Luke to be my father, to hold me in his arms, to somehow raise me? I don't think so. I was too large to hold. I was already raised. All I wanted was for him to say he was my father. And after that, I thought, I would be happy to never see him or speak his name again.

"No answer?" said Luke, his voice a little cruel. We had made our way up to the top of a sizable mountain. Well below us, through a break in the trees, was a farm, with its doll-sized house, patchwork fields, and cows the size of flies. Luke turned the car off to the road's narrow shoulder, right next to a sign signaling yet another dangerous curve, and he turned to me, his icy blue eyes flashing like diamonds. "You've been following me, calling me, writing me, talking about me to people, you've been using my name like it was public property, and now when I ask you what you want—you've got nothing to say?"

"I didn't say I had nothing to say."

"I ought to just kick the shit out of you," Luke said.

"I wouldn't try. I'm bigger than you and I'm stronger."

"Woo. I'm scared." Luke made a burlesque out of pretending to be afraid, but I could tell he wouldn't be bringing up that business about fighting me again.

"You're a constant in my life, you know that?" said Luke. "You're a fucking lodestar."

"I could say the same about you, Luke."

"All the folk music people are gone. I got a wife who got remarried and now I can't remember her name. The Lower East Side is full of lawyers eating Spanish tangerines; the West Village—man, I wouldn't be caught dead there. They got a McDonald's in Kyoto, you gotta stand in line behind the Buddhist monks to get your McFuck Me and fries. Communism's collapsed, the Soviet Union is a fucking yard sale. Everything has turned into what it promised it would never be. The Beatles are gone, the Stones are a joke, even they know it. All that remains the same is you, coming around, telling the same old story. And you know what? It ain't true. This thing that goes round and around your head? It's a story, man. Maybe your mama told you, maybe you made it up by yourself. But it just ain't true. Never was, never will be."

Luke got out of the car. I didn't know what to do. He was my father and I didn't know if he wanted me to follow him out of the car or to sit here and wait, and this not knowing, and the vast emotional ignorance to which it was connected, pressed down upon me, hard. Luke walked to the edge of the hill—a few more steps and he'd have been tumbling head over heels through underbrush and granite. He stood there with his hands behind his back, swaying, looking down at that farm below.

After a while, he realized I wasn't with him and he turned and gestured for me.

His eyes looked lonely. I had never seen anything so lonely in my life.

I got out. The high thin air held the sunlight and heat, but tentatively; the moment the sun went down it would be cold here. A shadow passed before me. I looked up and saw a couple of hawks circling. My legs felt unstable; I was still so nervous, being with him. I didn't know what I felt. I had an impulse to put my arms around him, but it didn't seem quite real; it seemed maybe something I just wanted to do, to accomplish it.

"I came here a couple days ago," Luke was saying, as if I'd been standing next to him for some time. "Can't stand to be around people, some of the time. I came here to breathe a little mountain air, but down in the spa, the air's all used up."

"I thought you came here to lose weight and deal with your dependence on painkillers."

"Don't believe everything you read, Billy."

He called me by my name. I felt a trickle of sweat roll down my spine.

"See that farm down there?" He pointed. His finger wore a silver ring with a black stone etched in a Chinese character. "I've been dreaming about that farm. I did that benefit concert to get the farmers some money a few years back—"

"I know."

"And this picture of a farm got into my head. And it's that farm, right down there. It's weird. I dreamed about this farm in Switzerland, man, in Singapore. Everywhere I've been going, this farm has been going with me. And now here it is." He looked at me and smiled. I felt the heat of that smile, understood how people had come to love him so abjectly, how cast off they felt when the smile turned off. "I'll bet you the skin off a cat I'll stop dreaming about it now."

He put his arm around my shoulder. My heart slowed, stopped, like an animal that senses danger. The toes of my shoes were an inch from the edge; all it would take was one shove and I'd go over. Who knew I was here? Natalie? How long would it take her to call in my disappearance? I felt the wind at my back. What capacity for killing lurked in Luke's weather-beaten, drug-infested heart? Did he think I might drag him into court, steal his fortune, besmirch him in some way? Was he even capable of thinking at all? For the past thirty years, there were always people around him ready to clean up the mess—cover-ups, payoffs, friendly persuasion.

They say I've murdered many men
And wore their scalps upon my belt
Okay, you got me, I've done that—and worse
And no regrets have I felt
Because after I lost my lover
After I lost my one true love
Oh Mama
I didn't care Who I hurt . . .

—"Howsoever You Shall See Me,"
recorded 1984

I moved away from him, or tried to, but his grip tightened.

"This country used to be just one farm after another. We lived with the seasons, the soil. A man loved his country then; it meant something. It was the source of his food, his livelihood. You defended your country because your country was where you worked, right deep in its soil. American dirt, man. You know what I mean?"

It was the name of his latest album. It seemed sort of cheesy for him to work it in like that.

"Billy?"

"Yeah." My fear was reaching a pitch; I could feel its engines roaring inside me. My legs wanted to tremble.

"I'm not your father. I know you think I am. I know you're just aching for it to be true. But wanting something that isn't real, something that can never happen . . . it just twists you around, man. And you know what, Billy? You ain't the only one. Everyone wants something. My money. My mind. An ex-wife of mine has twins. I put them straight, just told them the truth, I'm not their father, and the matter was fucking dropped. Why can't you do the same?"

"Then how do you explain—"

"Man, I never explained nothing in all my life. Okay? Do you have work?"

"Do I have a job? Yeah, of course."

"What do you do?"

"I teach." I tried to step back from the ledge, but he wouldn't let me.

"What do you teach, Billy?"

"School. Little kids. I teach in New York, in the public schools, uptown."

"That's good. I always wished I could get to be a part of something like that."

"Teaching school for a year and making a tenth of what you make in one concert? Yeah. I see where that could be tempting."

"You're doing something. A teacher. Or a doctor. Save somebody's life. That would be something."

"Then do it. Get a job as a teacher."

He smiled and said, "It ain't that easy."

"Well, you've done pretty well, despite your having been deprived of the pleasure of trying to teach a classroom filled with heavily armed, hyperactive ten-year-olds."

"What do I have to show? I wrote some songs."

"Which the whole world loved."

"But didn't understand."

"They loved you, too. They still do."

"You think they'd love my dental floss when I pull it out from between my teeth?"

"Yeah. They'd love your floss. Your floss would go for serious money."

He laughed. He seemed relieved to hear it, and I realized that somehow the conversation had turned and I had been put into the position of reassuring him.

"I'm getting old—I'm rotting inside and out, like a truck left on the side of the road."

"I didn't come here to feel sorry for you, Luke. Think of what you did to my mother."

"I loved your mother, Billy."

"Think of how you denied me."

"You were asking me for something I did not have. You were asking me to be your father."

"You were my father. You are."

"Do you know how many people there are out there, man, how many who say I'm their father—in every sense of the word?"

"I don't care about them."

"What do you want from me, Billy?" Luke asked, squeezing the back of my neck and half-whispering the words right into my ear.

I wriggled free of him and stepped back. I fixed him with my stare.

"I want one thing, and one thing only. Dad. I just want you to say you're my father. I don't want your money. I don't want anything else. I want you to believe me."

Did he roll his eyes? You bet he did. Did he heave an exasperated sigh, did he shake his head, more in sorrow than in anger? Absolutely. Did he suggest that I spend some time in a first-rate psychiatric facility? Yes, I believe there was some mention of that. But the point is, he did not throw me off the mountain, nor did he leave me there as he Volvoed back to Wellspring. He invited me to come back there with him.

We drove through Lenox, past Cafe Organique, past Natalie's Mustang—I didn't want to break the spell by suggesting he drop me off there and let me follow behind. We drove straight through the gate to Wellspring. The guard made a little mock salute as Luke sped past. We went to his cabin—vaulted ceiling, cedar paneling, a single bed, several bottles of water, magazines and CDs spread over everything, an acoustic guitar standing in the corner, clothes in a pile, a Walkman, a Watchman, a small reddish barbell, a green glass vase stuffed with flowers, a soccer ball, binoculars, two tennis racquets.

"Do you play?" he asked me, gesturing at the racquets.

I shrugged, afraid he'd send me home if I said I didn't play.

Luke grabbed a shirt off the floor and as he snatched it up a syringe fell out. It clattered onto the bare pine planks and we both stood there and watched as it spun around once and then shuddered to a stop.

"I thought you took the cure," I said. I felt terrified for him, as a son would for a father, and I felt something base as well, felt that I had caught him in a lie, a piece of hypocrisy.

"Long ago," he said, picking up the syringe and tossing it onto a pile of clothes. "I'm taking vitamin B-12."

"Yeah, right."

"Every other vitamin is worthless, and some do you serious damage. Vitamin B-12. You can't take it in a pill. Just don't work that way. You should try it," he said. "You look like shit."

Luke changed into his tennis clothes: dark blue shorts, brand-new tennis shoes—crossed bands of orange and turquoise, buttons and pumps at the fore and aft, the soles like waffle irons. His legs were slim, muscular, and tan—how many men at fifty have time to tan their legs?—and covered with a soft, smooth coat of mahogany fur. He put on wristbands, a headband, an elastic ankle support.

And then he brought me onto the clay courts, where he grunted and cursed and tried to win every point. I felt ridiculous in my long pants and street shoes. But I gave it the best I had, hitting the ball hard, when I could get to it, and hoping it would stay in bounds. My scoring so much as one point a game made him miserable. I had somehow contrived to believe that the great Luke Fairchild would see the absurdity of competitive sports—I, myself, was completely without interest in or hope of winning—and would somehow play cheerfully, amusingly, making shots behind his back, between his legs, blooping the ball, saying "Whooops!," laughing. Especially since he was playing with me—a pale, black-clad urbanite, who had been on a tennis court perhaps ten times in my entire life. But his ground strokes were wicked, his volleys thunderous, and he served to me with such velocity that most of the time I watched the ball whiz past me without even having time to move my racquet. Whatever became of "I've got nails on my bat, skin on my spikes, blood on my laces / No run, no hits, no errors, nobody left on bases," which many took to mean that our national obsession with sports was connected to some collective thirst for violence? (There were other interpretations of "Ballad of the Three Faced Woman"; see especially Gardner Leopold in the spring 1982 issue of *Fairchild Quarterly*.)

I felt like quitting. There was little fun in chasing after his shots, and the obvious glee he took in slamming the ball past me only made it more maddening, more humiliating. I was beginning to glow with resentment; yet the irritations of the lopsided match were mediated by the pleasure of his company, and the sense of flattery and relief that he was finally spending a little time with me.

Was this, finally, the experience of having a father, being a son? I could not keep my eyes off him. I looked at the dark mahogany fur on his navel when his reaching for an overhand smash tugged up his T-shirt. I looked at his large, slightly rabbity teeth when he made little slice shots near the net and bit his lip, striking a pose of cunning and concentration. He was my genetic scout; he was my predecessor, my author. He was my father. In a world of fatherless children I had been, perhaps, luckier than some. I could at least read about him. I could learn the minutiae. I had read interviews with his grade school teachers. I knew when he had measles, the mumps. I knew what he liked to read, or at least claimed to have read. (I believe there was a real difference between the two; Luke was insecure about his pedigree as a poet and claimed a level of erudition far in excess of what he had really attained.) There were journalists who clawed through his garbage so I could learn about what he was eating, what cold and sinus medications he used, and that he preferred the suppositories he brought back from Paris. Yet for all the information I had about him, I did not know him.

The sky darkened and the lights around the court came automatically on. He continued to slam his shots past me. I had never read about this mean-spirited, win-at-any-cost, shooting-fish-in-the-barrel side of Luke. He had never written about it in any of his songs. On the contrary, his persona in his lyrics was either hapless, hoboesque, as in "I'll be sleeping beneath the stars / Where the windows have no bars / And my alarm clock is a dog that licks my face," or so cool that not only would he not worry about winning or losing, but concepts such as hot versus cold, legal versus illegal, up versus down, or sane versus insane would fail to engage him, as in "It's time to split 'cause life's getting dull / Forgot to steal a hat so I guess I'll tip my skull." No, what he was showing me now was a Luke Fairchild he had not preened and perfected, uncadenced, unrhymed, and really quite unattractive.

Yet despite my hunger for him and all the emotional greed I had brought to this moment, I had my limits. I just could not chase that fucking ball around the court another minute. I could not swing my racquet at that fuzzy little round thing and have it hit the frame and dribble off to the side or else bounce high off the strings and go sailing not only over the net but over the fence. And I could certainly not bear Luke's frequent taunting remarks ("Oh-oh, it's Uncle Squiggly").

I dropped my racquet and said, "I have to stop."

Luke rushed the net, a look of concern on his face, as if he truly liked me, as if his welfare tottered on the pinnacle of my own. This legendary tenderness of his had an equally legendary unexpectedness. It was the antithesis of a lash of temper—he had dizzying, overpowering bursts of compassion.

"I'm fine," I said. "I just don't want to play."

"God, the way you dropped your racquet. I thought . . . I don't know."

"I'm fine. I don't really play tennis."

"Well, you should, man. Tennis is the answer. It's got the symmetry of a Grecian urn, and the strategy of grand master chess, and the warrior heart of karate, and the mindless mind of Zen, it really does. It's better than praying. It's sure a whole lot better than drugs. Believe it or not, it's better than money and better than women, because women don't know how to love us anyhow, any more than we know how to love them. Tennis. You ought to get into it. It's what keeps me going. It's all there is."

"I don't have your enthusiasm," I said. "You get totally into things and then you end up disappointed and just drop them anyhow."

"Yeah. That's what they say about me."

"Isn't it true? Isn't that why you left my mother? Isn't that why I had to grow up without a father?"

"You really ought to get more exercise, Billy."

"I'm too young to exercise. Living exercises me."

"Yeah. That's what I used to think." He slapped his gut. The press had made a big deal about how portly he'd become, but, really, he looked to be only five pounds over his normal weight. "But it's a matter of building habits to last a lifetime."

"You're kidding me, right?"

"No. I'm not."

"What are you, on the President's Council on Physical Fitness?"

"What'd you come for, Billy? Poetry? Sur-fucking-realism? I'm at the end of people expecting things from me. What do you want? Entertainment? The Truth? A guide to the cosmos? You haven't even bought a ticket, man. And anyhow, I've been picked clean."

He pointed to the racquet and I picked it up and handed it to him. In my own way, I was packing in a lot of father-son material, but it was, unfortunately, of the father–ten-year-old-son variety. He checked the racquet's frame to see if I'd nicked it in my pique, satisfied himself that I'd done no damage, and then turned quickly on his high-tech heel and walked off the court.

Was I supposed to follow him, chase after? I had no idea.

"Don't you even want to know about my mother?" I shouted at him, as he let himself out of the little redwood gate and faded into the darkness that surrounded the floodlit brightness of the salmon-colored clay courts. I could hear his footsteps crunching on the path, getting softer and softer.

5

I STARED at my mother's closed eyes, willing them to open, until visiting hours were over. With a nurse overseeing my departure, I rose slowly from the chair and gestured toward my mother. "I'll be back in the morning," I whispered.

I drove back to her house, through the moonless, inky night, down her steep driveway, inciting riots of gravel, and toward the house that now looked so eerie, so empty and alone. I'd left the door wide open when I raced out that morning. I was afraid to go in for a moment, and when I did, I frantically switched on lamps. As soon as the house was blazing with light, I collapsed on the sofa and fell asleep remembering something Esther once said, when I was in college. She was reading Simone Weil, whose work and life moved her so deeply. She quoted something Weil wrote: "The present is something that blinds us. We create the future in our imagination. Only the past is pure reality." I didn't remember what point Esther was making, but the words kept repeating in my mind.

There is a magazine published by a nerd named Pete W. Pfeifer, out of Roanoke, Virginia. The magazine is called *LF* and it devotes itself entirely to articles about Luke—analyses of his lyrics, discoveries of unreleased tapes, biographical reconsiderations, and fanzine gossip about what Luke is up to now, including any and all concert appearances. *LF* has a 900 line where, for $2.99 per minute, you can find out where Luke is (or is rumored to be) on any given day. I reached for the phone, and, knowing the number by heart, I figured I'd splurge the five or so dollars—Pfeifer always dragged out his message with a lot of money-wasting marginalia—and find out where the old Wandering Jew was while the woman who was supposedly the great love of his life hovered over a pit of nothingness.

"Luke is staying in his Malibu mansion," said the seemingly sultry woman Pfeifer had hired to read his piffle in her moronic phone-sex voice, as if we were all supposed to jerk off to Luke's whereabouts. (Pfeifer always had a woman reading the daily announcements, and word on the Luke circuit was that he had slept with each of them. It made me shudder to think of that goggle-eyed, greasy-haired little parasite using his microscopic connection to Luke to drum up a little sexual action for himself.) "Some time soon he will be heading back to the recording studio—call back tomorrow for a confirmation on that, and for the location of the studio. Oh, and last night, a delivery truck from California Dreamin', a local organic produce outlet, was seen pulling up to Luke's house, and so we can say with certainty that Luke's vegetarian regime is still in force. . . . Mmm. Yummy veggies to make his blue eyes shine."

So he was in Malibu. Just so happened I had the number, memorized. (The hole in my life left by his refusal of me was plugged up by a rat's nest of facts and figures.) Luke was staying at the seven-million-dollar beachfront glass-and-redwood modernist monstrosity bequeathed to him by Tim Bowman, former president of Manor Records—Bowman, dead of AIDS at forty-four, released all of Luke's Middle Period records, and

Luke's jumping ship for a lucrative deal at another label apparently left Bowman's ardor for him undiminished. Luke rarely used the Malibu house. He didn't enjoy the ocean, and he was too reclusive for walks along the beach. The specter of natural disasters—earthquakes, mud slides, wildfires—spooked him. He worried about his own death, but usually in the context of some greater apocalypse. It would, in his mind, take more than a burst blood vessel or a cancerous lung to kill Luke Fairchild—death must come with the ocean in flames, the ground split open like an overripe melon.

I sat on the sofa in my mother's living room and dialed the 310 area code, and then, for a moment, dialed no further. Did I really want to call him? Did I want him at Esther's bedside? Would she want him there? And if he didn't appear, did I want to feel the grinding fury? Oh well, fuck it. (It's what I always said when approaching him; it was my "Geronimo!") I dialed the number and a machine picked up on the first ring. The outgoing message was recited by a computer's voice. Not very outgoing. For a moment, I wasn't certain I'd dialed the right number.

"Luke," I said, "Esther's been in a serious car accident. She's in the Leyden Hospital and I'm at her house." I recited the numbers. "Call when you get a chance."

What did it feel like to be so profoundly sought after? How did it affect the flow of blood from heart to hypothalamus to know that at any given moment there were at least ten thousand people listening to your songs, wishing you would ectoplasmatically float from their stereo speakers and take form in their living room? Luke's entire concept of time must have been far from the mundane tick and tock of us mere mortals: time for him was something to protect from the nearly psychotic hunger of others; time was something he bestowed upon you in discrete little packages, if he so desired; time was money, but huge amounts of it—a second was a thousand dollars, a minute was a Rolls-Royce, an hour was a new liver and a little angioplasty thrown in, an afternoon was a ransom, a week was the national debt. Okay, maybe that was an exaggeration. But it didn't matter, since the precise truth was an exaggeration, too.

Luke tempted them to believe he was an oracle, that he could see around the corner just up ahead; he all but insisted he could do it. But then, when he got what he wanted, all that adulation turned so quickly and uncontrollably to hysteria, and if the pressure of all that he promised and all that he appeared to be could have that effect on ten or twenty million people, just think what the reflection of that adoration beamed back to its source could do to just one. I used to think what it must have been like to get twenty phone calls in an hour, how the rush of popularity would turn to harassment, and besides that there were people knocking on the front door, the back door, they were jimmying open the windows and trying to climb in, telegrams were arriving, FedEx packages of soft shell crabs that had to be cooked within the next five minutes or they would explode into a stench that would kill the Japanese elms for which the gardeners were at that very moment digging holes with their screeching groaning backhoes, and then your mother dies, and your dog bites the neighbor's adopted Costa Rican two-year-old on the lip, and you just won the Publishers Clearing House grand prize, and the IRS guy who looks like Elvis Costello is on the sofa to discuss your audit, and then multiply the feeling of all that by fifty, pump it up with helium, pump your own sorry head up with helium too while you're at it—and then you can approximate what it felt like to live one minute of my father's life.

There. Said and said and said. My father was too busy for me. And he would probably be too busy to see my mother.

I wished I had never made the call.

. . .

THE NEXT morning, on my way to my mother's room, a nurse intercepted me in the hall and silently beckoned me to follow her into an empty nurses' station. She spoke in a low, conspiratorial voice, with startling fervor.

"You're her son, aren't you?"

"Yes. What's going on? Is she okay?"

She gestured, as if to say, Who knows? I looked down the hall toward Esther's room.

"Has anything changed?" I said. "Please. Tell me."

"What have the doctors told you? Have they told you anything?"

"Not really. That it's too soon to know."

"Did they tell you that when a great deal of bone matter has been crushed that there is a danger of some of the marrow getting into the bloodstream? Did they tell you that this marrow can cause a life-threatening embolism? Did they tell you that?" She sneaked a nervous glance over her shoulder; she knew she was out of order. Then she heard footsteps and she hurried away, leaving me shaking, with my heart slamming against my chest like a handball against the wall.

I made my way toward Esther's room. As I was about to go in, two doctors were coming out. The senior doctor (Carey) was in his forties, tall, long-haired, daytime-TV handsome; the other doctor (Jawal) was younger, Indian, with bad skin, mournful eyes, and orthopedic shoes. (He reminded me of the cardiologist at St. Vincent's Hospital, where my mother took me when I was twelve and had passed out cold in my seventh-grade history class.) The doctors were unhappy to see me; they were on rounds and didn't want to take time to answer any questions. This taboo against asking questions has its effect, even if you try to ignore it. It keeps the questions short and makes you so nervous you forget to ask half of what you meant to.

Nevertheless, I introduced myself and asked how my mother was doing.

"Stable," said Dr. Carey.

"Has she regained consciousness? When is she being transferred to another hospital? There was talk about a medevac."

"Oh no, not today," said Dr. Jawal. He glanced at his clipboard.

"She's been in a coma for almost twenty-four hours," I said.

"That's not unusual," Carey said. "Her vital signs remain strong. . . . Umm. I was wondering. Is this the Esther Rothschild I think it is?"

"Yes, actually."

He smiled, shook his head. "I was a total Fairchild freak," he said. "And you know that album, I guess it was his third, with that picture of Fairchild and—that's your mother, right?"

"Yes."

"Fairchild and your mother walking down Bleecker Street, with their arms around each other. Man, that picture was everything I wanted my life to be. Anyhow, my kids are listening to that record now."

I felt myself capable of simply saying: I'm Luke Fairchild's son. That picture was taken six months before I was conceived. In this case, my aim was not to present myself in a more interesting light, but to focus this doctor's attentions more vividly upon my mother.

"She and Luke," I said, with a shrug. "She was the love of his life."

"I know—he wrote those beautiful songs."

"Seventeen songs. More songs about my mother than about the atom bomb."

"Does she ever see him?"

"Oh yeah. All the time. I'm sure he'd be very grateful—to you, I mean. Saving her life. Just, you know, doing the right thing by her."

Dr. Jawal frowned at me, perhaps knowing I was not telling the truth, or resenting the weird little bribe, but Carey seemed delighted.

"Can I ask you something?" he said. "Is he like his songs?"

"Which ones?"

"Yeah, right. I guess I mean, you know, hip, cynical, angry. Fairchildesque."

"Oh yes, he's all those things." I smiled. Was this doing any good?

"Did you ever listen to Luke Fairchild?" Carey asked Jawal.

"I'm from Madras, not Mars," the young doctor said.

Together, they started to move away.

"Is she going to be all right?" I asked, quickly.

"She's getting good care," said Jawal.

"A nurse was telling me about marrow in the blood. Is that something to worry about?"

The greenish light went on over the door in the next room. Somebody else wanted something.

"It's wait and see," Carey said, moving away. He caught my expression. "But that's not as bad as it seems. Time is on our side. And, Billy, the nurses here have got their panties all twisted up over some union matter. They're a great bunch of gals, but you shouldn't listen to what they say about medicine."

When I entered my mother's room, I found she wasn't alone. Sitting in a chair at her bedside was a woman with abundant graying convulsions of hair, wearing a black and red shawl, and smelling of incense. She turned as I came in. Her violet eyes swam behind granny glasses. With her pointy chin, small but heavily lipsticked mouth, and long nose, she looked like one of those madwomen who inevitably come up to you on the street to sell you a rose ten minutes after you've broken up with your girlfriend.

"Billy?" She reached her hand toward me; her fingers were plump, each one wore a ring. "I'm Maya Trotman?" Her voice went up, turning each sentence into a glissando of interrogation, the way some teenage girls speak, full of humility and uncertainty and a nervousness about being taken too seriously. She waited to see if the name registered. "Your mother's friend?"

We shook hands. Maya's grip was slight, her hand little more than a cool shadow in mine.

My mother was in her bed, breathing steadily. A machine irrigated her. Every piece of equipment in this hospital seemed a few years out of date—clunky, discarded, bargain-basement life-saving technology. I wondered how many people had already died in that very bed.

"How did you know my mother was here?"

She blinked at the bluntness of the question.

"I heard it on the radio?" she said. She breathed in through her delicate nose, the nostrils closed like the petals of a touch-me-not.

"Oh no," I said.

"It was just a mention? If you're worried about publicity—"

"I am worried about that."

"Oh, please don't. It was just a mention at the end of the news? On a really small station?" She was full of solicitude toward me. "I know—" she stretched the word out, discovered rivers of complicity in the globe of the vowel—"how much you'd hate to see reporters and all finding out about her, and turning this into a media event? But what about Luke? Are you going to call him?"

"It doesn't matter. He wouldn't respond."

Maya shrugged. "I haven't told anyone about your mother being here or her relationship with Fairchild. Your mother's feelings about Luke were something she shared with me, and I have respected her privacy?" She got a chair from the other side of the room and placed it near hers, and now she gestured: Sit, sit. "Esther and I met at the Catskills Women's Center? I was there for a Molds and Yeast Workshop and Esther was learning karate." A smile. This was a well-worn irony, smooth and pleasing as beach glass. "We've only been friends for a few months, but she's a hell of a lady. I guess I don't have to tell you that."

"My mother was taking karate?"

"Her goal was to get a black belt by Christmas?" Maya looked over at my mother, silenced, wrapped, hovering, and then she looked back at me, teary. "I guess she'll be getting that belt a little later than we hoped." She patted the side of the bed. "Won't you, Esther? Won't you." Suddenly, she took my hand. "Your mother talked about you all the time? She was so proud of you, your teaching, your travels. And you were always so good about calling her, and coming to see her? She appreciated that, Billy, she really did."

"Thank you."

She glanced toward the door and then lowered her voice. "What do the doctors say?"

I shrugged and felt, suddenly, as if I might cry. Give in to it? I tried to cover my sorrow with words, but my mouth had its own agenda. It didn't want to answer questions. The corners turned down, the lips trembled. I turned away from Maya, but she kept hold of my hand, squeezing it, trying to comfort me. In fact, she was comforting me.

"The doctors are noncommittal," I said, but judging from the look on Maya's face, my words were barely intelligible.

Just then, someone new came into my mother's room. It was a woman, about my age, tall, thin, a little awkward, with buzz-cut hair, four or five earrings, baggy green shorts, black tights, and dirty yellow construction boots.

"Mom," she said, "Tobias called and said if you're not in the office in an hour you're fired." She seemed used to breaking things to Maya.

"Well, I must thank him for his compassion," Maya said, standing up. She rested her hand on my shoulder. "Billy, this is my daughter, Rosa? Rosa, this is Billy Rothschild."

"Hi." She shook my hand. Her skin was exceptionally smooth and cool, like soapstone. She smiled. I had an irrational thought: Why doesn't Joan smile like that? Joan! I hadn't yet called her. And she hadn't called me.

"I'm sorry about your mother," Rosa said to me.

"Thank you."

"What's the latest word?"

I shook my head. She let it go at that.

"Come on, Mom," said Rosa. "I'll take you to work."

"I was born and raised on Avenue A," Maya said to me. "I don't drive?"

"I could teach you," Rosa said, clearly for the fifty thousandth time.

"Your mother was a truly excellent driver," Maya said. "I can't imagine what happened. She was one of the best drivers in the Hudson Valley." She rose up on her toes and gave me a kiss on the cheek. "Just think positive thoughts? I know everything's going to be all right?"

As they left, Rosa looked back at me. "See you," she said.

See you. I thought of Rosa, her earrings, her boots, her life. What would it be like to know her?

And then I was alone, and my solitude was immense, ferocious, and familiar. "Hi, Mom," I whispered. I covered my eyes with my hands and just sat there. There was no one in the world to whom I could turn.

A nurse came into the room, a red-haired woman with a small, scrubbed face, stout legs. She checked the readings of the machines that monitored Esther's vital signs. She was accompanied by another nurse, an angular, older woman with thinning hair and wire-rimmed glasses.

"How does it look?" I asked.

"Steady," she said. "It's fine."

"Are they going to move her soon?"

"I don't know. You'll have to ask her doctor that."

"I don't really know who her doctor is. People just come and go."

The older nurse looked at her clipboard. "Dr. Heilborn."

"Oh yeah. Him." I made a sour, skeptical face. I just assumed the nurses disliked the doctors, just as we teachers disliked the school administrators, the people who had the right to give us a hard time while we did all the real work.

"Dr. Heilborn is an excellent doctor," the older nurse said, narrowing her eyes.

"Fine. If you see him, let him know I'd like to talk to him. I have no idea what's going on."

I turned back to my mother and said, "She's gone now, Mom."

Oh please answer me.

A WHILE later, I went to the lobby and used the phones near the gift shop. I could no longer put off calling my grandfather. Since my grandmother's death, Grandpa had been living at the Shoreview Home in Little Neck, New York, in a congested, kind of tough part of Long Island. He was unhappy there, but there was nothing to be done with him. He refused to move in with my mother and he couldn't very well sleep on the sofa in my apartment. Besides, he was deemed to be in need of constant attention (forgetting, falling) and a special diet. He often wished he was dead. Nearly all his old left-wing buddies were already gone. The books of philosophy, history, and literature he had so vigorously cross-referenced in his table talk had by now faded from memory. His mind was a burned library—the spines and their titles still facing out from the shelves but the pages within turned to ash. He hadn't been able to work as a general practitioner in ten years. He was bored senseless. His skin crawled. His bowels were petrified wood.

The switchboard at the home transferred me to the fifth floor—last time I called, just a week ago, Grandpa was on the third floor, and I couldn't help feeling this change was not a good sign. A Jamaican woman answered after several rings. I told her I needed to speak to Irv Rothschild. She said he wasn't feeling very well and she'd rather not bring him to the phone.

"What's wrong with him?"

"Just having one of those days."

"Well, I need to talk to him. His daughter's in the hospital. This is his grandson."

There was a long pause while she thought it over. Wasn't there a procedure for this? Why was everything run so shoddily, as if people were just making up things to do as they went along? The hospital, the nursing home. It wasn't as if these stages of life were unpredictable, something that happened out of the blue and then called for improvisation and emergency measures. Being ill, getting hurt, growing old—this is what happened to everyone. Why did rent-a-car offices run more smoothly than nursing homes? Why did banks seem cleaner and more filled with solicitude than hospitals? "I'll see if he can come to the phone," the woman said at last.

My grandfather Irv sometimes made the case that everything tragically wrong with this last part of the American twentieth century (and perhaps, by extension, the entire world) could be blamed on Luke. People who knew us, and who were privy to the secret history of our family, tended to assume that

Irv's ferocious analysis of Luke's historical importance was just a father's mock-Hegelian defense of a deserted daughter—a lot of fathers have complicated opinions about the guys who get their daughters pregnant and then disappear. But in Irv's case, the wrongdoing was intensified by the fact that not only did Luke leave Esther, but their breakup was public and protracted, and there were songs about it, songs that millions of people knew, titles that countless strangers would request in concerts: sing "Forgetting You Is Easy"! Sing "Everyone Makes a Mistake"! Sing "Fourth Avenue Fugue"! These songs made millions of dollars and helped to finance Luke's voyage through a world of willing women. And then add this to the stew: not only did Luke leave Esther, not only did he put their intimacy on the hit parade, but he left her pregnant, he left her with a son, a son who he would never admit was his, and whom he did next to nothing to support.

Irv was a Communist. He and Grandma were a part of that Red subculture of old New York, and they'd had a pretty fine time of it through the thirties and forties. They were convinced they were on the winning side. They were surfing on a gigantic historical wave. Their meeting halls were filled; every day was an adventure—a socialist America seemed a real possibility, believe it or not. During the war, there was the heady rush of having their own country in alliance with the Soviet Union; you could almost imagine that you were living in Moscow, the fates of our countries seemed so entwined.

But after the war, after Hiroshima, the Cold War began, and soon after that anything that smelled Soviet was considered deadly poison. American Reds were being slammed into jail. They were getting kicked out of the colleges, kicked out of Hollywood, run out of the unions they had helped to build. "They call it the McCarthy era," Grandpa often said, "but that's just to get everyone else off the hook. You think one drunken crybaby senator from Wisconsin can do that much harm? Everyone was in on it—Meany, John L. Lewis, Nixon, Eisenhower, General Electric, you name it."

The Reds had to run for cover, and one of the odd places they ended up was the folk music scene. It gave them a chance to stay political—those songs about cold-hearted mine owners could be taken as odes to expropriation and the songs about the American Civil War could be construed as pleas for racial justice and even as memorials to the heroes of Spain, if sung with a certain knowing fervor. And while the Red hunters might easily track down Communists, ex-Communists, Com-symps, and fellow travelers at MGM or CBS or Time-Life, they were not so likely to monitor hootenannies and the little folk music broadsides, where, under the covers of musicology and ethnology, the causes of unionism, brotherhood, and peaceful coexistence could be modestly furthered in relative privacy.

This was the world in which Esther was raised, a world she still revered when Luke came into her life. Luke was fascinated by it—to Dad, Communism was like Rosicrucianism, or membership in a Masonic lodge, a secret society, full of its own language and rituals and hand signals. It appealed to him on so many levels: it was despised, it was dangerous, it proposed an upside-down future. It was predictive, like astrology; it was as American as a tall tale. It embraced the blacks. In those early days with Esther, Luke was an eager student. The Scottsboro boys, the novels of Richard Wright, the passion of Paul Robeson: it all held such appeal for him. But his avid attention, his enthusiasm did create a misunderstanding. Those old Reds didn't realize that the voracious appetite Luke brought to their songs and legends was the appetite he brought to everything that was new. He was restless, his attention was easily distracted; his idealism was rather delicate, easily crushed. And when other influences came into Luke's life—drugs, film, the Top Forty, motorcycles, Zen—my grandparents (and, I suppose, Esther as well) scoffed at him, treated him as if he were a dilettante, a child, and Luke, in turn, responded to the withdrawal of the initial approval with a kind of violence that took the form of ridicule and scorn—as if Hegel, Marx, and peace in Vietnam were suddenly irritating and old-hat. They were no longer ideas but impediments that the old bunch were throwing in his path, things he had to kick out of the way as he went for whatever it was he wanted next.

"I know it seems meshuga now," Grandpa said, last time I visited him at the Shoreview Home, "but we were so excited to have Luke learning our songs. It wasn't just the coffee houses with the beatniks, you know that, don't you? He was playing and singing progressive songs about the injustices in life, in front of thousands of people. They weren't just concerts anymore, they were mass rallies. With good songs and a feeling among the young people that they could really change the world. They looked up to Luke. He could have changed the world. He could have done something. Something huge, like no other singer has ever done. It was in his grasp. And he let it go. That Steinberg came waltzing into his life, with the rings on his fat fingers and the smug little grin like he just cornered the herring market, and he told Luke, 'Hey, why are you wasting your time with these people? You should be making gold records.' And Luke, goddamn him, he listened. Oh boy, did he listen. Peace wasn't so sexy anymore, it wasn't interesting, it wasn't spangly and sparkly, and the same with sit-ins, and economic justice. The sonofabitch was more interested in singing about his pot dreams. I could wring his neck, with his 'obsidian umbrellas in a church with no name.' What kind of pud-pulling reactionary bullshit is that? He didn't just leave your mother, the sonofabitch, he left all of us. He left decency. The little punk signed on with Steinberg and joined the capitalist class! And then what does he do? Use his influence and his talent to get that no-goodnik murderer Sergei Karpanov out of jail!"

At last I heard footsteps on the other end of the line, and then Grandpa's voice, full of vigor and annoyance.

"What's going on?" he said. "Where are you calling from?"

"What did they tell you, Grandpa?"

"They tell me to eat my carrots and drink my juice. Now you tell me. What's going on?"

"Mom was in an accident. She's in the hospital."

There was a long and awful silence, that kind of emptiness that gives us a glimpse of death. And when Irv finally spoke, his voice was like a spray of gravel.

"Is she all right?"

"Yes. She's all right."

"I want to talk to her."

"She can't talk right now, Grandpa." I let that sink in. "She's in a coma. The doctors—"

"Yeah, yeah, the doctors." I pictured him as he was the last time we were together. When I came to the home he was in his room, eating his lunch off a tray, in bed. He was wearing a light green hospital gown; his long legs were skinny and hairless and his toenails had grown monstrously long. Yet he was strong. His embrace was powerful, and he kissed me so hard on the cheek my jaw ached.

We talked on the phone for a few more minutes. I gave him an honest report of what had happened, the shape she was in, inasmuch as I could. And I told him where exactly we were, the address, the phone number.

"I'm coming," he said, finally. "I'll hire a car. Tell her I'll be there in four hours, maybe five, maybe six. But I'll be there. Just say it right in her ear, never mind the coma. Often they hear. Often."

"I will."

"Keep checking on those doctors. Those goddamned country doctors."

"I will."

"The things that can go on in those places. Someone can put the wrong tube in her, or give her a pill that was supposed to be for someone else. You don't know."

"I'll stay here."

"Where are you now?"

"At the hospital."

"In her room?"

"No. In the hall. She's sleeping, I didn't want to call from there."

"Okay. I accept that. But keep an eye on things. I charge you with this responsibility."

"I can't stay there all the time."

"Billy. I'm not asking you for that. I asked you for a nickel, not a thousand dollars. She's all I got. And you. Everything else is over. Even history."

"She's going to be all right, Grandpa."

"I had to watch the death of socialism. Okay? And I did it. I had to watch the death of my beloved wife. And I did that, too. But I will not be alive for the death of my child. I draw the line there."

"She's going to be all right, Grandpa."

"And Billy? Don't tell him. Okay?"

"Don't tell who?" I said. It was a loony question. Of course I knew. Grandpa spared me the answer by hanging up.

THE LAST time my grandfather and Luke had seen each other was the day Sergei Karpanov got out on bail. Grandpa put the blame squarely on Luke and called him as soon as the news broke. Luke's phones had been going all day, but he hadn't picked up once. Grandpa, however, called in on Luke's private line in New York; Luke had given the number to my mother, years ago, telling her that if she ever needed to reach him, day or night, three hundred and sixty-five days a year, the call would be forwarded to wherever he was. (I assume there were others who had this secret number, but in my researches I've come up with only one other person who had the power to make that little white phone in Luke's bedroom ring, and that was a woman disc jockey in Tampa named Holly Whitehurst, with whom Luke spent a little less than eight hours and to whom he gave the secret number on a despairing sort of whim.)

"Is that you?" said Grandpa to Luke. It was about ten at night. Irv was in the kitchen. The only light was from a sputtering fluorescent over the sink. He was in his brown slacks, an old green cardigan—old-fart clothes, he called them. His fine white hair was wild from the electricity generated by his running his fingers through it over and over.

"Irv?" Though Luke hadn't heard Grandpa's voice in years, he had a perfect recording memory for sound.

"I want to talk to you. Face to face."

"Now?"

"Yes, now."

"It's kind of late, Irv. I'm in bed."

Luke had just worked out, taken some steam, a sauna, poured some of Sergei's vodka into his tall glass of cranberry juice.

"I'll be over in twenty minutes. It's important."

"Irv. I was really sorry to hear about Lillian. I wanted to call you. Did you get my letter?"

"No."

"I liked her very much, Irv. Lillian was—"

"And what if she didn't like you?"

"I'll have to live with that."

"So? It's all right? I can come over?"

"You're an old man, Irv. You can't go running around in the middle of the night."

"Okay. Then you come here."

There was a long pause. Grandpa figured if Luke was giving it this much thought, then he had him.

"All right," Luke finally said. "Give me an hour."

"I don't have an hour. Come right now."

"Irv. I'm doing you a favor."

"Come right now!"

Luke's driver, Carmine Manzardo, lived just a few blocks away, on Crosby Street, and Luke's car was garaged on Houston. They were set to go in fifteen minutes. Over the Brooklyn Bridge. The neon from the Watchtower Building reflected in the East River, backward mirror writing; a mysterious-looking ship with a flag Luke could not recognize was being loaded under floodlights in the Brooklyn Navy Yard.

"Everything okay?" Carmine asked.

"Just drive, Carmine." Luke stared out the window. A lit cigarette furled its lilac plume around his fingers.

They drove through slipping-down neighborhoods. Large limestone houses long ago divided into cramped apartments. Shopping streets with most of the stores closed forever. A streetlight shining down on emptiness, circles of stark, shining emptiness leading them deeper and deeper into Brooklyn.

"If I'm not out in fifteen minutes," Luke said, getting out of the car, looking at Grandpa's virtuous old house, "come in and get me. Say I'm late for something and we gotta go."

There was a fence, a gate, a little swatch of lawn, like a sample from the yard store. The streetlight reflected in the dark, curtained window. Luke had never been here at night; this was a house of afternoons, sitting in the parlor with Esther, shooting the breeze with the Rothschilds and their Commie friends, looking at Esther, letting her know with his eyes it was time to go, to a party, to make love. Leaving, as often as not, with an armful of food and another armful of pamphlets—Negroes, Cuba, peace. (See "Burning the Pamphlets of Yesteryear," recorded 1989.)

Luke knocked at the door. The house was dark, and after a few moments' silence he wondered if the old man had fallen to sleep in the time it had taken Luke to get to Brooklyn. But just then, the porch light went on—amber, its etched glass casing a sarcophagus for fatally ardent moths—and Irv was standing there, dressed in a blue suit, an unbuttoned white shirt, leaning on his wooden cane. It was almost as thick as a baseball bat, and its rubber tip was the salmon color of a brand-new eraser.

Without a word, Grandpa opened the door to Luke and gestured him in. Luke turned and signaled Carmine, a touch to the forehead.

Carmine felt confused. What did that mean? Everything's okay? Or Come and get me?

Irv turned on lamps and he led Luke into the parlor. He indicated with a sweep of the arm that Luke should sit in an oyster-colored easy chair, next to a fancy little end table, piled high with unread newspapers, still rolled tightly and bound by the paperboy's rubber bands. Grandpa had yet to say a word, not even hello. His breath was noisy. His cane thumped heavily on the fading carpet.

Luke sat, glanced at his watch—Sergei's actually, a Bulova, which the Russian thought was fancy because he had heard of it, seen ads.

"Do you listen to the news very much, Luke?" Grandpa said, standing near Luke, looming over him.

"Hello, Irv."

Grandpa nodded, waited.

"I like to know what's going on," Luke finally answered.

"Why?"

"Listen today."

"I don't know."

"Tonight, I mean." Grandpa leaned on his cane. Used his free hand to pat his chest hair. It was slick with sweat.

Luke shook his head no.

"All-news radio? Ten-ten on the dial?"

"I don't think so, Irv. No."

"Well, I do. And you know what I learned? They decided not to extradite your murdering friend back to the Soviet Union. He'll stand trial here. In fact, he's out on bail. Orders direct from the State Department."

"So be it."

"Yes. So be it. But such a lot of money, for the bail. They're talking half a million. I wonder how the weightlifter had so much money at his disposal." Irv pointed his cane at Luke and then brought it down again with a thud. "You must be proud of yourself, Luke."

"For what?"

"Oh please. Your modesty stinks of cowardice." That last word hissed out of him. Grandpa's hands were starting to tremble. He took a deep breath to bring himself under control.

There was a gentle pat-pat-pat across the carpet. Ditmas, a fat, one-eyed calico cat Lillian took in shortly before her own death. Irv had objected to the cat moving in, but now he doted on it. She rubbed against Grandpa's legs and then leapt into Luke's lap. Luke scratched her behind the ears, until Grandpa shooed her off with a poke of the cane.

The cat disappeared into the cabbagy darkness of the house.

"Did you know Katarina Karpanov?" Grandpa asked.

"Look, Irv. I came here in the middle of the night, for old

times' sake. But I didn't come here to answer your questions, or for you to try and twist whatever I say into some grand scheme of yours. I didn't have to come here, all right? I've got a million people tugging at my sleeve and I'm pretty good at not paying attention."

"It's a very simple question, Luke. Did you know her? Did you know Katarina Karpanov?"

"No, Irv. I didn't. Did you?"

"She was in this house. A beautiful woman. Selfless. A doctor like you dreamed of being, on your first day of medical school. Yes. I knew her."

"And do you know Sergei?"

"I would never want to. Never."

"Well, there it is. You in a nutshell. Good guys and bad guys. It's because you were raised in the city, man. You never got to play cowboys and Indians, never got to get it out of your system."

"So now you're a psychoanalyst. Added on to your other wonderful talents: fiancé, father, comrade, and now a head-shrinker. But of course none of this, none of these great talents, matches your gift for creating a tidal wave of public support for a man who cold-bloodedly murdered one of the finest young women I have ever met."

"He didn't murder her."

"Oh yes he did. Yes. And you will not pretend to know what you cannot know. Have you done an investigation? Have you studied the police reports?"

"Have you?"

"You, with your fancy lawyers. Of course, you bend the law whichever way you please. Make it a pretzel. Make it a bow. Put the bow in your hair and dance naked under the moon, you piece of shit."

"Irv," said Luke, getting up.

But Grandpa pushed him down into the chair, using the tip of his cane.

"Do you hate progressive people so much that you would do this?"

"Who are these progressive people, Irv? I'd like to meet them."

"You have met them. Here. In this house. What is my daughter to you—a reactionary? What am I? You came here, you ate our food, we taught you everything. What were you before? A little nobody from nowhere, smelling of the subway, with scum on your teeth. And you were such an eager student. You have that gift, you must know that. This gift, this terrible, corrupt gift to become anything you choose. You're a chameleon, and just as cold-blooded. Katarina's blood, soaked into the carpet, hours later, was warmer than your blood is right now."

"Irv, you've lost your fucking mind," Luke said. He glanced at his watch and made another move to stand up. He didn't even want to make eye contact with Grandpa; he was probably afraid of what he would see, afraid of making Irv even angrier. But something caught his attention, a shadow.

Grandpa had raised his cane high over his head, holding on to it with both hands, as if it were one of those wooden mallets you use to ring the bell at a carnival. He brought it down fast and hard; it hit Luke in the shoulder, and it hurt.

Instinctively, Luke grabbed for the cane, but Grandpa wrested it free. He brandished it, clearly intending to use it again.

Luke rubbed his shoulder, keeping an eye on Irv. He got up slowly, his hands now fists.

For a wiseguy, a man who had insulted so many people, and spent so much time on the road, Luke had had very little experience fighting. He was pretty much of a mouth guy. And since his early twenties, there was always someone around to stop the fights or fight them for him. Fatherless himself for most of his life, he hadn't had those boyish sparring matches with Daddy, hadn't closed his eyes and unleashed pinwheels of punches, only to be corrected, shown the proper form: defend with the left, attack with the right, keep your hands up, keep your eyes open.

Not that he couldn't have taken a seventy-five-year-old retired doctor. Pound for pound, the smart money would have been on Luke. But Grandpa struck first, and Luke was slow to react—when you've had a rough-and-tumble life, those first punches come quickly, but if you haven't, then you waste time wondering if it's really come to this, or if there's just been some stupid misunderstanding.

"You bastard—you bastard!" Irv shouted, and he hit Luke again with the cane, on the side of the head, and then once more, in the chest.

Luke dropped to one knee, covering his head. He looked at his hand. Red.

> *The old man cracked a river*
> *In the middle of my head*
> *I was the reddest man alive*
> *Now that Stalin is dead . . .*

—"Over the Bridge,"
recorded 1989

Luke grabbed for Grandpa's legs, missed, and then slumped onto the floor. There was knocking at the door. Grandpa stood there, paralyzed with confusion. Who could be calling at this hour? The police? Was Luke so wired into the police that they knew he was in trouble? The knocking continued. Grandpa looked down at Luke. Luke was getting up again, or trying to. He was on his knees, his head hung down and his tongue lolled out, as if he were playing at being a dog.

Finally, Carmine just let himself in. He saw Luke, ran to him. He lifted Luke easily. He held Luke in his arms, at the shoulders and the backs of his knees. It was how an unconscious damsel in distress would be carried out of an evil castle.

"He'll be all right," Grandpa said.

"I got nothing to say to you," Carmine said.

"I'm a doctor. I can look him over. Put him on the sofa."

"Nothing to say," Carmine repeated.

The next day, in bed, aching, Luke wrote "Land of the Dead," one of his most successful songs since the fertile days of the mid-sixties.

> *Late at night I received a call*
> *Went riding into the land of the dead*
> *Been through the prophets from Marx to St. Paul*
> *But only your name lived inside my head*
> *Every time I think I'm free*
> *Something about you happens to me*
> *Your memory beats like a drum and burns like a coal*
> *Tracks me down like a wolf and eats my soul*
> *Pushes me through your daddy's door*
> *To put it mildly, he didn't like me no more.*
> *Oh. Oh. Oh—*
> *Only a fool*
> *Like me*
> *Would want to be a lover*
> *In the land*
> *Of the dead . . .*

—"Land of the Dead," recorded 1989

The logical thing for Luke to do would have been to see a doctor. He was pretty banged up. The skin over his heart was luridly discolored; he had a wrenching, dizzying headache; and his scalp leaked where it had been split by Grandpa's blow. But he chose not to, probably out of embarrassment. Carmine looked in on him, as did Carmine's mother. Luke had a large supply of painkillers on hand, everything from Tylenol 3 to opium. He covered the pain; he relaxed in the narcotic bathysphere of the drugs. Nights became days; the curtains were drawn tight. He spent hours on the phone; people weren't certain why he was calling, or what he meant to say. He was in a stream of semiconsciousness.

The news shows and the papers marked Sergei's release and credited Luke and *American Shakedown*. Normally, Luke wouldn't have paid any attention, but in the days following Grandpa's caning, Luke pored over the newspapers, watched the news on TV. If he'd been packing, he might have Elvis'd the set, because a few commentators took the occasion to decry the influence of celebrities on our civic life. A guy named Monty Gray, from the local ABC affiliate, in particular, expressed outrage. "Mr. Fairchild obviously regrets missing the era when a folk singer had genuine martyrs to sing about. So, lacking a Sacco or a Vanzetti, or a Medgar Evers for that matter, he comes up with a bargain-basement victim in the person of Sergei Karpanov—and then foists on a gullible public a whole record of songs about a Russian lout who may have bludgeoned a woman to death in a New York City hotel room. If there's anyone out there who doubts that that thing called 'the sixties' is over, Luke Fairchild's songs for Sergei should be proof enough."

Finally, Sergei came home—to Luke's house on Washington Square, which was the only address Sergei had.

I have done everything I can to imagine what happened

between them, but only they know, and neither of them will tell me. As far as I can make out, Sergei asked Luke to loan him money, probably a great deal of money. He may have invoked their friendship, he may have claimed Luke owed him money for all of the weight training, he may even have demanded a share of the money generated by *American Shakedown*—a Soviet shakedown, so to speak.

But one thing is certain: Sergei had no intention of awaiting his New York trial, no interest in clearing his name, and, in all probability, no confidence that his name would be cleared.

The man who sold Sergei a false passport was named Terry Menegon, and when he was finally arrested, in Brooklyn, years later, he admitted selling Sergei a Dutch passport for three thousand dollars, which Sergei paid for in cash. Of course, this money came from Luke, either as a gift or stolen. There was usually cash lying around, rings, little *objets*. Then Karpanov disappeared over the Canadian border. He was spotted in Montreal, and then in Quebec City, where he was said to be wearing a long fur coat and spending freely, drinking in prole bars, gorging himself on smoked meats. But the rumors did not stop there. Sergei sightings were reported from Nova Scotia, Reykjavik, Lyon, and Prague. There was a story that had him secretly coaching the Romanian weightlifting team. And then: nothing. He seemed to have completely disappeared. That is, until shortly after the dissolution of the Soviet Union, when Grandpa got a letter from an old friend traveling in Russia. The friend said he thought he had seen Sergei sitting with a tableful of thugs in a newly opened restaurant, near the Kremlin. Shortly after that, Grandpa fell in the shower and shattered his hip, and when he got out of surgery the next stop was the Shoreview Home, in Little Neck.

6

ON THE WAY back to my mother's room, I heard someone call my name. I looked up and there, dressed in white cook's garments, was Little Joe Washington, who, despite the end of his career and a weight gain of at least a hundred pounds, still called himself Little Joe. His face was dark, round, bathed in kindness. He was my mother's near neighbor, the man who winterized her house every November, gave her long (and obviously futile) lectures about alcohol, loneliness, the secrets of nature, a man bound to Esther by true affection, but also by the shared experience of having been shortchanged by Luke.

We embraced. The smells of Joe's kitchen—garlic, butter, vinegar—rushed toward me. I felt wispy and insubstantial in his arms.

"She's going to be all right, Billy," he murmured to me. "Doctors these days, it's amazing the things they can do."

"I'm really glad you're here, Joe. How'd you find out?"

"Word gets out. People who need to know, know."

Having been raised near musicians, I had learned to ignore my essentially empirical nature and to accept those vague little homilies as a form of rational discourse. People who needed to know knew? Fine. Maybe Joe and my mother and all the droopy-mustached bass players and the beret-bedecked would-be songwriters, maybe they were right and I was wrong and it was the feeling of a thing that mattered, not its sense.

Little Joe Washington always accepted my claim to be Luke's son, and now, as I walked back toward Esther's room, with Joe's fleshy, ponderous arm draped over my shoulder, I felt a comfort in his warmth, his manly fragrance. The truth is, Joe himself had a few unclaimed kids left along the way; but now, in his ethical old age, when he could least afford it, financially speaking, he had embraced four of these children, ponying up for tuitions, weddings, even hypnotherapy for a daughter who wanted to quit smoking. His support of my claim was not without its own complications. Aside from his own experiences of inconvenient offspring, Joe's belief in me was also a belief in Esther, whom he met shortly after I was born, when Joe's career was starting to fade and Luke was on the cover of *Time*, and Joe's idiot brother-in-law lawyer first brought forward the somewhat plausible but incompetently handled plagiarism suit against Luke.

Upon Luke's suggestion, Luke and Joe met without their lawyers in the townhouse Luke was renting on Horatio Street, the semilegendary and notorious House Nine, where rumor had it so much pot was smoked you could get a contact high just driving past in a taxicab with the windows rolled up. Luke's fourth record had been out for a month. There were still plenty of people who didn't think he was particularly important and even a few who had barely heard of him, but their time was coming to an end. It was getting more and more difficult, and sometimes even a little scary, for Luke to go out in public. He had moved twice in the past few months, and the place on Horatio Street was full of security, and usually full of Luke's sudden entourage, a nervous, flattering, conniving bunch—musicians, lawyers, promoters, dealers, writers, politicos, painters, Tarot-card readers, women with dark circles under their very young eyes.

When Joe arrived, it was one of the rare moments when Luke was alone. The place was bursting with badly spent money: pricey Persian carpets that in Luke's possession suffered more wear and tear in a month than they had in the centuries before his purchase; pop-art paintings bought at the peak of the market; massive TVs; gargantuan stereo speakers; dozens of guitars; trippy Tiffany lamps; sofas covered in silk brocade and spotty with cigarette and joint burns; a ninth-century jade incense burner from China; et cetera, et cetera, ad nauseam.

"It looks like the world is treating you nice," Joe said, plucking a striped caftan off of a black leather chair, seating himself with an *uumpf*, crossing his legs and letting Luke eyeball the lightbulb-shaped hole on the bottom of his shoe. Like many a wily old lion, Joe felt no loss of pride exaggerating his own weaknesses—what he could no longer get through speed and strength he would gain through sheer cunning.

"Oh man," said Luke, too high to dissemble. "It's been too much. Too weird, too fucking weird."

He gestured around the room. Records were strewn everywhere. Christmas baskets of fruits and flowers, some nearly as high as the ceiling—gifts from promoters, his record label, his lawyers, his accountants, his public relations experts, his tailor, his cobbler—were piled up in the corners of the room. Christmas cards hung from the white marble fireplace, bent at the corners and slipped beneath the weight of Egyptian statues. A lilac disk of pot smoke hung in the sun-struck air.

"You took from me, Fairchild," Joe said, giving Luke's name a lurid, sarcastic twist. "And what did I ever do to you? Give you a job? Give you a break? A little national exposure?" Little Joe raised his fist and brought it down fast, as if plunging a knife into someone's back.

"Wait a minute, man. You came here as my friend, so why don't you bloody well act like a friend?" Luke was hanging around with a few Brits at the time—among them Jennifer Cotswold, who went on to write a dozen songs about him and who now, her career in total eclipse, is making the cable-talk-show circuit telling stories about Luke, particularly how he came to imitate her accent.

"How much money you making this year?" Joe asked.

"I don't know. I'm writing songs, I'm on the road. I'm not in some room counting my money."

"Well, I *am*, you dumb-as-shit motherfucker! I am counting out every *penny*. And you want to know *why?*"

"No, man, I don't want to know why. I don't need to know why. All right? Knowing why is something *you* need."

"Because I'm trying to make a dollar out of fifteen motherfucking cents."

"You know what, Joe? I should have listened to my lawyers. I never should have agreed to meet with you. I asked you here because I love you, and, you know, old times' sake. You're here because all the birds have flown south. Man, I've been walking a road that ain't even been built. I've been seen places I ain't never been to. Man, they've snapped my photo in the queen's palace, and I was sleeping under a waterfall two continents to the left. But if you're going to keep on claiming I ripped off one of your songs . . . I mean, I write eight songs a day. Some of them take five minutes. I shit songs. I come songs. What do I need with ripping you off? Everything that happens in this century, man, comes through me. The atomic bomb went off and I was born and that's all there is to it. I've got souls inside me, millions of souls, and they're all working overtime. What do you want from me? Money? Take some money. You used to pay me, so now I'll pay you. How much would you like? What would it take to make you happy?"

"I'd like fifty thousand dollars."

"Hey, who wouldn't?"

"In cash."

It was just then that Esther knocked on the door. There was a security camera, and Luke saw her on the TV screen, bundled up against the winter winds that came swirling off the Hudson River. Luke was visibly agitated to see her. Barefooted, he walked to the door. He wiped his hand against his pants, as if to dry his palms.

Esther came in in a fury. The ice of the Canadian prairies rode the back of her cape; she was a troika full of snow demons. Her black hair was frozen at the tips; she had wrapped a red scarf around her chin and mouth. Normally cagey in her anger, content to hint at it, somehow trusting that her point would be made and would prevail, with Luke, especially of late, Esther was subject to fevers of temper, practically malarial bouts of fury.

You ask me why I'm shaking when you know you want me dead
The twenty-fifth hour of the thirteenth month
*   and a burning Eskimo sled*
A crack in the sky, a catch in my throat,
*   pull my lever and cast your vote . . .*

—"Orange Julius Blues," recorded 1968

"You have to get Jerry Mayo to leave me alone, Luke, and I'm not kidding," Esther said. She stood in the doorway: behind her, icy blue sky, the nerve endings of a bare tree, the hood of a brown Mercedes. "He can't get to you so he comes after me." She turned, closed the door, hard. The stained glass rattled in its pane.

"Jerry Mayo is a squirrel who forgot to gather acorns," said Luke. His pale face showed a burning rash of color.

"It's not just Jerry, Luke. It's everyone. It's Eliot Shore, and it's Barbara May Sellers, and that stinkbomb bozo with the codpiece on the outside of his pants—I can't remember his name."

"Wilson."

"What?"

"Wilson. His name is Wilson. The bozo."

"Look, I don't care what his name is, or even if he has a name. The point is, I want you to, I need you to, I just totally *demand* that you tell all these people that you don't live in my apartment, that you never visit me there, and you have no intention of *ever* visiting me—"

"But I do."

"Well, don't."

"I may even visit you there tonight."

"Luke, I'm serious."

"I may climb the sycamore tree outside your window and sing to you like Romeo on speed. 'Esther, Esther, wherefore art thou, Esther.' "

"Those are Juliet's lines, you jerk. Luke: listen to me. I'm losing my mind. I need sleep. Billy keeps me up all night long. He arches his back and howls like he's possessed. His poop is green."

My mother told Luke these rather unappetizing things about me because she needed to dramatize her predicament (exhaustion, isolation), and she also wanted, perversely, to increase Luke's isolation from me. If he would not be a willing father, she would deny him the future opportunity to become a repentant father—no, not quite deny him, but impede him. The road to forgiveness would be blocked—not destroyed, not even barricaded: it would just not be easy. That was as far as she could go.

"What do you want me to do?" Luke said—a standard

reply, by the way. He was always helpless in the face of other people's problems. It was never his fault, never his business, never his place, never within his power to do anything about it. He saw Visions of the Four-Gated City, but he couldn't tell you how to get to Thirty-fourth Street. "I don't talk to those guys. They're a bunch of energy vampires."

"Tell them to leave me alone, Luke. They hang out in the hallway. They eat all their meals at Armando's because of that one table where you can see my window. They're getting fat from all that linguine. It's sort of sad, but it scares the hell out of me, mostly."

"What are you scared of? Those guys are harmless. All they want is to be me."

"That's what I'm scared of. That's much more scary than some guy with a gun who wants money because his kids are hungry or he's addicted to smack. I can deal with that. It makes sense. But a bunch of people—I don't know, how many are there now? a hundred? a thousand?—trying to be you, and hanging around me because I used to know you—"

" 'Used' to know me? Come on."

"I can't handle that. Some of them get girlfriends with hair like mine, or they make them wear wigs—can you believe it? And they dress the women up like I was, on the album, and the men are already wearing clothes like yours, and they walk up and down the street. I really do think they believe they're us— at least the guy thinks he's you. The girl most likely doesn't have the faintest idea who the hell she is. I know I didn't."

"You knew who you are from the day you were born."

"How do you stand it? It's all so out of control. It's just songs, music. Don't get me wrong, Luke. I think what you do is lovely. You know that. But it's not . . ." She gestured, which Luke took to mean *It's not socialism, it's not freedom for the oppressed, it's just entertainment.* "You can't take something that's supposed to be this size—" she described a grapefruit with her hands—"and then make it *this* size—" she threw her arms wide open—"without distorting it."

"I'm just writing the songs and singing them. What less can I do?"

"Oh, I know, I know." She touched his cheek. She was still wearing her gloves, red wool. "It's not your fault. But let's face it: even the songs have changed."

"Oh, man, not this again." He put his hand on his chest, batted his long, girlish lashes. "Everybody's got advice for Fairchild. Sing about the bomb, sing about the Negroes getting hosed by Bull Conner. Sing about the farmers and the workers. Well, what about Woody Guthrie, okay? He sang about nothing but farmers and workers and I didn't see no one around his bedside when he was dying, none of those workers and farmers, man, no one holding a lunch pail, no one with dirt under his fingernails, or even a union card, unless it was for the Screen Actors Guild."

By now, Little Joe had gotten tired of simply eavesdropping and he'd left the living room and stood in the foyer, behind Luke. Luke didn't know Joe was there, and my mother just figured Joe was a bodyguard or a musician.

"I'll do what I can, Esther. What more is there? I'll write a song that'll put all those soul-Xeroxing motherfuckers in their place. I don't want them knocking on my door."

> *Little Jack Horner and Billy the Kid*
> *Lost everything they didn't keep hid*
> *Won't let the same thing happen to me.*
> *Oh man, you fakers, get away from my door*
> *No matter what you heard, I don't live here no more.*

—"Keep Away," recorded 1966

"If you don't, Luke, I'm serious, I'll never talk to you again. This ride you're on, I don't want to be on it."

"Don't say that to me, Esther. It hurts me." Luke's voice wobbled. He was slight to begin with, but getting high day and night and traveling from one concert to the next and now having to be careful of fans—a new kind of fan, nothing at all like he was used to from the old days on the folk circuit, old days that were little more than a year behind him, but felt like decades ago—had whittled him down further. He looked forlorn even when he was having a pretty good time, and when he was unhappy he looked as if he wanted to die.

He stood close to her, bowed his head. She made damn sure she did not touch him—there had already been five or six reconciliations between them, and each one left her feeling worse than the one before. The pattern was depressingly predictable. He would humble himself before her, as if that was what she wanted, rather than what she truly needed from him: recognition of her. This self-abnegation was just another way of keeping the spotlight on Luke. But nevertheless, this is what he liked to offer her: the bowed head, the teary voice, the declaration that he was nothing without her. Luke, my mother had said, more than once, this isn't only about what you are and what you are not and how I can make you better. This is about me, too, isn't it? And now it's about Billy. But that never stopped him, and often enough it didn't stop Esther, either. She had ridden a bus all night from New York to Austin when he was in the midst of a three-night stand and the hecklers were making him so frightened he lost his voice. She had let him into her (our) apartment when he showed up high on mescaline and remembering the time his father had held him by the shirt and slapped him twenty times across the face. "If my mother hadn't died—and I killed her, you know, I did, I killed her when I was coming out of her and the A-bomb was dropping . . ." He wept, as Esther held him and waited for him to calm down. She wasn't even sure the story was true, but it didn't matter. Ben Kramer was already dead. She had never seen a birth certificate, he had no driver's license, so who really knew when Luke was born? Maybe Hiroshima did explode the moment of Luke's first breath. Who knew? He was a fiction, like Huckleberry, or Henderson. She made love to Luke anyhow, with me staring at the blistered ceiling from my crib in the next room, and soon after he was his old self again: moody, critical, out for a pack of smokes, gone. No, she would not touch him. Not now. Not today.

"Hold me, baby," he murmured. "If you don't hold me, I think I'm going to fall into a million pieces."

"You know this man was going to give me some money before you walked in here?" said Little Joe Washington.

"Can we have a little privacy, would that be asking too much?" said Luke. He brought what he knew about stage presence to the moment, what he knew about staring down an audience, making a line of lyric give ten thousand people the chills just by the way he said it, the way he cocked his head, sneered. If Luke had learned nothing more in the past year, he had at least learned how to create an effect.

Joe just looked at him, said nothing in return.

"Esther," said Luke, taking her arm.

She overreacted, yanked back from him. Her eyes flashed, she rubbed the spot where he had touched her.

Luke was stunned, hurt, appalled, and, because of the way his life was now arranged, disappointment was simply unacceptable. Disappointment was for the people without reservations, for has-beens, freelance journalists, folk singers. Luke had entered the first chamber of that vast haunted house of celebrity in which you got what you wanted—and got it quick. One of the directors of the Museum of Modern Art arranged for Luke to see the Picasso show all by himself, after the museum was closed for the night, so Luke wouldn't be disturbed. There was always someone around to get him what he wanted, whenever desire struck: runs to Chinatown for shrimp in black bean sauce, to Brentano's for a *Dictionary of Slang*, to Gramercy Park for Acapulco Gold, to Spanish Harlem for a papaya juice—not to Eighth Street, mind you, which was just a short walk away, it was too watery there, not even to Seventy-second Street, a friend of his found a cockroach in his cup there; no, it had to be the one particular stand on 112th, run by the skinny one-eyed guy with the gold tooth and a Che Guevara T-shirt, he got the sweetest fruit out of Hunts Point, and that's what it had to be, and Luke knew the difference so don't try and give him any of that downtown papaya. There was no longer an intermediary, not so much as a speed bump between his desires and their fulfillment. The world was his. That moment in a thousand movies when someone gestures out toward the twinkling lights of the City and says "Someday all this will be yours," that immigrant dream, that loner's wish, that unreasonable, unseemly, absurd desire for wealth and power—it had already happened to Luke, the City was his. He could barely be blamed for thinking that in the end people would be as procurable as fifth-row seats on the aisle, or that young cop's horse, which he gave over to Luke two o'clock one Tuesday morning so that Luke could gallop wildly through Central Park, singing "Trust Fund Mama" at the top of his lungs.

And, let's face it, people *were* procurable. They were moths drawn to his flame, and if that wasn't enough, Luke had gained authority: he could actually achieve his ferocious horny teenage dream and go into a bar, find the most appealing woman, and just point at her and she'd be his, at least for the night.

Girls on the road, what are their numbers
I don't know, I won't even guess
They see by my spurs that I am a cowboy
They ask me Are you lonely and I tell them: Yes.

They offered me diamonds, they offered me gold
A trip to Kyoto and Viennese shortcake
In a world of illusion they showed me their dreams
They stole my spirit but left me the heartbreak . . .

—"Girls on the Road," recorded 1977, 1992

Yet all the personal power Luke had gained over the past year had no effect on Esther. In fact, his wealth and fame and the beginnings of his deification only distanced her further. If she had been concocting a way of making herself distinctive to him, or of increasing his obsession with her, she could not have chosen better: he was so used to leaning back when people approached, it had changed his center of gravity. Yet with Esther he had to lean forward, and that made him lose his balance time after time. Yes, it might have been some sexual tai chi she had devised, or it might have been how she really felt. Most likely, it was a lucky combination: a true feeling she could summon and emphasize, a personal reality that also had considerable usefulness.

"Esther," he said. "Don't do like that."

"Forget it, Luke. I came here for one reason."

"And I think I know what that reason is." He smiled and started to reach for her again.

"Don't force yourself on me," she said. "Don't grab me, don't pet me, don't even touch me, okay, don't even fucking touch me!"

Ah: but that was her mistake. The repeat at the end, the

expletive undeleted. Luke knew her well, and desire makes certain people clever. Her voice might have been flat as a floor, but he suddenly sensed where the trapdoor was, the shortcut to the depths of her.

I think of them standing in there, the windows the color of an onion's inmost heart, the smell of marijuana in the air, my parents' eyes flashing across the foggy harbor of the foyer, and unfortunate Little Joe Washington stuck in their force field. He's already told me how much he wanted to leave, the embarrassment and irritation he felt—but he was transfixed by fascination, and of course there was the money. (He was right to worry that maybe his best chance to get a cash settlement from Luke had already passed—he was closer to getting that quick fifty grand the moment before Esther knocked on the door than he would be for several years.)

And—where was I? Home on Sullivan Street, but with whom? Grandma? That runty little pothead babysitter Esther used only because she lived in our building? (Sorry, Carol, but really, you were the worst.) Was I even on Esther's mind? Did she think: I better cut this short and get back to Billy? Believe me, I'm not insisting. What do I know of the Sisyphian task of raising a child? I'm sure she longed for breaks from me, longed for privacy and a life of her own—and how many million times more engrossing was this life as Luke's ex, the muse and obsession of the man of the American hour; how much more riveting it was to relive their passionate past, the memories of daybreak hotels with the sounds of the street cleaners shush-shush-shushing the cobblestones beyond the shuttered windows; there were lights in their past, cheers, screams, limos nosing through the throngs like the prow of a ship through heavy water, the water in some flipped-out painting, in which every wave is full of human faces. Fame had just begun for Luke, though at the time it didn't seem to anyone that it could get much bigger, much crazier. How could this, the memory of it, the hatred of it, the proximity to it, how could it help eclipsing her difficult, somewhat lonely life? Luke was so much more exciting than her real life, or real life in general.

"You never really cared about me, did you?" And do you know who said this? Not my mother, not Esther the Abandoned, not the one living in a rent-controlled walk-up on Sullivan Street, not the one who slept alone while the other went from lover to lover. No. "You never cared about me" was what Luke said: Luke.

"Not this again," said Esther. She turned, went for the door.

But he spun her around, forcefully.

"How many people did you sleep with when we were together?"

"This is the great Luke Fairchild? Mr. Hip?"

"I know you slept with Peter Baumgarten. Who else?"

"I'm not doing this with you, Luke. I came here—"

"You know he appears in fuck films. You do know that, don't you? Porn musicals. *Breast Side Story*—he was in that. *Eat Me in St. Louis*."

"Look, Luke, Peter—"

"Oh, it's 'Peter' now, is it? Peter."

"Would you prefer it if I called him Mr. Baumgarten?"

"I would prefer it if you never slept with him. If you didn't make a fool of me up and down the street. The downtown boys were laughing, the uptown girls were rolling their eyes."

"This is ridiculous," said Esther.

"Who else were you balling, besides Peter?"

"Fuck you."

"Oh, sweet. How like a lady."

"Is this because you want me to say Billy isn't yours?"

"He isn't. He couldn't be. I'm sterile and you know it. Radiation sickness. And you know what else? I don't want you to say whose he is. I don't even think you *could* say."

"Because I'm such a whore? Oh my God, I can't believe I'm being sucked into this conversation. By you, of all people. I must be out of my mind. You. The most unfaithful person."

"I never gave my heart to anyone but you."

"Your heart? Since when did the human heart have anything to do with your life?"

"I'm never going to get my money, am I?" said Joe. He had just about made up his mind to call it a day, give it back to the lawyers to solve, when Luke fell to his knees.

"Why don't you just kill me, okay?" Luke cried, throwing his arms out wide. "Why don't you just fucking kill me?"

"Do you think I haven't thought about killing you?" Esther said, her voice going up like fireworks. Most likely, Luke expected remorse, or even some mongrelized whimper of sentimentality; he hoped at least that his histrionics might awaken a feeling of love in Mom. But she knew him too well, and she had been hurt too deeply. Suddenly, she was a shark, incited by even stage blood. "You've got the loyalty of a flea," she said. (See "Flea Circus Lament," recorded 1970.) "If I live a hundred years, I'm *never* going to be treated as badly as you've treated me. Never! Look what you've done to me! Do you ever even think about it?"

"I think about you all the time. What do you think I think about?"

"That's not about me. It's about you. Everything's about you now, Luke. You don't care about Negroes and civil rights—"

"I don't believe I'm listening to two white children talking about Neee-groes," said Little Joe, throwing up his hands.

"You don't care about the bomb," Esther was saying, "or even freedom. Except freedom for you. And then you do this thing, pretending you care so much that you can act like you don't give a shit. But it's not an act. You really and truly do not care. You're a sellout and you know it. Look, there's nothing wrong with getting high. I like to, too. But you're high all the time. You're high right now. It's just another way of cutting off from the world. It's masturbating."

"I assume you mean that to be a bad thing," said Luke.

"When was the last time you talked to Sandy Golden? Or put your name on a petition? Or spoke out about what's happening in this country?"

"What'd you do—swallow your father? Is he down there, shouting the words out through your throat?"

"All you care about is getting high and getting your dick wet."

"Which reminds me," Luke said. He got up, took a step toward her. She raked her fingernails across his face.

He grabbed her by the wrist. She tried to pull away, kicked him in the shin. His shins were almost like his balls, wildly sensitive. He lunged at her, tackled her from around the shoulders, sent her reeling back into the wall. Her head hit the mirror; a spooky spiderweb crunched into the glass. She touched the back of her head, checked her palm for blood. Her thick raven hair had cushioned the blow.

"You fucking bastard!" she screamed, and rushed him, flailing her arms. Luke did his best to cover himself; his aggression was already spent, and now all he wanted was to survive.

She pummeled him. But a left-wing Brooklyn girlhood hadn't been much of a preparation for the real dirtiness and violence of life. Her blows were weak, poorly aimed, and ambivalent. As a mother she was incapable of administering a spanking. All she knew how to do was what had been done to her: she could make you feel guilty, or a little corrupt; in a pinch, she could pinch you. She was mild, she lacked force, perhaps she even lacked some element of passion. She lacked that quality that you need to be savagely on your own side, that desire to prevail, to win, to have the greater share. She had a temper, true, but it came from grief, frustration, not anything truly vital. She slapped at him, punched him, but did no damage, caused him no pain.

Just then, three of Luke's crowd appeared on the doorstep, dressed in Afghan jackets—raw sheepskin painted purple and white, tufts of coarse, spotty fur around the collar and the sleeves. They were holding bags of groceries.

"It's the Party People," one of them called out.

"We are the Party People, we are the Party People," the other two sang.

A gangling girl with curly red hair was the first one in. She wore knee-high lace-up boots; despite the winter, her coat was open. She was a model, flat-chested, dreamy, sexy, and amused, with the confident air of someone who always gets invited to the party. "Oh!" she said, seeing Luke and Esther in the foyer. "We bought meat on Little West Twelfth Street, from a real butcher, right off the hook."

Behind her stood Winston Scattergood and Alan Silverman. Winston was a fleshy, flaxen-haired kid, stoned and sweaty, who was then a driver/gofer/companion/court jester for Luke, and who ten years later would be a hot-shot movie executive, and who twenty years after that would be dead of AIDS. Alan Silverman was wiry, dark, always cranked up on speed. He functioned as a kind of cultural commissar. His job with Luke was to know where the best parties were, the best drugs, the newest bands, the best clothes, and he did it well. "Comrade Silverfish," Luke liked to ask, "what's new and how do I get to be a part of it?" (Alan's flash forward is medical school, marriage to a beautiful, deaf Kenyan, heroic good works in Africa.)

Luke took Esther's hand and they walked up the staircase to the second floor. Esther did nothing to resist; they would have a momentary truce, based on their common interest, which was to get away from the trio of *La Bohème* revelers.

"Hello, Esther," said the red-haired girl. "Are you around now?" She said this to my mother's back, and my mother to this day doesn't know that girl's name. Of course, that was part of being around Luke. There were always so many more people than you could ever hope to keep track of. People who thought about you and wanted to take your place.

What happened when Luke took my mother upstairs? I can't say with any certainty. My knowledge of this moment comes primarily from Little Joe, who was downstairs looking at the ceiling, which throbbed like a plaster heart beneath their footsteps. "Leave me alone!" my mother shrieked. And then, a minute later, she was heard to say, "Take your love and shove it up your ass."

Years later, after Joe had retired from the music business, moved upstate, and opened up his restaurant in High Falls with the money he got when his plagiarism suit against Luke was finally settled. "About half an hour after your mother left, Luke came down," he told me. "His eyes were all red. He wasn't talking. He just sat down at the piano and wrote three songs in an hour. Real bitter shit, meaner than hell. And then he started singing this really sad song, but it was in French. French! Man, I gotta say I was impressed."

"I should have taken her keys away from her that first night," Joe said to me as we stood by Esther's bed, watching her oh-so-slowly breathe.

"The keys to her car? How would she get around?"

"I don't know, Billy. I've got time on my hands. I could have driven her."

"Very nice. *Driving Miss Esther.*"

He shrugged. His eyes looked half angry, half sorrowful.

"What do the doctors say?" Joe asked.

"You try getting a straight word out of any of them."

He nodded. A lot of his life has been about not getting a straight word out of people—club owners, promoters, record-label execs, agents, lawyers. It had given him a sense of communication based on silences, lies, double-talk, and it made him, in his late middle age, taciturn.

We stood there, keeping what was left of my mother company. The hospital, with its urgencies, its frustration, truculence, and small meannesses, faded behind us, and for a timeless time it was just the three of us, an aging soul singer, a comatose woman, and her son, there, silent, at the edge of some secret universe, in the washed-out faded unwholesome dying light of a hospital room.

For years I had been grateful that Joe and my mother found each other and became friends; I thought he would keep a kindly eye on her. But it never quite dawned on me that he might look out for me as well. What would life had been for me if Joe was my father? What would I look like? How would I feel? The search for Luke would be taken away from me, and what would fill the great emptiness left in its wake?

I had to a great extent ruined my life, defaced it. I was standing next to my mother, who right now might have taken the bait and was now slowly being reeled in by that great fisherman Death, and though I should have been thinking of her and her alone, these thoughts about myself and what I had done to myself continued to rain within me; that persistently gloomy inner weather would not stop. It was always inclement and I wanted to ask for some clemency. Very bad joke, but true.

Finally, Joe put his arm around me and we left the hospital. He had to get back to High Falls, back to Little Joe's, his restaurant, where, despite his many employees, he oversaw every detail.

We had time for a coffee, which we took at a desultory little diner called Smitty's, on Leyden's small-town version of

Broadway—Country Gal Clothiers, the Pipe and Pouch, Norma's Notions, that sort of thing. The trees along the road were in bloom. The mountains to the west were pale green, the sky denim blue. How could a world in which my mother was dying be so beautiful?

"Bring us a couple of cups of coffee, will you, Micky?" Joe said to the waitress. Joe called nearly everyone by name. He had taken a memory course advertised on TV and it really worked for him—he always had good luck responding to those late-night TV offers, the food dryer, the tummy flattener. He hoped to one day sell a *Little Joe Washington's Greatest Hits* collection on TV, to do an ad in which he sang snippets of his songs while the titles scrolled by and an 800 number blinked off and on at the bottom of the screen.

Joe brought his coffee cup to his nose, sniffed it professionally. The menu at Little Joe's said "The Best Coffee in the Hudson Valley," and Joe worried that someone would come up with a better tasting cup than his blend of chicory, French roast, Café Bustelo, Brown Gold, and Droste chocolate. Ah, but he was safe here. He took a noisy, aerated sip, put the cup down, dried his lips with his napkin. Aging had brought out some latent daintiness in Joe, he had become an Old Gent, and though he could still be counted on to tell stories of the road, the raunchy fifties, all-nighters in the colored motels throughout the South, bourbon right out of the barrel, marijuana so rich with resins you had to smoke it with the end stuck into flame to keep it lit, he recounted these tales now as if they had happened to somebody else, a wicked twin.

"Do you think she's going to live?" I suddenly said.

Joe leaned back, gave some evidence of thinking about it— as if this were a matter of logic, or prescience, as if either of us could say.

"She's going to be all right," he said. "She's strong. She's going to fight back. You'll see."

I buried my face in my hands for a moment.

"I called Luke, to tell him."

"You did?" said Joe. He looked truly surprised. "Why did you do that?"

"We were talking about him, right before the accident, Mom and I. I don't know. It just seemed the right thing to do."

"You have to cut him loose, Billy. Just cut the man loose."

"I know."

"What did he say?"

"I left a message."

Joe shook his head. "That won't do much good."

"What else can I do?"

"He's a million miles out of her life now. And if you want to know, you think about him more than she does."

I felt a sudden clumsy, clattering grief falling through me like an avalanche of cups and saucers. The sunlight that slanted through the Venetian blinds of Smitty's Diner had moved from the dented tin cap of the sugar shaker to the tips of Joe's fingers.

Just then, someone rapped on the window. Startled, I looked out and saw a woman—familiar, good-looking, but who? I recognized her, but for an instant I couldn't remember her name or where I had seen her before.

She smiled, waved, her gestures jokey, exaggerated, shy.

Rosa. What was different in this picture? She still wore the tights, the boots, the hoop earrings—ah: she held a child's hand. A dark little Franz Kafka of a boy; I put him at four or five. His hair was long and wavy, his eyes almost black, curious, charged with irrepressible energy. He looked like what mothers call "a handful," one of those turbo-tots for whom you need patience and a sense of humor. He was on his toes, trying to see for whom his mother had stopped.

With more enthusiasm than I expected, I gestured for her to come in.

"You know Rosa?" Little Joe asked.

"A little. Is that her kid with her?"

But before he could answer, she was there at our table. I was remarkably disturbed by her presence, but I wrote it off: my heart was a stray dog just then, liable to follow anyone home, especially if they slowed down, glanced at me.

"Edgar!" Joe said, as Rosa's boy scrambled into the booth next to him and patted Joe's pockets as if he were quite used to finding treats in them.

"Nice manners, Edgar," Rosa said. Then, to me: "We meet again."

"I kind of like this small-town life," I said. And I knew it was not just my imagination, she did look at me with a kind of full-throttle frankness, and I was seized by this vivid, carnal sense of her.

She gestured toward my side of the booth and I slid over, making room. She was exhausted. She put her elbows on the table, ran her blunt, boyish fingers through her hair.

"Two jobs and no life makes Rosa a dull girl," she said.

"What do you do?" I asked, a little too quickly, with some of that New York Prove-It in my voice.

"Accounts receivable for this guy who sells blue algae pills mail-order—"

"Algae!" shouted Edgar, still engrossed with patting down Joe.

"And I work at the recycling center. I operate a backhoe."

"Really!" I said, with quite a bit of enthusiasm.

"Knock knock," Edgar was saying to Joe.

"Who's there?" answered Joe.

"Edgar!!" Edgar shouted, his laughter rising like a flock of birds exploding from a tree.

"Plus I freelance for the local papers."

"That's three jobs, then," I said, displaying my fabled ability to count one, two, three.

After frisking him thoroughly, Edgar gave up on Joe as a

source of hidden treasures and slid out of the booth—plucking a tuft of batting from the torn seat as he went—and began to roam the diner, greeting some of the other customers, and spinning the bright red stools along the counter. Rosa looked at him out of the corners of her eyes.

I turned, gestured for the waitress. I didn't want Rosa to leave; a cup of coffee would slow things down.

"What'll you have?" I asked her, as if this were my table and I was in charge.

"Oh, Micky will know," said Rosa.

And sure enough she did. She appeared a few moments later with a cup of hot water and a slice of lemon. Rosa took a tea bag out of her purse, dropped it into the hot water.

"I am now one of those women who carry their own tea bags. I never thought it would happen." She poked at it with the tip of her spoon. It bloated and rose to the top like a corpse.

"You pull that in my restaurant, I'll charge you for the water," said Joe.

"I can't afford your restaurant," said Rosa.

Joe reached for her, took her hand. "Hey, I was just kidding."

"Hey," said Rosa, "so was I."

She linked her fingers through his and they smiled with the ease of old friends. It did not seem that they were lovers, or had ever been, but it was clear that they had shared secrets and late-night talks and meals and confessions and tears, and that they had toasted each other with cheap wine and at other times with wine so expensive it was really more than they could afford. They had traveled together, gone to funerals, tried and then given up on meditation, helped each other quit cigarettes, donated blood for a mutual friend in the hospital. They were part of a circle of friends, a family of their own choosing. I felt rapturously alone, ridiculously isolated.

Rosa craned her neck, looked at someone sitting in a front booth.

"See that guy sitting near the register?" she asked.

I followed her eyes to a guy in his late forties, early fifties, a great gray brute of a man in a leather jacket, holding a carefully folded newspaper in one hand and a tall glass of neon-bright orange soda in the other. Joe didn't bother to turn around.

"He looks like that old Russian weightlifter friend of your father's," said Rosa. "Sergei Karpa-something."

"Karpanov," I said. In fact, the man in the booth did bear a disturbing resemblance to Sergei. He was thickly muscled, rigid; his steely, close-cropped hair seemed to cover a brain that churned out simple commands: eat, fuck, kill, hide.

"No way in the world that Russian is going to show his face in the U.S.A.," said Joe, fixing the pockets that Rosa's boy had pulled inside out.

"Maybe we shouldn't be talking about this," said Rosa, looking at me with concern.

"It's okay. I'm surprised you remember it. It was a long time ago."

"I guess I know a lot about Luke Fairchild. Not like an insider or anything. But I just love his stuff. Did they ever find Sergei?"

"Not yet," I said. "Every once in a while a story surfaces about him being back. Why he'd want to come back here, that's anybody's guess. He had some good times here, but that's hardly a reason to risk arrest. Then there's the Luke as Victim school, which has it that Sergei wants to find Luke, rough him up, crush his skull, whatever. Me, I'd love to talk to him."

"Well, maybe this is your chance," said Rosa.

"I doubt it. Why would it be him? There's no statute of limitations for murder."

"But I thought he was supposed to be innocent."

"I don't think so."

"Well, I love the song," she said. "The whole album was great."

We were silent for a moment, and then, to my horror, Rosa said his name in a kind of piercing, accosting whisper: "Sergei!" We watched, but the man in the front booth didn't move a muscle. And then he put his orange soda down on the table, and moistened the tips of two of his fingers, and methodically turned one of the expertly folded pages of his newspaper.

"Are you busy for dinner tonight?" I asked her.

7

ROSA drove Edgar to her mother's house, and from there she was going to pick up a bottle of red wine and come back here to have dinner with me. I was in the kitchen, marinating the vegetables, squinting at the directions on the box of Texarkana Rice—no Minute Rice for Mama, no Indian River, no Carolina: only obscure brands with six extra steps in the preparation. There was nothing in her cupboard that could be purchased in a run-of-the-mill supermarket, and certainly nothing that was advertised on TV. Bewildering varieties of Instant Karma soup, each costing nearly four dollars—Pumpkin Miso, Chinese Tree Ear, Oregon Fruit, Peruvian Potato and Cod. Bags of dried Japanese mushrooms. A jar of Austrian hazelnut butter. Boxes of risotto mix.

On a corked bulletin board near the kitchen phone was a long scroll of adding-machine paper, upon which Esther had written important telephone numbers. Fire. Police. Ambulance. Suburban Propane. Billy. The Shoreview Home. And then, at least fifty friends, most of them unknown to me, though I did see Joe's name, and Maya's, and Rosa's. There were a couple of churches, a synagogue across the river in Kingston, a women's shelter, something called Family of Woodstock. I knew my mother did volunteer work. But who were the others in this tribe? I'd had no idea she was part of such a vast network. Nearly all of them were just first names, except where there were repeats, and then only the last initial was tacked on. So they must have been intimates, real friends. How had she done it? How had any of them pulled it off? What did they give to each other, and what were the thousand varieties of love they shared—love that was as odd to me as the soups in my mother's cupboard? They had made themselves a family, a community, while all I had done was to perfect my solitude. My eyes scanned the list. Margie, Florida, Beth, Aaron, Annie L., Annie B., Dominick, Rudy, Marcus, Allen, Jorge, Debby V., Debby Z., Warren. The names sounded within me like an incomprehensible prayer. And then, in the middle of the list, I saw: Felix, Tess. My half-brother and half-sister. Their New York City numbers were crossed out and the new ones had an 802 area code. They were both in college at Bennington.

I stood there, stunned, my cheeks scalding. What were they doing on her list? How did they know each other? Why did they stay in touch? Whenever I tried to hook up with the twins, they avoided me; I could only have a word with them when I took them by surprise, when I lurked, and stalked. What language of connection was I missing? How had I gone so many years and remained emotionally illiterate?

The lid on the pot of steaming rice began to shake and clatter. I turned off the stove, checked the time. Rosa would be here very soon—Rosa with whom I had contrived to bypass conversation and head straight for sex.

I took a quick shower to get rid of the sharp smell of the hospital. My mother's tub had a rubber shower attachment. The window sill was filled with fragrant soaps, bottles of lotion, purple geodes, pink crystals, a big red sponge like Satan's brain. The water was barely warm; the drain was sluggish, and by the time I was finished I was standing in water above my ankles.

I had been wearing the same clothes since leaving Father Parker, and now that I was clean I felt there was no choice but to dress in my mother's clothes. I realized it was not a good sign when a son nearing thirty gets himself decked out in Mom's duds, but my mother and I were similarly built, and many of her clothes were boyish. I chose a white turtleneck, a blue cotton sweater, Gap jeans. I checked myself out in Mom's bedroom mirror. I looked fabulous. Her clothes fit me better than my own.

Rosa arrived a few minutes later, carrying two bottles of wine, looking nervous. I sensed in her excitement, in her jokiness, her playful, pushy, teasing manner, in her slightly too loud laughter, in the feverish glitter of her eyes, that some time while she was shopping she had made the decision to sleep with me.

Yet something happened while we were eating dinner that almost completely derailed the Erotica Express. Rosa gave me one of those squinting hey-wait-a-minute looks and said, "Are those Esther's clothes you're wearing?"

"Well, as a matter of fact, they are."

"May I ask a follow-up question?"

"I'm counting on it."

"Is it meant to be exciting?"

"To me?"

"Or me. Either of us. Anyone."

I shook my head, reached across the table, and touched Rosa's hand. I had a little hedgerow of humor to hide behind. "No part of me considers dressing up in my mother's clothing exciting."

Wine. More wine. And wishing for still more. I was aware, very aware that my mother was swathed in antiseptic bandages just a few miles away and I was here in the meanwhile flirting with a woman whose acquaintance I had just barely made, and this awareness burned in me like a yellow light, not stop, not go, but caution, watch it, look both ways, consider your life.

Why do we take off our clothes and introduce our sexual organs into those of people we barely know? Is it the mating urge? Hardly, I would say, since most of these moments of congress, were they to result in the beginnings of a new life, would cause us boundless misery, and we therefore generally take precautions against procreation and even go so far as to root the little bugger out, if it comes to that. Is it, then, a failure of wit that sends us racing into the sack, a sinking feeling that we cannot keep the conversation going another minute? I confess to having had sex because I couldn't think of anything else to say. Is it loneliness, a need to curl up like a child next to a warm body? Is it some sinister desire for power over another, a clammy curiosity over whether or not we can get so-and-so into bed with us? Is it boredom, is it anxiety, is it that lowliest of desires that expresses itself with a shrugging "Why not"? I was attracted to Rosa, liked her haircut, her shoes. She smelled nice, asked good questions, listened well, spoke well, cracked a couple of jokes—but could that possibly add up to our committing acts that others wait years to consummate, and even then only after long courtships, arrangements of dowries, familial negotiations, ceremonies that last all day and half the night, and then up to the conjugal bed, and next morning rip off the wedding sheets and hang them over the sunstruck cobblestone courtyard, where the children play and the hens cluck and the neighbors let out with a loud, good-natured, slightly smutty cheer to see the bloody red stain in the sheet's center, the hymen's maidenly evidence?

My being so adept at these hasty couplings might well have been inherited from Dad, who was (and probably remained) one of the champs of the quick seduction. He was—well, men have a phrase for it and it's rather embarrassing, but we say "successful with women," which casts a rather cold and unflattering light on the enterprise, revealing the empirical core of our sexual self-assessments: how many attempted, how many completed, a quick calculation and voilà, a passing average. According to Luke:

> *I've been with thousands of women*
> *Can't remember their names*
> *The jingle-jangle of their bracelets*
> *The circus smell of their perfume*
> *It all seems so distant*
> *It all seems so sad*
> *Pathetic, absurd*
> *Can it really have happened?*

> —"It Takes a Man to Crawl,"
> recorded 1982

Even when Luke was Stuart Kramer he wildly appealed to women—and, really, when you see those early photos you have to wonder why. He was skinny, unkempt, with teeth like a crumbling stone wall. His fingernails were long, each one a terrarium. With his hair short, combed with a part on the side, he looked geeky, outpatientish, and you could see that his head was wider on the bottom than on the top, like a buoy. He was a motherless child, with the emotional cunning necessary to meet his own needs. He knew how to make girls care about him, and feel powerful and protective around him.

Luke's powers of seduction were not of the big-man-on-campus variety, nor of the brooding bronzed Adonis, nor of the hissing snake in the tree of knowledge. And to say he got women into bed, got them to take off their clothes, peel off their undergarments, open their thighs and offer their sacred darkness, their unprotected, unprotectable softness—really, quite a remarkable thing, under any circumstances—by dint of his sheer neediness is to practice reality reduction to such a degree that it surpasses miniaturization and becomes sheer distortion. That long, long string of women who loved Luke did not go to bed with him out of pity or even concern. They wanted him. Why? He was on his own, he was often in trouble, and he was a troublemaker. He was the virtual prototype of the boy parents warned their daughters against. When Luke was young, fucking him was like running away from home, or maybe even joining the circus. He was wild, he was strange, the smell of freedom was all over him, that mixture of smoke and wind and cheap wine, as redolent as peanuts, sawdust, and elephants.

Yet it was not only freedom he offered; it was acceptance, too. He did not care if you were a little heavy, or if you were skinny, or if your breasts were small, or if your pubic hair percolated straight up to your belly button, or if you had a little shadow of mustache over your lip, or a hooked nose, or wore glasses, or if your hands were manly, your feet immense, or any of the other ten thousand things that young girls worry themselves sick over. He did not care if you were black or white or brown or yellow. And if there was something strange in you, that was fine; there was something strange in him, too. He talked about piss and shit and pimples, his own bad breath, his b.o. There was nothing you could do to turn him off, and he let you know it—and that was tremendously effective for him, back then, when he was just a runaway teen living in the storerooms of St. Louis record shops.

And let's not forget the other important ingredient that allowed him to rack up such a staggering number of lovers in those pre-sexual-revolution days in the late fifties and early sixties—he was a bulldog of desire, never letting it rest until he had what he wanted. And he was a despot of cool. If you did not follow him wherever he wanted you to, he made you feel narrow-minded. If you did not do things his way, he made you feel awkward, pathetic, frightened. Though functionally an orphan, never having known his mother, his pale, sunken-eyed and suicidal father in and out of hospitals, shock treatment, Luke concentrated on middle-class girls from Ozzie-and-Harrietsville, girls whose breath he could literally take away with the danger and cunning of his own life and whose occasional words of demurral he would not hesitate to assign to bourgeois cowardice. "Don't go bourgeois on me, baby," he'd say.

He knew where all the best parties were; he knew about the Douglas Bake Shop, which gave you free samples of warm bread if you were there when they took them out of the oven at five in the morning. (Listen to "Free Samples," recorded 1963: "*St. Louis morning like a sky full of biscuits....*") He was forever off on an adventure, and that was part of the deal, too. If you slept with Stuart Kramer, you not only got the best sex he could give you (in those days he was ardent, animalistic) but you got to share in the drama and ramble of his life as well. And he did make the helter-skelter of his days—in and out of school, no real address, more days on friends' sofas or even park benches than in the little narrow bed in his own room—seem daring and desirable. He was Tom Sawyer (another Missouri kid) painting the fence of his own life, whistling, making up songs, making it all seem so irresistible.

By the time Stuart became Luke, he had slept with about two hundred girls—Dad's own bragging is the helium that has filled this Macy's Thanksgiving Day Parade float of a number, but the estimate turns out to be reasonably accurate. Which, naturally, raised in me the inevitable question: putting aside my half-brotherhood to Felix and Tess, how many other demi-sibs have I got out there? (And if they have married and bred, then how many demi-nieces and -nephews?) And this speculation always brings me to the oft-broached yet nevertheless eternally sensitive subject of Luke's undescended testicle and his low, low, low sperm count. Even if we accept his inflated rhymes about his genitalia ("*It took fifty firemen to unfurl the hose,*" "*Come on mama climb the Eiffel Tower,*" etc., etc.), there is no question but that as long and thick as it may (or may not) have been, it was, on a simply reproductive level, a wan thing. If semen were orange juice, then his was made from concentrate: seedless. If semen were cream, then what he was putting out was not even milk, it was not even two-percent, it was skim, it was lactose-free, watery bluish-gray, practically transparent. Et cetera. Thirsty little devil, he drank significant amounts of beer, wine, Coke, water, and his ejaculations, no matter how frequent, were large and wet: but it was a river without fish. In all probability, his low sperm count was the result of his one-ballishness. His right ball was a kiwi, but the apartment next door was vacant, a little shrivel of sac, a droopy hirsute fringe. I always thought of this absent friend as "undescended," which was how the biographers would have it, but really it was only Luke's assumption that the right nut was somewhere up there, hiding out in the maze of guts like an outlaw in the badlands.

> *Through the fog in the plaza in the heart of Barcelona*
> *Blows a one-way ticket to Never Can Be*
> *I wander this world in boots of illusion*
> *The lie of generation . . . oh, it ends with me*
>
> *Christ on His cross left no sons behind him*
> *Buddha was childless, Mohammed lived free*

Ten million soiled souls cry out for salvation
The crime of generation . . . ah, it ends with me

The earth is a vault that the robbers have plundered
New York dumps its dead into the sea
The orchards are deserts, the fountain is empty
The sin of generation ends with me.

—"Cancel My Reservation," recorded 1985

Not only was Luke resigned to his sperm's lack of motility, but in fact he made it a virtue. He came to view, or at least portray, himself as somehow too spiritual to breed (see "Recreational Model") and his dick itself too magical to be confused with mere mortal members (see "Hunt for the Unicorn"). The inability to breed was evidence of having advanced to an elevated rung on the evolutionary ladder, like not getting your wisdom teeth, it meant delicacy, airiness, and gentility—a word that is next-door neighbor to "gentile": while the ethnics bred like bunnies, the Wasps were like pandas. If we take Luke at his word—and there were a number of medical reports to back him up—then my conception could be viewed as something of a miracle. For years, for practically a decade (so we're talking here at least twenty-five hundred nights of ejaculations), Luke used no form of contraception, and he encouraged in his legions of lovers the same attitude—though clearly there was nothing he could do about it if any of his many one-night stands was taking birth-control pills or sported an IUD. But a condom was out of the question ("Puts a hood on his Johnson, like he's in the KKK"—"Naturally," recorded 1970), and he would not tolerate the gels and delays of a diaphragm, and foam was a turn-off, too, like spraying insulation in there, and he wasn't going to lie to you and tell you he'd pull out before he came because he wasn't going to do that, he wasn't going to puddle himself on your stomach. "With me, you don't have to worry," he'd say, and apparently he'd say it the same way each time: winking, raising his forefinger, tilting his head to the right, as if he might be trying to lighten up something intrinsically sad, confessing to a deformity but not making you uncomfortable, heading your pity off at the pass. And in the words of Derek Arthur, the portly, stammering, tobacco-stained British Lukologist whose bloodless, doe-eyed child bride hiked up her miniskirt and let Dad screw her in an (attended!) elevator at Brown's, "He was bloody well believed—not just by the Sluts and the Plaster-Casters and the Pathetic Groupies and the Drugged-Out Skanks, but by women of some quality who ought to have known better."

I always assumed my mother would have made it into Arthur's category of Women Who Ought to Have Known Better (though his own wife was relegated to Pathetic Groupies, in his book's British hardcover edition, and then to Drugged-Out Skanks, in the American paperback), but I think the fact was that Esther half believed Luke when he told her that he would not and could not make her pregnant, and she also half desired a child, though emotions as conflicted as these don't generally divide themselves neatly in half—perhaps only twenty percent of my mother wanted a child, or maybe it was even ten, but it was enough for her to go along with months and months of contraception-less sex, wild, practically compulsive couplings that took them in and out of bedrooms all over New York—in her old bedroom in her parents' house, on her nubby, nunnish little bedspread, in the Albert Hotel, with the sounds of Chuck Berry singing "Roll Over Beethoven" and another copulating couple echoing in the air shaft, further uptown at the Warwick, with the smell of room-service roast beef sandwiches in the cool air, in Chelsea, in Harlem, on the Lower East Side, and straight across America, while Luke toured to larger and larger and wilder and wilder crowds and I, unborn, hung pinioned on radiant spears of starlight waiting for the moment when one of Dad's lackadaisical little sperm proceeded from his one working ball, squiggled to the epididymus, and then with an *I think I can I think I can* somehow figured the way to Esther's ovum.

It, I, was a miracle—but a miracle no one particularly wanted, with the ambivalent exception of my mother. Even her parents wanted her to get an abortion, though abortions were then illegal and both my grandparents, as a reaction to McCarthyism and the execution of the Rosenbergs, were terrified by the idea of breaking the law, any law—they even paid full price for me at the movies when it could have easily been said that I was eleven. When I asked Esther what Luke's feelings were when she told him she was pregnant—and I came to ask her often—she never said much more than "He wasn't there for me." He wasn't there for you? Then where was he? But my mother did talk to Neil Schwartz—and here I may as well take the opportunity to admit (to myself) that Mom and Neil almost certainly were lovers—and I have it on his authority that when she realized she was pregnant she immediately went to the Port Authority and with her customary frugality took a bus to La Guardia Airport, and then (flying standby) caught American Airlines flight 44 to Chicago, where Luke was at the end of a three-night engagement at a toney North Side club called the Gate of Horn.

The following, then, comes from Neil's most recent, and perhaps final, piece of Lukology, a massive work called *The Gospel According to Luke:*

> By the time Esther finally tracked Luke down, it was already evening. Luke had moved out of the Conrad Hilton, where he had been made to feel unwanted, and

was staying with so-called "sick comedian" Lenny Bruce, in an apartment of a drug-dealing friend of Bruce's, on Rush Street, an easy walk to the Gate of Horn. By the time Esther arrived, she was exhausted and beginning to doubt the wisdom of having made the journey. "I kept on thinking that maybe I just should have called him with the news or waited till he got back from his tour," Esther said, years later. "But I was pretty freaked out and I really wanted to see him."

When Esther knocked on the door to Apartment 7G, she was met by Lenny Bruce, whose pale swollen corpus was covered by nothing but a bath towel and a pair of calf-high black socks. Bruce had been expecting a drug delivery and was struck with surprise when he threw the door open to the elegant, dark Miss Rothschild.

"Who the hell are you?" Bruce asked, clutching his towel.

Esther was well aware of who Bruce was. In the late Fifties and early Sixties, Lenny Bruce was one of the most well-known comics in America, and to the hip set he was the only stand-up comedian worth listening to. Luke had two of Bruce's early records (*The Sick Humor of Lenny Bruce* and *I'm Not a Nut—Elect Me*) and he often played them for Esther, frowning at her when she failed to laugh. Her taste in humor went toward the menschier grooves of Mel Brooks and Carl Reiner, with their jokes about Jewish cavemen and nectarines, and she found Bruce's rat-a-tat riffs about hookers and airplane glue abrasive, and even a little depressing.

Still, her reaction to seeing Bruce was a feeling of happiness for Luke. She knew Luke admired the middle-aged comic and that Luke liked nothing more than the chance to actually meet someone whose work he admired. (In fact, Rothschild recalls seeing a master list of the people whom Luke wanted to meet—Jacqueline Kennedy, Thelonious Monk, Willie Mays, Tuesday Weld, and Jean-Paul Sartre were some of the names, and Bruce's name was on there, too. When the celebrity was finally met, Luke put a check next to his or her name.)

"Is Luke here?" Esther asked, but before Bruce could answer, Esther heard Luke's laughter coming from the front room of the disheveled, odoriferous apartment. Bruce must have known what was going to happen next, because he did his best to impede Esther's progress— taking her gently by the arm and fixing her with a soulful stare. (A few years later, when Bruce died of an overdose, Esther attended his funeral services, a lone black-clad figure standing off to the side in the rain.)

Luke was sitting on the floor of the airless, fantastically disheveled bedroom, sharing a joint with jazz guitarist Roland Dougherty, Luke's own backup guitarist "Boona" Baker, and folk diva Wendy Crabtree. In folkie circles, Luke and Wendy had been linked for several months. They had played several festivals together, and Wendy had recently recorded several Fairchild songs along with her usual program of English, Irish, and French-Canadian ballads. But this was the first time the usually sanguine and sexually self-confident Esther had seen them together—in fact, Luke and Wendy had just become lovers—and the sight shook her to the core. Wendy sat with her back to the unmade bed and her long bare legs stretched out before her. She wore a buckskin dress and a sleeveless blouse; her skin was very dark and her black hair was long enough for her to sit on. Esther stared at this woman who was suddenly her rival and Wendy, despite her reputation for fearlessness, lowered her eyes in embarrassment.

"What are you doing here, Essie?" asked Luke. Bluish marijuana smoke came out of his nostrils as he spoke. He didn't seem particularly upset and not even all that surprised. "No one told me you were here."

Whatever possible answers to Luke's question flickered through Esther's mind, all she could say was the plain unvarnished truth. "I came here to tell you I'm having a baby," she said.

It's interesting to note her choice of words. She did not say "I'm in trouble," or "I missed my period," or even "I'm pregnant." She said "I'm having a baby," which clearly revealed her intention to bear this child, and Luke, whose very personal brand of empathy generally allowed him to hear everything that a speaker intended and often a great deal which the speaker wished to conceal, understood from this moment on that the woman who was, to that point, the love of his life and who was, arguably, the love of his entire life, was about to take a step into a realm which every fiber in Luke's being forbade him from entering himself.

He was silent for a few moments. "I remember waiting for him to say something," Esther recalled, years later. "I remember the pot smell mixed with the come smell and the dirty laundry in that room, and I remember Mr. Bruce standing behind me just touching me lightly on the small of my back because I think he was worried I might pass out, and I remember poor Boona jiggling his knees, he was so nervous. But most of all I remember Wendy Crabtree's black eyes darting little looks at me and this mysterious little smile on her face. I remember wanting to kick her, which was nothing I had ever felt about a human being before, or even a stray cat."

Luke finally took Esther to a nearby Chinese restaurant near Sixty-third and Stony Island Boulevard, a little storefront joint beneath the timbers and iron of the overhead El tracks. Esther was content with a pot of tea but Luke, who ate with huge, though infrequent bursts of appetite, ordered egg rolls, wonton soup, sweet and sour shrimp, and several other items from the menu, asking that they all be brought out at the same time. The table was laid as if for a feast for ten people; Luke gave no sign of noticing that his girlfriend wasn't eating a bite.

Luke ate ravenously. His chin, which was sporting the beginnings of what even at its full flower would be a wispy beard, shone with grease. All his life, Luke had tried to control his environment by making certain his reactions to events were offbeat. Just as he dissolved into a fit of hysterical laughter when he learned of his father's suicide, or stuck a penknife into the meat of his thumb when he learned that his second album for Epoch had sold one hundred thousand copies in its first week on the market, now Luke reacted to the news of Esther's pregnancy with a display of gluttony that would have embarrassed King Henry VIII.

Finally, poor Esther could bear it no longer. "Don't you have anything to say?" she wailed.

"I'm trying to be a gentleman here," said Luke. "Any other man would be giving you the third degree, but I figure when you want to tell me who the father is, then you will, and in the meantime pass the shrimp, little darling, can you do that for me?"

"Tell you who the father is? What are you talking about? You're the father."

THE RICH MAN'S TABLE

"Oh man, it would be so fucking cool if I could only believe that."

Over the next few months, as Esther Rothschild became more and more pregnant, larger, more easily tired, and certainly less interested than ever in being a part of Luke's increasingly high-profile life, Luke tried to convince her to abort the child and go back to the relationship they had enjoyed in the past. "I miss you, Essie," he'd say, shaking his head, staring at the bulge in her stomach, and sometimes even falling to his knees and weeping with loneliness—though Esther suspected these crying fits were an excuse for Luke to put his head against her stomach and listen for signs of the child within.

I never intended to quibble with Neil Schwartz or the Neil Schwartzes of this world, of which there are legion—the half-truth brigade. Isolating some favorite, fetishized facts in favor of other, less lovely or less exciting, ones is really a kind of intellectual pornography. Neil could only go so far in portraying Luke's selfish panic at the news of my inception; Neil, who despite his many, many kindnesses toward me (guitar lessons, skates, Yankees games, Pelé autograph) was just another Lukologist. The so-called exposés of my father were done in the spirit of a farmer harvesting a field: even as the cotton is picked, new bullshit must be spread for next year's crop. The unwritten law of professional Lukology is never to go so far in exposing the truth that people will stop wanting to read about the great man, thus ending the whole industry.

What Neil failed to include in *The Gospel* was that my father mounted a wild and constant campaign to convince my mother to have an abortion. The son of a bitch wanted me scraped out. The thought of Luke, with all his powers of persuasion, using everything from his hipness to my mother's adoring attachment to him to convince her to terminate me, and the bravery of her resistance to him, has made me, over the years, practically swoon with an endlessly reenacted sense of danger and rescue, danger and rescue, danger and rescue—the great drama of my life, played out before I was born.

Birth control. As Rosa and I staggered and stumbled toward my mother's room, though I was wearing my mother's clothes and about to make love to a friend of my mother's, in my mother's bed, I was primarily worrying about birth control. Rosa threw herself onto the bed, fun-loving thing that she suddenly was, and landed flat on her back. I knew the unwritten choreography of these moments well enough to know that now I was supposed to fling myself upon her, break my fall with my hands so that my body hovered just over hers, and then kiss her deeply, while I gradually lowered myself onto her, the journey of a push-up but not round-trip. But I just stood there, grinning inanely—though with a humiliatingly hard erection.

"Are you on the pill or something?" I said.

She had already begun unbuttoning her blouse. Her breasts, as if anticipating their impending freedom, seemed to grow larger. "No way," she said. "Are you?"

"I don't believe they've perfected the male contraceptive pill yet," I said.

"Well, they haven't perfected the woman's pill either, but that doesn't stop doctors from handing them out."

"Point taken," I said.

Her fingers stopped unbuttoning her blouse, but she was still smiling. "Anyhow," she said, "you have to wear a condom. Safe sex and . . . well, you know."

"I don't travel with condoms," I said.

"Darn."

"Darn?"

"I'm disappointed."

"I was sort of hoping *you'd* have one."

"I'm old-fashioned. A man invites me for dinner, I bring a couple bottles of wine, but that's about it."

"Well. What should we do?"

"There's always a cold shower."

I must have looked more disappointed than I realized. She got one of those "Aw, whatsamatter?" looks and reached up toward me.

"I can give you a hand job, if you like," she said, but softly, with a kind of purr in her voice, so it didn't sound that bad.

"I don't really want a hand job," I replied, hastily, without weighing my options.

"I don't mind. I've even given them to my dog."

"Now that's an enticement. Which hand did you use?"

She looked at both of her hands, laughed. I spooned next to her, stroked her hair, following the curve of her skull, and then massaged her neck.

"What's your dog's name?" I whispered.

Her body tensed. She raised herself on her elbows, glanced (guiltily?) at me.

"Why'd you ask that?"

"I'm just kidding. It's . . . it's a non sequitur. It's something I do."

She dropped flat onto the bed again. Silence. Inactivity.

"Well, now you've made me curious," I said.

"Luke," she said, resigned.

"You're kidding." But, really, I ought to have been grateful it was just her dog and not her son.

Rosa looked away. I followed her eyes; she seemed to be looking at the framed photo of Esther, Grandpa, and me on my mother's night table. She was trying to figure a way out of what had suddenly become an uncomfortable situation. She felt she had hurt my feelings, and also she had exposed a certain rather grotesque groupiness in herself. But what to do now? She decided to sweep it all under a carpet made of sex. She turned over to face me, so close her features were a womanly blur. She ran her fingers through my Lukish curls. She nibbled at my long Lukish earlobe. I forgave her. The temptation of celebrity was too strong. And Luke was more than a star—he was a prophet, a god. I was probably as close as Rosa would ever come to touching immortality. Why did I think she was better than that? I was no better than that.

"If you promise to be careful, we can make love anyhow," she whispered directly into my ear.

"I can sing Luke songs while we do it." I think I must have been trying to queer the deal. I think I wanted to talk, to befriend her, to start building my list of names of people I could call and who would call me, rather than just add another woman to my list of ludicrous conquests.

"Shhh." She gave me a shut-up kiss.

What happened to her child, her child's father, her mother, her past, her boots, her privacy and dreams? The particularity of her was being blown to bits like a little Hiroshima of the soul, irradiated, cooked by the ten thousand suns of Luke's fame.

"What if you get pregnant?" I said.

"I won't."

"Famous last words."

"Well then, what?" She pressed her pelvic bone into my hip.

"Hand job?" I said, more or less joking.

She was silent for a moment and then she said, "Do you want to go first? Or can I?"

She took my hand and guided it to her crotch. She rolled onto her back. She spread her arms, her legs. She looked like an X on my mother's bed. She held me in place and moved herself against my palm. Et cetera, et cetera. Fade to black.

8

Rosa was still with me when I got a call from the hospital, informing me that my grandfather had arrived and was insisting upon seeing Esther, which was of course impossible, and he wouldn't budge, which was of course typical of him, and would I please come right over and collect him.

Grandpa Irv was sitting in the reception area when I arrived. He was erect, taut as barbed wire, with a little plaid suitcase, such as a child would carry, at his feet, and his cane leaning against the wall. His eyes were closed. There he was, the man who had always symbolized for me logic, unflappability, and tireless hard work. Irving Z. Rothschild—the Z stood for nothing, it was just a letter his mother stuck in there to distinguish him from another Irving Rothschild who lived in their building on Hester Street. Grandpa seemed to be asleep. "Grandpa!" I called out. I had left Mother's house somewhat irritated by his sudden arrival and the trouble he was causing at the hospital, but now that he was before me I was so deeply grateful to see him.

He snapped to. Years on call had left him with a well-oiled nervous system. He sprang to his feet, unconsciously reached for something—perhaps his doctor's bag, that old brown leather satchel that used to be at his bedside, holding a stethoscope, tongue depressors, syringes, pills, and little pamphlets about socialized medicine he gave to certain of his patients, the ones he felt needed political education.

"Billy!" he said, opening his arms to me.

We embraced. He had shrunk, but there were still five feet and eight inches left to him. Yet he was hollowed out now; his bones were like soda-shop straws. He patted my back, clasped my hand. Looking at me overcame him for a moment, and to keep himself from crying he impulsively pulled my hand to his mouth and kissed it, a weird, courtly, yet somehow hysterical gesture.

Blessed as I felt by my grandfather's kiss, so rescued, so loved, the moment he touched his lips to the back of my hand I remembered I had left the house without washing, and my fingers might still be cunty. Grandpa had a sense of smell like a bloodhound, and as the other senses faded, his olfactory genius only increased. He could smell the ocean when we were miles away from it, burned coffee across the river in New Jersey, shoe polish on a passer-by, sesame noodles when we were still six blocks from Chinatown. I gently dislodged my hand and then pretended to scratch my nose—sure enough, they were redolent of getting Rosa off.

"How'd you get here?" I asked.

"A friend. What difference does it make? Who's the attending physician? I have to talk to him."

"You can't do that now."

"Does he know he's dealing with the daughter of a physician?"

Actually he, or they, did not. It struck me: Esther, to the people in this hospital, was the woman who used to go out with Luke Fairchild. That her father was a doctor was as unknown to them as the sachets of dried lavender in her dresser drawers, or the way she moved her hand in front of her face to obscure her slightly gummy smile, and it hadn't occurred to me to mention it.

An elderly woman in a pink quilted robe came up to us, supported on an aluminum walker. She wheeled an IV tower along with her; her left hand was purple from the bruises of needles going in and out. She was freshly lipsticked, with a strangely young, wild look to her—like a country girl on a boozy Saturday night.

"I want to thank you for all your good advice," she said.

"That's perfectly all right, my dear," Grandpa said, the strain in his voice suddenly submerged beneath the savory baritone of his professional voice, that mixture of kindness and condescension he used for forty-four years in his ministrations to the Brooklyn left and the Brooklyn poor. "Just remember the folks in this hospital have bought a lot of very, very expensive equipment and they want to use it at every opportunity. You follow me, dear? They order up test after test, cause you a great deal of discomfort—but remember: they tack it onto the bill. You have the right to say no. So you make sure they explain every procedure."

"Oh, I will, I can promise you that," she said. It looked for a moment as if she wanted to touch Grandpa, but she was as unstable on her walker as an uncooked egg and she didn't dare.

As the woman clumped away, Grandpa gave me a brief but unmistakable "So there!" look, as if it had been my idea to close up his practice, put him out to pasture in Seizure World.

"Let's get out of here," I said.

"Why? You don't like it here?" He smiled; his teeth were large, unevenly placed, Druidical stones. "You were always so squeamish."

"You must be exhausted."

"I'm fine. Soon, I'll be asleep for eternity. Now I like to keep my eyes open. Are you at Mommy's?"

It had only been since Grandma's death that Irv had taken to calling his daughter Mommy.

I picked up his suitcase. Together we walked toward the door; as we approached the front desk, the night nurse quickly busied herself with something on her computer. Grandpa must have given her hell before I got there and she clearly wanted to avoid even looking at him.

Outside, in the hospital parking lot, the night air was chilly, but nonetheless fragrant with the shy, hesitant spring. Honeysuckle, wet earth. Above, the sky was so full of stars it seemed as if some of them might spill to earth. Grandpa stopped to look up, holding on to my arm for balance.

"Now there's a sight," he said, softly. "Look at all our relatives out there." It had been one of his consolations during my fatherless childhood, how we were all originally descended from matter, the same matter that made the Big Dipper, Cassiopeia, and every other star in the sky.

"She's going to make it," I said, inanely, but meaning it, too. I was now one of those people who believed in the sympathetic magic of the well-meaning sentiment. And why not? What else do we have? The clenched fist eventually becomes crossed fingers.

"Which one's yours?" he asked me, gesturing with his cane to the little knot of cheap sedans gathered in an otherwise empty parking lot.

"That one," I said, pointing to a dark green Ford Probe.

"That's your car?" I didn't know if he meant it was too good for me, or not good enough.

"It's rented."

"So you've got a credit card," he said.

"Yeah, I've totally sold out to the corporate machine. Moloch's my main man, now."

Grandpa nodded, waited for me to open the door for him. I

stood there helplessly, watching him negotiate the series of bends, twists, and slides necessary for him to get into the car. He looked like someone trying to walk down a narrow flight of stairs with a wide-open umbrella. Everything was such a hassle for him—his bones, his bowels, his eyes, his ears, gravity, history, memory. The last time I visited him at Shoreview, I found in his shirt pocket little slips of paper upon which he had carefully printed some of the names he had been forgetting of people at the home—the doctors, the physical therapists, the attendants. He hadn't bothered with the other inmates.

As soon as I drove out of the hospital parking lot, Grandpa closed his eyes, and a moment later he was asleep. There was comfort there, being beside him. He had been as close to a father as I had in this world. When I was very young, and consumed with shame over my fatherlessness, I sometimes pointed Irv out to others and claimed that dapper, elderly man as my dad. For the three months I was a Cub Scout, it was Irv who brought me to meetings—Esther tried, but my conformist urges were like fingernails on the blackboard of her emotional radicalism, whereas Irv, crafty old Leninist, believed in boring from within—and it was Irv who came limping along for the father-and-son camping trip to Bear Mountain. It was Irv who gave me my first glass of beer when I was fifteen, skunky Canadian brew which he poured as lovingly as if it were expensive Champagne: "Better than seltzer for after a meal." And it was Irv whom Esther assigned to give me a talk about sex—which he did in his office, complete with detailed medical illustrations—after which I was fairly well equipped to deliver a baby.

I pulled in front of my mother's house and gently shook Grandpa's shoulder to awaken him. He woke instantly, but the paleness of him, the caved-in quality of his mouth, the stunned emptiness of his eyes gave the impression of someone waking from death.

"We're here," I said, not much above a whisper. "Esther's house." I realized he was scrambling for an idea of where he was.

I walked around the car to open the door for him. The night, despite the avalanche of stars, felt like an abandoned house. I heard the shrill, unearthly cries of coyote cubs coming from somewhere in the invisible woods, manic, eerily melodic yips and howls—how Esther loved them!

"You need some help?" I asked, holding out my hand to him. He didn't answer, but he gripped me—his hand was cool, smooth, like a statue suddenly capable of movement. I gently tugged, and he allowed me to pull him to his feet, out of the car.

Grandpa secured his balance and then looked toward the house. The lights in the bedroom windows blazed like fires in the darkness. He looked at his stricken daughter's cottage in the middle of nowhere, far from Brooklyn, somehow even farther from Manhattan, far from theaters and galleries and meetings, far from the UN, far from Federal Plaza, and Grand Army Plaza, and One Centre Street, and all the other places where father and daughter demonstrated to end the arms race, or free Angela Davis, far from any life that Irv himself would consider worth living, her hideaway, her early retirement home, this slate-and-shingle crypt of keepsakes and diaries, with its cupboards full of esoteric teas, and the beams of its attic groaning from the weight of her boxes of photographs, and its basement the burying ground of all her empty liquor bottles—for though she drank in secret, she created a kind of sorrowing archaeology of every slip. It was a place away, an obscurity, an irrelevance that always irked Irv; but tonight, as it floated before us in a sea of darkness, he was unaccountably moved by the sight of it.

"What a pretty house," he said, and gazed at it as if it were a kind of paradise. "It's really pretty, isn't it?" His voice was quaking. Irv was an emotional man, but his feelings were often unpredictable to him—they ambushed him, or blew through him like sudden storms. His attitudes toward daily life were shaped by the rigors of medical science—measured, clean, methodical, dogged and pessimistic—and his sense of fate was entirely circumscribed by scientific socialism, a Marxist view of history as an implacable engine driving humanity to its destination: that paradise of freedom from money and property where everyone was a Messiah. But now he stood before his daughter's humble house, a house that in her absence had become her in his imagination, and I knew it was taking everything of his waning strength to keep him from sobbing out loud.

We walked into the living room. The remains of the fire that Rosa and I had made glowed like slag. A note was tacked to the pine mantel: "Was that You, Was that Me?? Call and discuss. R." I tore it down and impulsively tossed it into the fire.

Irv sat near the hearth and held his hands up to the flame, turning them this way and that, and I ducked into Esther's room. I sniffed to see if the scent of sex was in the air; the fact that I could not detect a thing gave me scant comfort. I plumped the pillows, opened the window an inch or two. I looked out into the darkness. It seemed that no matter what the circumstance, there was something I was trying to cover up, always rearranging the furniture of my life to hide threadbare spots on the carpet.

"You can sleep in Mom's room and I'll take the sofa," I said, rejoining Irv in the living room. He had slipped off his shoes and, with stiffened legs, held his feet up to the fire. They looked like tough, skinny, city squirrels in those gray ribbed socks.

"You aren't going to bed right now, are you, Billy?"

"I just thought you might be tired."

"I could eat."

We went into the kitchen. I warmed the last of the lasagna and poured him a glass of dark, cloudy apple juice, which, though it was an unfamiliar brand, I managed to assure him made no claims to be a curative or elixir of any kind. I poured a glass for myself and sat at the uncovered pine table with him and watched as he ate.

"Are they doing the right things?" I asked.

He shook his head—but not emphatically, he didn't want to completely terrify me. "We should get her out of there tomorrow. I know they want to send her up to Albany Medical Center, but I want her in the city. The name Dr. Rothschild still means a lot in New York City. We'll send her to Roosevelt Hospital and get this done right."

I nodded, and then took a long drink of apple juice, which tasted like some magical distillation of sunlight and decay. I had been trying to ask this question since her crash, but it kept eluding me, like an object in a dream. It was beyond my saying. "What are the chances of her dying?" I finally said. "I heard she might get an embolism or something from bone marrow in her blood."

"Who told you that?"

"A nurse."

"A nurse? She has no business playing doctor." As egalitarian as his politics might have been, Grandpa was rigidly hierarchical about medicine.

"But what about what she said?"

"Don't you worry about that, Billy. Okay?"

"It's too late for that, Grandpa. I already am worried. Just answer me, okay?"

"Telling you not to worry is an answer."

"No it's not, it's advice. What are her chances?"

"They're good."

"Good?"

"Good to excellent."

"But not excellent."

"What's wrong with you? She's had a terrible accident. She's in a coma. Do you know what that means, to be in a coma?"

"I'm really frightened."

"I know you are, Billy. But you know, you've always been frightened, you've been frightened your whole life. You were afraid of the dark, you were afraid of snakes. Grandma and I took you to Coney Island to see the fireworks one Fourth of July. Everyone was cheering, but you just pressed your face into me, closed your eyes, and covered your ears. And then after you got sick, you were even more frightened. You didn't want to play with your friends. You started wondering how much time alive you had left, and then if a ballgame was rained out or if you were sick on your birthday—"

"I don't think being frightened for my mother right now is an irrational fear. Do you?"

"Irrational? No. But not useful, either. Is there any more of this lasagna?"

After, we went back to the living room and Grandpa asked me to put another log on the fire and I walked out to the porch, where there were split logs stacked beneath a green tarp. I pulled out a couple that felt light, remembering that Esther had said these were the ones that burned most quickly, and then stood there for a moment watching the vapors of my breath race upward toward the full moon. I was sending smoke signals up to the gods: Save her, save us. No dying, no pain; no more pain.

I threw the logs onto the fire, igniting an explosion of orange sparks. Grandpa went back to warming his hands and feet—I wasn't sure if this was really necessary or just his idea of what one did in the country—and I sat behind him in

Mother's antique armchair, with its creamy satin cover and its needlepoint roses.

"Do you remember Little Joe Washington?" I said.

"Of course I do," said Grandpa. "Mr. Washington and Esther became very good friends."

"He came to the hospital today."

"Your mother has always inspired such loyalty—with the exception of You Know Who."

"Then Joe and I went to a diner in town and I had the strangest feeling that Sergei Karpanov was sitting up front."

Grandpa turned around and at the same time the fire began to rage, silhouetting him as he put his hands on his hips. "You saw Karpanov?"

"No, it wasn't him. But the guy looked a lot like him."

"Did you ever see him, the murderer?"

"Just pictures. Did you?"

"No." He pursed his lips and shook his head, regretfully. "But you know of course that his poor wife was a guest in my home. When she came to New York as part of the East-West Medical Friendship Committee. I was on the committee that helped organize the whole thing. Karpanov. I wish it had been him. I'd gladly kill him. Joyfully. I would whistle the 'Ode to Joy' and cut him to pieces."

He turned back toward the fire and held his palms up to the flames. And I sat there, overwhelmed by a memory that, while I ransacked others for their stories of Luke, I had, until this very moment, somehow lost track of.

Of course Sergei's wife had been to Grandpa's house. I knew that. My mother had been to the welcoming party, and I had been there, too. This simple fact had been obscured by my sudden accumulation of stories about my father, and I was amazed at this: how much more was hiding behind the warehouse of junk I had in my head?

Mother and I had taken the D train from West Fourth Street and twenty-five minutes later we were in another world, Brooklyn, specifically Ditmas Park, Taft-era bourgeois houses with their wide porches and leaded glass windows, their self-satisfied, almost fierce stolidity, with menorahs in some of the windows and Christmas trees in the others. We trudged through a light, stinging snowfall. It was Sunday, about noon; there wasn't another soul on the streets. The sky looked like a reflection of the pavement. This was far from unfamiliar territory for me, but Esther nevertheless pointed out her childhood landmarks: the Tudor house with the dead juniper bushes in front where her first boyfriend, Gary Cohen, lived; the synagogue that had invited Truman Capote to speak at their cultural program and where Capote arrived insanely drunk, in a dirty suit, by turns weepy and insulting; Mr. Michael of Brooklyn, where she had her hair shorn like Joan of Arc's; the candy store run by concentration camp survivors, who were so suspicious, so fearful of having so much as a Mary Jane pilfered from their shop that they glowered at every kid who shopped there and who were, in turn, hated and taunted, even by kids from devoutly Jewish households. "I feel so terrible when I think of how we treated them," she had said, holding her lamb's wool coat closed at the throat and linking her arm through mine. I was in college, home for the holidays, feeling at once superior to my old life as Esther's little boy and desperate to soak up every ounce of the love she gave me. I had snorted a couple small lines of coke that morning upon waking, and I had more in my pocket, stored in one of Esther's empty Midol bottles.

My grandparents' house was getting that run-down feel to it. The plants were drooping, the once crisp white walls were gray, the smudgy windows were like eyes full of tears. Every room seemed to be worried sick over Grandma, convalescing now and getting worse, her body a forest in which fires of errant white cells spontaneously burst into flames, burning bushes of cancer, blazing to proclaim the power not of God but of Death. In the past year, confined to the house, she had taken up painting, and her cubist canvases hung on every wall, paintings of graves, and headstones, and empty beds, and stars of David—Grandma was an atheist, but not in the foxhole of her own imminent demise. She was asleep when we arrived, and Irv was busy in the kitchen, instructing the caterers—whereas once he seemed barely to notice his surroundings, wanting only an easy chair, an unread paper, and a hot meal, old age had made him fussy about domestic matters, and he was upset that the caterers had brought coffee mugs and not proper cups with matching saucers. Esther slowly made her way through the rooms, dazed with the sadness of anticipating—she knew soon she would be losing her mother, with whom she had quarreled so regularly, who instinctively stiffened when Esther embraced her, who made cutting remarks about Esther's sexual adventurism, and whose criticisms of Luke had been so insulting, so irritating, and, in many ways, so on the mark.

An hour later, the house was filled with the progressive doctors who had ministered to Esther her entire life: walruslike Benjamin Goldfarb, her first gynecologist; mousy Ida Edelman, from whom she received allergy treatments; and there in the corner, with a dark blue overcoat draped over his shoulders, his hair turned silver, a shy, regretful smile on his shy, regretful face, was Peter Carbone, who twenty-five years ago had gently removed her wisdom teeth with no more effort, it seemed, than plucking a Chiclet out of a pudding. Under the tongue-loosening spell of the sodium pentothal, Mom had confessed her torrid teenage crush on Dr. Carbone and then she grabbed for his large amber ears so she might pull his face close and French him.

Soon, the Russians arrived in a caravan of Checker cabs. Under Irv's watchful glare, the waiters circulated glasses of

Champagne. Even Grandma appeared, looking quite mad, dressed in a navy blue artist's smock, holding a bouquet of paint brushes, her dark eyes pinned from the tincture of morphine Irv gave her for pain. Toasts were offered, first by Grandpa in his ultra-folksy mode, as if Jimmy Stewart were playing the role of a progressive Brooklyn doc, then by Eleanor Chumley, the white-haired, icy-eyed chairwoman of the East-West Medical Friendship Committee, and then the Russians had their turn. First to speak was a massive young doctor with a kind of Beatles hairdo, who said, "I bring you greetings from your comrades and colleagues in the Union of Soviet Socialist Republics," to which the Americans applauded and shouted "Bravo!"

Then, Katarina Gorky spoke. "We want to thank Dr. Rothschild for opening his home to us," she said. "Many of us were very frightened to come to the United States. But being in this home, and seeing such friendly faces . . ." She touched her fingers to her heart. She was a nervous, narrow-faced woman, with dark pixie-cut hair, inky eyebrows, dominating brown eyes. Katarina wore a blue suit, with a short skirt, high heels, dark stockings. Her voice was pure and strong, as if she had once studied to be a singer. But she had not studied voice, nor did she play the piano, paint, hike, camp, or ski, or sew, or enjoy the movies. Science and medicine were her great passions, all that she knew and all that she had ever cared about—until falling in love with Sergei, which she already recognized as a fantastic mistake. From now on, she must have thought, she would stick to what she knew.

"She was a lovely woman and a fine doctor," Grandpa said, turning away from the fire for good this time and sitting in a rocking chair. He rocked back and forth, back and forth, with the same this-is-what-you-do-in-the-country diligence with which he warmed himself at the hearth.

"Tell me what Luke was like when you first met him," I said, trying to be casual about it. I hoped Esther hadn't told him I was compiling information for a book or voiced her objections to my project.

"What for—that meshuga book of yours?"

"Because you're my grandfather and this is a part of your job."

"Really? Is that so."

"Absolutely. It's right there in *The Grandfather Handbook*."

Irv smiled and opened his arms, beckoning me to his side. I came to him on bending knees and wrapped my arms around his meager torso, put my head to his chest, and listened to the reassuringly powerful beating of his heart, while he lay his hands on my back and rubbed me up and down. It had always always always been this way.

"He looked like a little wet rat the first time your mother brought him home to us. He was already getting to be a big deal, but he looked like he'd been sleeping in doorways and only washed when it rained. He stunk, if you really want to know. And he had acute halitosis, like someone who is so hungry he's starting to digest his own organs. Plus, it seemed as if he and a toothbrush rarely crossed paths.

"You know, one day, when you have children of your own—I'm not pressuring you, but you know, in the course of human events—then you will know what it feels like to meet the man who your daughter tells you is the greatest thing on earth, Prince Charming and Eugene Victor Debs and Robin Hood all wrapped into one prize package. No matter how wonderful he actually turns out to be, you're going to be looking at him very carefully, because you, like me, will feel there is no one worthy of all that praise, and no one really worthy when you come right down to it, no one worthy of your daughter.

"But with this one, with this one it wasn't nitpicking, you

didn't need to dissect the situation to find that little bit of rot—with this one you needed surgery to find the good."

"But you liked him," I said, getting up—my legs were going numb.

"Liked him? Oh, I wouldn't say that."

"But you already have said it. Many times."

"When did I say that?"

"I don't know. Ten years ago."

"When I was young and foolish." He laughed and then was suddenly silent. He brought his hands together as if in prayer and closed his eyes. "But it's true. He did manage to charm me—but charm is a terrible thing, when you think about it. It's a trick, it's the way of the snake. Charm is salesmanship. Time and again, I'd see him at my bookshelves, running his dirty finger with its obscene long fingernail over the spines of my books, or else sitting like a yogi on the rug, reading."

"And you liked it."

"Who wouldn't? You know, your mother has the heart of a true progressive—the struggles of real people touched her so deeply. But she didn't like to read Marx or Lenin. Theories and her just never got along, and frankly not even history. Economics? I'd say it was Greek to her, but she learned Greek very easily. But Luke was interested in everything. I'd send him home with an A&S shopping bag full of books and next Sunday he and Esther would come to the house—ach! his table manners! the way he shoveled the food in and protected his plate with his arm like a jailbird—and he'd have them all read, every book, and understood, too, brilliantly, I mean like a born theoretician. But what was so goddamned refreshing about him is he didn't even like to show it off. He put himself below me, like my student. He wanted to know about everything I knew—and those days, before my mind started going soft, believe me, Billy, I knew a lot. I understood, for instance, Marx's theory of surplus value, and I could explain it better than Paul Sweezy or any economist. I'm not boasting. I don't know the first thing about the theory of surplus value now—I don't know if I forgot it or if I don't even believe in it anymore. It's just gone. The folder is still in the file, it's labeled 'The Theory of Surplus Value,' but all the papers inside are missing.

"Naturally, your grandmother had a different take on it. 'Of course he lets you do all the talking,' she used to say. 'Otherwise he'd have to stop feeding his face for half a minute.' But be that as it may, the fact is Luke—or Stuart, or whoever he was—he was a quick learner, and somewhere beneath that whole name-changing nonsense and the greasy blue jeans and the ridiculous hats and the ambition he wore like a sword in his belt—whatever!—you know you didn't have to be a Ph.D. in human nature to spot from the very first that this was a boy with big plans and no intention of ever, ever letting anybody or anything get in his way. I don't deny him his genius.

"He was an eager beaver, that was the thing about Mr. Luke Fairchild. If you knew something, he wanted to know it, too. So he falls in love with Esther, just naturally accepts her ways of thinking, maybe because he didn't have very many ideas himself, so there was no conflict, nothing to get in the way. And then she brings him to the house, and you know how it was—dinner conversation going from history to economics, Negroes, sit-ins, peace demonstrations, *Bread and Wine*, *Waiting for Lefty*—everywhere and anywhere and sometimes all at once. And there's the former Stuart Kramer from somewhere out there in the Midwest sitting and not saying anything, just playing with his food, but taking it all in, looking so intent, like we were a heartbeat and he was a GP listening through a stethoscope. He wanted to know what we knew."

"That's exactly how he is, though, isn't it?"

"I don't know how exactly he is. And I don't think anyone else does."

"I think I have some idea," I said.

"I'm not here to argue with you," Grandpa said, stifling a yawn. He took off his wire-rimmed glasses and rubbed his eyes vigorously with the heels of his hands. When he finished, his eyes were pink, opaque. Another impulse to yawn—this time he didn't suppress it. He opened his mouth wide; trembling strands of saliva connected his top and bottom teeth, shimmering like a spider's web. "It takes more than an ejaculation to make a father, Billy."

"I know that. But he is my father. He haunts me."

"He's a drug addict. He abandoned your mother. He abandoned you."

"Still. He is my father."

"But what do you want from him? That's what I want to know."

"I have no idea."

"There's nothing he can give you, Billy. Nothing."

"There has to be."

"What could he give you?"

"He could get off my back."

"He's not on your back, Billy. He won't even say he's your father."

"That's the weight."

Grandpa sadly shook his head. "What a treat that guy is. I hope you know that when I knocked him around with my cane, I was giving him hell for a lot more than Sergei Karpanov. One knock on the head was for Katarina, and then for Mommy, and another was for you, and then I gave him a good one for being such a goddamned Pied Piper and leading all those good young people away from progressive politics and into that fantasy land of electric guitars and drugs. Those songs he used to write—many of them he got the idea for at my table, from my books—were filled with meaning, songs of common people struggling for their dignity, the right to raise their families, to eat, to vote, to live without fear, and then he falls in with a new crowd and it's bye-bye Esther, bye-bye Freedom Riders, bye-bye immigrants, bye-bye Ban the Bomb. And for what? A music-business sharpie with fingers like knockwurst, smelling like a whorehouse, who tells Luke: You're wasting your time with these people. Come with me and get rich! Steinberg! Ach, that man, with his promises and schemes, so greedy he'd sell his own mother's shadow."

"He's ruined now, Grandpa. All his money has been spent on breach-of-contract suits against Luke. He hangs around Times Square in a dirty raincoat, unshaved, unwashed. He's mentally ill."

"It's small consolation, Billy." He yawned again and then abruptly stood. "Where do I sleep?"

"Sleep in Mom's room. I'll take the sofa."

"You sure?"

"It's where I always sleep when I come here."

"You're a good son, Billy. Your mother is always talking about you. She's very proud of you."

"My exciting career as a public school teacher?"

"For everything. For the love and concern you've always shown her. You're what keeps her going."

"I feel sorry for anyone who has to depend on me."

"Stop talking that way. Just stop it right now. Is that supposed to be modesty? To me, it smacks of self-pity."

I walked him into the bedroom. Indentations vaguely in the shape of Rosa's and my forms were imprinted on the Indian bedspread. Nervously, I smoothed it down and then folded it back, so Grandpa might easily slip into bed. I showed him the bathroom, turned on the reading light, and turned off the overheads.

Later, stretched out on the sofa and trying to sleep, I checked my watch. It was nearly 3:00 a.m. In Malibu, however, it was merely midnight. I scrambled off the sofa. The phone.

I moved quickly, determined to keep a step ahead of

my thoughts—which surely would have included self-admonishment, dire warnings about making this call. I dialed Luke's number with a flurry of fingers, like a court stenographer. I would not leave another message if his answering machine picked up the call, as it surely would.

On the second ring, the phone was answered—not by machine but by a human. A woman. Small, Asian-accented voice.

"Hello, who is this?"

"I'm looking for Luke," I said. My heart was beating so ferociously, I could barely hear my own voice. Was I whispering?

"He's not here. He went to New York, an hour ago. Who is calling, please?"

9

I CAN BARELY remember the morning. Urgent, burning urination, piss itself thick as honey. Helium-headed. Why? Who knows? Fluky heartbeat. Bad body. Shame on you, body. You can just sit in that chair until you're ready to behave. Pacing. Cereal. Coffee. The night had been cold, and a thin skin of ice had formed on the north window above the kitchen sink. I pressed my palm and fingers on it until I saw the hand-shaped world outside: a thumb of willow; fingers of sky, trees, grass, and garden; a bird bath floating in the pond of my palm.

It was just after seven in the morning when the first of the phone calls began. I thought it was the hospital and I answered immediately, before that initial sick twist of dread became a paroxysm. The first caller was a woman named Rudy. I remembered her name from Esther's call list. She had a light, porous voice, a Yankee accent, and she had no idea my mother was in the hospital. She was "just checking in," she said. Next came another name from the call list, a man named Warren, who had heard the news and was sobbing. I took the messages, one after the other, until the sixth call, which was from a guy with a smooth, confident voice and the easy, loping cadence that money can buy. I wasn't telling anyone that my mother was in the hospital because I was still fearful of the emergency becoming a media event. I simply told him Esther wasn't in and invited him to leave a message.

"Okay. This is her friend Felix. Will you tell Esther that Tess and I are driving down to the city in two days and we'd like to stop over at her place and say hi, or maybe just stay for a cup of tea, or whatever would be convenient for her?"

"Felix?"

"Yes. And Tess."

"This is Billy Rothschild, Felix."

There was a silence, in which I imagined him looking up at the soundproof tiles in his dorm room at Bennington, as if to register his annoyance with God.

"Hi, Billy," he said. "What's up?"

I felt ungainly, practically monstrous. Felix had gone to no small inconvenience to keep our paths from crossing—I never did learn what Annabelle Stevenson had told the twins to warn them off me—and I felt a little sorry for him to be so unexpectedly in my clutches.

"You know," I said, "I just learned last night you guys and my mother were friends."

"Yes, we are," said Felix, clearly worried where this was leading.

"That's sort of weird, though. Isn't it?"

"I guess."

"How did it happen?"

"We were Christmas shopping and Tess saw her in the sweater department at Saks. Tess recognized her immediately—she looked so much like she did on that old album cover. We were still all bent out of shape over . . ." His voice trailed off. He was reluctant to trigger me by mentioning our father's name.

"Luke?"

"Yes. I guess you know what that's like." He paused for a moment, perhaps wondering if he had just insulted me. "Anyhow, we went up to Esther, introduced ourselves. She was so great about it. When I thought about it later, I realized we were just coming out of nowhere and really imposing on her. But she was so open, so warm. And we've been friends ever since. I mean, you know, we call her, just to check in. It's just nice to know her. You know how she is. I mean, you know a lot better than we do," he hastened to add.

"Look, Felix," I said. "I've got some bad news—only I want you to keep it to yourself. You and Tess. Esther was in a pretty bad car wreck and she's in the hospital."

"Oh shit! Is she going to be . . . is she going to be all right?"

"She's pretty banged up."

"Oh no. Billy. What can I say? Where is she?"

"She's in the hospital in Leyden. But we're trying to get her to a better hospital. Albany, maybe."

"Should we come down? Is there anything we can do?"

"No, not now. I think maybe Luke's coming, though."

"Luke?" As if the notion were preposterous. Then, a short, cynical sound that would more or less pass for a laugh. "I think I'll give that a miss. I think I'll file that under Life Is Too Short."

His blitheness confused me on some childishly devout level. Felix didn't sound particularly angry with Luke, or filled with any real longing. He had better things to do; he wanted to keep his distance. He had somehow learned his lesson. He'd cut his losses, he'd found another way. Felix went west when I went east; he went up when I went down. What had consumed me, driven and defined me—and, it was beginning to dawn on me, had brought me to Esther's house, which in turn had probably caused her to drink, and then to crash her car—this wild-goose chase, this doomed children's crusade, was apparently to

Felix something of a waste of energy. He thought he would give it a miss? I felt like a pious little country priest whose parishioners have failed to come to Good Friday services because the daffodils are blooming on a hill outside the village.

"Do you ever see him?" I asked.

"Luke? No. I mean, not for a long time. Maybe ten years."

"Yeah. I know what that feels like," I said.

"It feels fine," said Felix. "He doesn't even admit to being our father, and we don't need his money anyhow—so the way we figure it, we're better off."

I heard the sound of an engine and looked out the window. A green Chrysler minivan with faux wood paneling was making its way up the driveway, its windshield wipers waving frantically, though the early morning sky was clear. At the wheel was a large, middle-aged woman with blond hair, wearing a beret and a multicolored Tibetan jacket, and in the passenger seat was a man or a woman, who was wearing a black leather jacket and who was unanimously bald.

"A car's just pulling in," I said to Felix. "I better see who it is."

"Okay. Will you give your mom our love? Can you call me or something and tell me what's happening?"

"Okay. But let me ask you a quick question. How are you better off?"

"I don't know. I just feel that way. I don't want to be Luke Fairchild's son. I don't want everyone looking at me that way. I don't want to have to live up to it, and I don't want to have to live it down. I just want to be myself."

We said our goodbyes and I went to the front of the house just as the blond woman was about to knock on the door. She knew my name, and she told me her name was Magda. She and her friend had just been to the hospital but had not been allowed to visit Esther. I wanted to know how she had found out about the accident, but I couldn't find a way to phrase the question without its sounding peevish or mean. I told her I'd tell my mother she had tried to visit, and then, right before she turned to go back into her van, she impulsively threw her arms around me and embraced me with such suddenness and such fierceness that it took me a moment or two to realize that I was actually being given love, that uncomplicated, unquestioning love we often claim to want and need and which we sometimes fail to recognize when it is staring us straight in the face.

Soon after, I went into the bedroom to awaken Grandpa. He slept on his back, with his long hands folded on his rising and falling chest, and one bare white violet-veined foot poking out of the covers—a sleeping trick he had once taught to me, a way of cooling down without tearing the covers off.

"Grandpa?" I whispered.

His eyes opened instantly and, remaining flat on his back, he reached for his eyeglasses on the night table.

"What's wrong?" he asked.

"It's time to go. To the hospital."

He emerged just minutes later, dressed in a brilliant white shirt, a red and royal blue tie, a dove gray suit. He must have packed his little suitcase with the care of an origami master. He put a comforting hand on my shoulder and we set out for the car. On the drive to the hospital, I wrestled with the notion of telling him I had called Luke the night before and that now I had reason to believe he was on his way—what else could "he went to New York just an hour ago" have meant? What else could have sent Luke flying east at such a late hour?

We arrived at the hospital with the words unspoken and we breezed by the reception desk without anybody noticing us. We took the elevator up to the second floor, along with two lab technicians, at whom Grandpa coolly nodded, as if his position of authority would allow nothing more, nothing less. On the second floor, I said a soft hello to the head nurse, who, when she saw Irv, quickly glanced at the little wristwatch to make certain the old man wasn't ignoring the rules governing visiting hours.

"Oh, Mr. Rothschild?" the nurse said. Both Irv and I turned to look at her, and she indicated she was speaking to me. "There's someone in with your mother now."

"A doctor?" Grandpa asked.

"A priest, actually," said the nurse.

"Billy," Irv said, grabbing my arm. His eyes were wide with what I first saw as fury and then as fear. "I don't want a priest in there. Who would do such a thing to us?"

"Okay. Okay okay okay." I moved quickly toward Esther's room. "All right, all right," I said, barging into the room. There was a welterweight priest sitting at my mother's bedside. Rosary beads and a crucifix hung between his widely parted knees. The blackness of his clothes made a hole in the world. There was a smell in the room—incense? tobacco? "I'm sorry, Father, but you're going to have to leave." There was a long silence. And then the priest turned to face me and he was Luke. Father indeed.

"Luke," I whispered. It took me but a moment to realize he had come in clerical drag as a way of guarding his privacy. He looked mad, his sun-baked face as creased as a walnut, his graying hair hidden by a sporty little checkered homburg, such as Bing Crosby might have worn, his tea-and-tobacco-stained teeth, so determinedly resistant to wealth and fame, showing for a moment in an uneasy, pleading smile.

Luke stood up, squinted at me. I could feel the grief that was in him. His eyes were a blur of red; the evidence of his despair moved me so suddenly and so powerfully I felt my knees weaken. He lacked the insecurity and desire to please upon which is based much of what we call good manners, and so he made absolutely no attempt to conceal the fact that he was momentarily uncertain as to who I was. But really it was merely a matter of logic—who else could I have been? Even putting aside the quarrel as to my paternity—whose mother was in that bed? Who had called him in Malibu? Luke glanced back at my mother, who slept motionless in her barred bed, the hydrating and—one could only hope—pain-killing liquid trickling into her through clear plastic tubing, her oxygen supplemented by the hissing butterfly clips perched at the edges of her nostrils, like noseplugs for a long-distance swimmer, which once, in fact, she was, and now, in some miserable, metaphorical way, she was again.

"Billy, right?" he said.

But whatever was to come after that was lost to Irv's entering the room. To my amazement, Grandpa made Luke the second he laid eyes on him.

"What the hell are you doing here, Luke? Is this supposed to be—what? A happening? A . . . put-on? Or have you really sunk this low?"

"Hello, Irv. Glad to see you're not carrying a cane."

"As well you should be."

"You want to sit down?" Luke asked, offering the chair he had just vacated.

A passing nurse, elderly, with immense eyeglasses and thin, chablis-colored hair, stuck her head in the room, "Only two visitors—" she said, and then cut herself short, seeing that the third visitor was ordained. By now, Irv already had Mother's chart in hand and was scrutinizing it, with frequent glances back at Esther.

"What's the story, Irv?" Luke asked. "What's wrong with her and what are they doing about it?"

"They're waiting to transfer her."

"Well, that's good. This fucking veterinary clinic ain't no place for her. But what's wrong? What happened?"

"So. All of the sudden," I said, "you're interested. Where have you been?"

"Been? Why?"

"You're getting here kind of late, aren't you?"

"You know that gospel song?" Luke said. "God may not come when you want him—but he's right on time."

"You're not quite God, Luke."

"She crashed her car," Grandpa said.

"Your grandson here told me that over the phone."

Grandpa glared at me for just one radiantly scornful moment, and then went back to reading Mother's chart.

"Bleeding internally," Grandpa said, blunt, factual. "Multiple fractures. Third-degree burns on back, legs, torso, and face."

"Oh, fuck," said Luke. "Her face."

"Yes," said Grandpa. "Her face. Let's see. What else do we have here? Liver function, fair. Heart, good. Respiration . . . hmm. EEG normal—excellent. I was worried about that."

"Why haven't they moved her already?" asked Luke.

"That's what I'm trying to find out," said Irv.

"I heard that the medevac helicopter service they use went out of business," I said, "and the one they use at Albany Medical Center is broken."

"Man," said Luke, shaking his head.

"I don't want her going up to Albany anyhow," said Irv. "I want her going to Roosevelt, in the city. I have many friends on staff there and she'll get the best."

"Yeah," said Luke. "New York. It's gotta be good for something, right? Anyhow, my lawyer's brother is chief of plastic surgery at New York Hospital. It's already set up for her. That's where all the society women go—not to mention foreign dictators. All we gotta do is get her down."

"Plastic surgery—that's your priority?" said Irv.

"For her burns," I said.

"And—" said Luke, raising one finger, and looking for a moment not only mad but strangely endearing in his habit, "the doctor who treated me after my car wreck is in New York and I talked to him, and he'll be there, too."

I felt my pulse quicken. Luke was referring to Dr. Sanford Peck, very much a call-me-Sandy sort of wavy-haired hunk, who became an orthopedic surgeon originally out of his love of skiing, but then moved to L.A. because he had an unruly and unrequited crush on a movie exec named Sherry Lansing. I'd interviewed Dr. Peck twice, once by phone about five years ago, and then in person, while he was in New York attending a professional conference at the Sheraton, less than a year back. He told me Luke didn't have much of a capacity for pain but then added, with an inside dopester's smirk, that he did, however, have a large capacity for painkillers. "I mean, here's a guy who can get whatever he wants, whenever, and he's hustling his doctor for a few extra Percodans. You know what I mean? He has a kind of streety, King of the Gonifs quality."

I didn't want Sandy to see me, didn't want him to let Luke know about the interviews. If Dr. Ski Slope saw me with Luke, he might very well make some reference to our interview, like "Hey, Luke, your meshuga kid here grabbed me last year and grilled me like a lamb chop and it was all about you." I wanted to hold off about Luke knowing about the interviews, the notes, the book. My plan was as it had always been: to publish the entire story, call it *I Am Luke Fairchild's Son*, or *My Fucking Hero*, or *The Rich Man's Table*, and send him an advance copy, cushioned in bubble wrap, via third-class mail.

By the time I was paying attention again—and surely no more than a few moments could have passed—Luke was telling Grandpa that he would arrange for a private ambulance and Grandpa was saying that he would get the paperwork started so we could get Esther out of Leyden as soon as possible. Irv turned to leave and suddenly my father and I were, for all practical purposes, alone.

Luke made sure the door was firmly shut and then he threw his arms behind him and locked his hands, and then rapidly raised and lowered them, up and down, like the handle of a jack. A moment later, his spine made a series of alarming cracks and pops. "Oh, man," he said, with evident satisfaction, closing his eyes. His eyelids were dark, thick as alligator skin; you could barely make out the bulge of the eyeballs beneath. Once, he'd been the kind of man who needed to shave but two or three times weekly, he was once so fresh-faced, almost pink, but now he was weathered as a stump. Over the years, his face had grown and shed at least a dozen beards: a pirate's unruly fringe, a Russian mystic's long black tusk, a stylish Vandyke that lasted not nearly as long as the double chin it had been grown to conceal. Now, shaved clean, he looked worn, almost ravaged. Gravity tugged insistently at the corners of his once arrogantly curled lips, giving him the look of a man who when asked "How's business?" sourly replies "Don't ask." If you'd taken the crucifix and the round collar away, he would have looked Jewish from across the street; people would have been able to spot his Semitism the way Grandpa smelled the sea. His ears had grown, and so had his nose. In a caricature drawn on the CD cover of one of his bootlegged concert performances (Geneva, Switzerland, 1980), the artist had drawn Luke's schnoz as long as a baguette, bent at the end, making him look like an illustration of the Jew Without Scruples from some Nazi pamphlet.

Mom used to say (though never to me) that Luke was an innocent, a child, beneath it all. Well, that innocence was long gone, swallowed by the muck of ego, entitlement, and drugs, revelation, conversion, and tantrum, blow jobs, anal sex, private showings, his pick of the litter, and a thousand and one rarefied pleasures and perversions I could barely imagine. He was paying the price for his life, organ by organ. And somewhere within him was the terrible sad panic of a once holy man starting to realize that, despite everything, his body might out-live his soul.

"Do you remember when I came to see you at that spa?" I asked.

"Which spa was this?" he said.

"The one around Lenox, Massachusetts. Last summer, for Christ's sake."

"Last summer?"

"It doesn't matter. Do you remember when I saw you on Martha's Vineyard?"

"Is this a test? What do I get if I answer correctly?"

"I can't believe you don't remember," I said.

And with that, my time alone with my father was com-pletely squandered. Grandpa came back into the room, his face registering frustration. I ignored him for the moment.

"I came to see you in Lenox, Massachusetts," I said to Luke, in the overenunciated, syllable-obsessed way of the petulant son to the absent father, a voice I had never before had an opportunity to use, but which came to me full-blown, like your first sneeze. "You were at the Wellspring Lodge. You insisted we play tennis together. That was a lot of fun. That was a real first-class treat. I can't tell you how much I enjoyed chasing the ball around in the sun and—"

"You know he has a bad heart," said Grandpa. "He had rheumatic fever when he was a child."

"Grandpa. Please."

"Bad heart's better than a bad conscience," said Luke. "Bet-ter than bad breath, too."

Silence, except for the beep of Mother's monitor, marking time like the digital clock in a bomb.

"She was still protecting you, did you know that?" I asked.

"What in the hell are you talking about?" Luke was getting angry. He wasn't used to being pressed; for all his perfected spontaneity, his man-of-the-people poses, he was used to huge helpings of deference, he was used to that old devotion being slathered on with a snow shovel, he was used to the sibilant chorus of Yes surrounding his life like a swarm of locusts.

"I'm talking about the woman you supposedly loved."

"What are you trying to do, Billy? You want to fight with me? I'm just a couple buckets of blood, and bones for the dogs. This 'me' you want to fight is really something in your own head. Why don't you try fighting with yourself?"

Luke's voice was startlingly low, a honeyed croon, so unlike his usual nasal, wise-ass, reedy kazoo of a voice that it caused me to wonder if he had just become a different person, or if his soul was like one of those flashlights that can shine red, white, green, yellow, or blue, mediated by a simple plastic dial over the face of it. But then I realized: this was his Nashville timbre, the almost comically resonant style he affected after he had repudiated the paisleyed psychedelia of the sixties, and began to boyishly idolize the cowboy singers, beer-bellied, eagle-eyed middle-aged men in string ties, the Nashville old guard, terse, tough guys with barroom scars on their knuckles, or a bitten-off ear, a shattered knee, guys who spent more money on drugs than the Grateful Dead and Blue Cheer and the Stones put together.

"How are you planning to get her to New York?" Grandpa asked Luke.

"We're just talking about money here, is all," Luke said.

"What else is new?" said Grandpa.

"Well, we don't want Esther waiting around all day," Luke said.

"Of course not," said Grandpa. "But they seemed to think there would be no problem in removing her by seven this evening, at the latest."

"And if they fuck that up we're here for another night." Luke tepeed his fingers and . . .

And I remembered that one of the last things Esther said before the crash was that was a gesture Luke and I shared, a bit of chromosomal legacy more mysteriously transmitted but no less distinct than brown hair or soft teeth. I watched his fingertips tap two by two and I felt for a moment almost overwhelmed by an emotion for which I had no name. It was like being nailed to the wall and soaring like a bird at the same time.

"If Esther sat up in bed right now," I said, in a voice that I was certain sounded serene, "do you know what she'd say? She'd say, 'Luke, I want you to meet your son. Billy, say hi to your father.'"

"Not now, Billy," said Grandpa. "First things first."

But of course he would feel that way; he was Esther's father. His first allegiance was to her, her well-being, her happiness; it was only natural. He was her father.

"Let me ask you something, kid," Luke said. "Why would I ever be so wicked or so blind? If the flesh of my flesh stands before me, who am I not to embrace the child?"

"Is that from the Bible or something?" I said. "And anyway, how can I know why you're wicked or blind? How can I know anything about you? You never came to see me. And when I track you down, you never seem to remember who I am, or when you last saw me, or what I want."

"What you want? You know how many people walk in and out of my life, wanting something? Wisdom, old rags, reasons to believe? I don't have what you want, and you probably don't even know what you want. You just want what you don't have."

"I know what I want," I said. All the decks had been cleared, every competing reality had been set aside, everything, and now all there was was this, this moment, this room, this man standing before me, this man whom I had chased and dreamed of all my life, this shadow of a shadow, this dream of a dream.

"I want the same thing I wanted when I came to see you at Wellspring. I want the same thing I've wanted my whole wasted goddamned life. I want you to say you're my father."

Grandpa put his hand on my shoulder. Was there something in my voice that alarmed him? Was he worried? Repelled? I could not bring myself to exactly care.

Luke, too, seemed unnerved. And I thought to myself, with an almost paranoid singularity of focus: Aha! He's afraid to answer! But even then, in the freezing, hollow, echoing madness of the moment, I was obscurely aware that Luke's face did not register fear so much as pity. I thought, Well, that is just not going to work. But his suddenly soulful eyes slowed me down, nevertheless. And this moment's hesitation proved fatal—my heart began to clatter and bang like a tin man falling down a steep flight of stairs. My hands and feet were turning icy. The world was a Lichtenstein painting, a transparent world of bubbles and dots.

"What's wrong with him, Irv?" I heard Luke say, in a voice that sounded like the distant ocean when you are in a hotel room, half-asleep in your bed.

"You're giving him a heart attack, is what's wrong with him," Grandpa said. And then: "Billy? Can you hear me? Billy?"

I looked at him. How old he seemed, how frail. I forgot to speak; I thought I had said something, but I hadn't.

Luke dragged a metal folding chair to the middle of the room and Grandpa, loosening my belt, guided me down into it. My tongue felt huge in my mouth. My hands, made of lead, dropped into my lap.

10

"ARE YOU SURE you feel all right driving?" Luke said, as we pulled out of the hospital parking lot. I had been thoroughly checked over, pronounced in sound albeit neurotic health, and released. Now Luke and I were on our way to Kingston, on the other side of the Hudson, where he had somehow secured not only an ambulance but an attendant who would accompany us as we transported Esther to New York. Luke was vague when I asked him how all this had been arranged; I suspect he himself was not sure. He had a number of people on his beck-and-call brigade, people who tended to his menagerie of needs and whims. Needless to say, he did very little of the labor of his own life. It had been at least thirty years since he'd changed the sheets on a bed, or changed a lightbulb, or stood impatiently in line for popcorn, worried the movie would start without him. Yet despite his twenty-four-hour coddling, he still maintained his angry, alienated sneer, he still wrote as if he were somehow an outlaw. He wrote, I suppose, from some proletarianized spirit, a disenfranchisement of the soul. Or perhaps his memories of being beneath the heel of society were still so vivid that they seemed more real than the Malibu-Monaco axis upon which his current world so luxuriously turned.

We drove over the bridge spanning the Hudson. The river trembled blue and white as the wind raked at its surface. Luke seemed uncomfortable; my rented Probe was probably the shittiest car he had ridden in in at least a quarter-century. He stretched his right leg out and massaged it above the knee. Years after shattering it in a spin-out on the Pennsylvania Turnpike (at nearly the exact spot where the jazz trumpet legend Clifford Brown fatally crashed) Luke's leg often ached. (It was the leg that led to his addiction to painkillers, and then to heroin.)

"Still playing a lot of tennis?" I asked him.

He simply shook his head no. So much for tennis.

He remained silent, coiled deep within himself. His snubs, of course, were notorious, and I had heard of them from several women who were involved with him. Annabelle Stevenson told me that Luke once didn't utter a single word to her in eleven days. Even Esther, who was slow to speak against Luke, at least to me, said that once Luke had come to her bed near dawn, his drugged-up eyes no more expressive than olives. He perched on the bed like an incubus and stared at her until she awakened. Once she was up, he continued to gape at her, as if she were some bizarre creature beyond his comprehension, a sport of nature who not only bewildered him but who had done him direct harm. When Esther finally cracked and cried out—she was not wholly unaccustomed to these staredowns, but she had her limits—Luke threw up his hands and stalked out, as if she had just proved his nutty, nocturnal point. As for me, I was thus far unfazed by Luke's legendary silence. I preferred it to his also legendary tongue-lashings, bullying sarcasm, and general shittiness.

His silence in the Probe had been broken only by his musing out loud about the possibility of dropping in on Eliot Shore, who was living near Kingston. Eliot had once been so

many things to Luke—jester, yes man, messenger, general fac-
totum, occasional confidant, and Luke's partner in that horri-
ble parlor game they called "Blake," which amounted to
nothing more than mercilessly teasing some hapless victim
until he or she blushed, trembled, or burst into tears. They
called the game "Blake" after the William Blake line: "Opposi-
tion is true friendship." By which Luke meant he was looking
for someone who could stand up to him.

The game would go something like this: Some awestruck
person, reduced by the nearness of Luke to abject adoration,
would be drawn into a mock argument between Eliot and
Luke. The argument would be about something absurd—
should a purse snatcher be given the electric chair, does aspirin
make the penis larger, that sort of thing. Finally, the bystander
would be pressed into expressing an opinion; with some regularity, the victim would take Luke's side, at which point Eliot
would say, "You're on his side because he's Luke Fairchild,"
and with that the trap snapped shut and the person would be
caught in a verbal maze, with Eliot and Luke willy-nilly
exchanging positions, back and forth, with trick passes like the
Harlem Globetrotters, until the victim didn't know what she
believed, or if she even had beliefs, and then—if it was the
penis-enlarged-by-aspirin riff—Luke and Eliot would whip
out their cocks and ask her to guess which of them had regularly been taking Anacin. It was the sort of nasty joke for which
people are rightfully accused of sexual harassment these days.
Even then you needed more than insensitivity to get away with
it: you needed power, and you needed to despise the isolating
force of that power.

"So," I said, "I meant to ask you." I paused for a moment, to
let him wonder. Then: "How are your kids? How are the
twins? Felix and Tess."

"Don't see them much as I'd like to."

I felt an icy twist of humiliation at the pit of my stomach, in that dark and tender place where we store our aloneness and terror. I had expected him to deny that the twins were his, yet somehow he had not.

"But they *are* yours. Right?"

"Do we have to do this now?"

"We may not have another opportunity."

"Opportunity? You call this a fucking opportunity?" He shook his head and looked away.

We were nearing the Van Fleet Lodge, once a turreted mansion of some social distinction, a place of formal picnics on the east lawn, evenings of chamber music, and long dinner parties that included the Roosevelts, John Dos Passos, and Arturo Toscanini, and which was now a private hospital for substance abusers. (Esther had once considered checking in for a week or two: I saw now I ought to have done more to encourage her.) Our route took us past a few used-car lots; a boarded-up mini-mall; a trailer park whose muddy entrance was flanked by two monumental plaster lions; a drive-in called Kountry Kone; a batting cage, driving range, and go-cart complex called Eddie and Bo's Fun City; and an automobile graveyard, where thousands of compacted cars were piled on top of each other like slabs of dried and salted meat. ("I see the people cut out of the deal / The wind blown trailers, the twisted steel"—"Standard of Living," recorded 1988.) I knew the sights well; I had been on this road a few months earlier, when I came to interview Eliot Shore on the raw, gray day after Thanksgiving.

"Eliot lives down that road," I said, pointing to a sign that read Block Factory Road. Green metal, rusted, riddled with bullet holes.

Luke was taking off his crucifix, his beads. He unfastened his priest's collar—it sprang to life as soon as it was off of him.

Then he unbuttoned the top two buttons of his once pious but now suddenly stylish black shirt. His wrinkled, sun-spotted hands. His sad eyes. The faint wheeze of his long, slow breaths. Father.

"Eliot Shore?" he said. "That's weird. I was just thinking about him."

"I know."

"How do you know?"

I was about to say: You said his name, you wondered out loud if he was still around. But some strange and unexpected sense of tact prevented me. I thought it would embarrass him, and I did not want to. All my life, I had wanted a father who was pledged to protect me, and now that man was next to me and I needed to conceal from him the secrets of his own aging, just as I never mentioned to Irv the little crib sheet of forget-table names I found in the breast pocket of his shirt.

We passed the rotted carcass of road kill on the side of the highway, a raccoon, perhaps, or a large cat. A trio of gigantic crows, their oily feathers bright in the sun, pecked hurriedly at the matted fur, looking for the morsels that remained.

"How's he doing, poor crazy Eliot? Still hungry?" Luke said.

Hungry? The question unsettled me. What did that mean? I had spent hours with Eliot Shore. I had taped him, answered his phone when he suspected it was creditors on the line, listened to his poetry, taken his supposedly pregnant cat to the vet and then had to come back with the bad news that Octavia was not pregnant but had cancer. I could have thought of many words to describe Eliot—"elusive," "paranoid," even "perverted"—but "hungry" would not have occurred to me.

"Maybe we should stop in and say how'dya-do," Luke said, turning in the seat and looking back toward Block Factory Road.

The back of Luke's neck was red, deeply wrinkled. It was in these passing glances of him, in these stolen looks, that I found myself loving him just as I had over the years, when I heard his voice on a record and sensed within it something brave and unprotected. It was in those odd moments, when I very least expected it, that, as the Sufis say, my heart had wings, and it flew from the cage of bone and self, away from the prison of the actual and into the ether of the possible.

"Do you want to?" I said, slowing down.

"No, no, we better not. It's dangerous visiting the past. And anyhow, we better get the ambulance."

The sunlight coming through the car savaged his face, it just seemed to chew him up. It was astonishing how poverty-stricken he could look. Of course, he would have been mad to go for the skin peel, the cosmetic dentistry; the surviving seediness reminded everyone, including himself, that he was still an outsider, and it gave him the right to sing about refugees, broken men, and outlaws.

"Eliot likes young girls, always has. Of course, when he was twenty-three, nobody paid attention to him balling teenagers. Was he with a young girl when you saw him?"

"Fifteen years old."

"And he was pawing her, always keeping her engine running?"

"Yes." I remembered how I tried to look away, and not quite being able to, as he groped poor pale pudgy Paloma beneath her embroidered tunic, and the look in her blue eyes as they locked onto mine—that expression of blank defiance: Like you wouldn't squeeze my titties if I sat on your lap.

Luke smiled, twirled the crucifix around like a little silver lasso and let it wrap around his hand.

"He's still so entirely loyal to you, though," I said. Stop flattering him, I thought to myself. You're not just another courtier.

"Eliot let me down. I thought there was more to him. I thought he was going to go all the way."

"All the way where?"

"If I knew, I'd go there myself."

I took the turn at the blinking light.

"What were you doing at Eliot's?" Luke asked me.

"Talking about you."

He did not pursue it. He did not want to risk having to listen to me going on about his being my father, a topic we had tacitly tabled since my little attack in the hospital. We drove in silence for a few moments, until I saw a small sign indicating a right turn toward Van Fleet Lodge. A narrow, black-topped road, bordered by lilac bushes, their blossoms rusted from rain and age, proceeded by a series of curves toward a dark red brick mansion, set between two towering maple trees, on a hill. In front, a small carved sign bearing the lodge's name was surrounded by red and yellow tulips, some with their soft mouths opened wide, many of them past their bloom, with just their charred stamens remaining on their drooping stalks. Several people were on the porch—middle-aged for the most part—seated on wicker chairs, with drawing pads balanced on their knees. Their model, an old woman draped in a bedsheet, sat on a high, three-legged stool.

An unpaved parking lot was off to the side of the house, where there were several modest cars, a small yellow school bus, and the ambulance. Washing the ambulance was a guy about twenty, skinny, but with broad shoulders, and an exceptionally small head. He wore brand-new blue jeans and an orange Syracuse University sweatshirt. He had long hair, down past his shoulders. As he moved the spray of the hose along the side of the ambulance, his face remained expressionless, almost entranced.

My stomach turned. That ambulance was for my mother. It was big and boxy, like an armored truck used to pick up the money bags from a small-town bank in 1960. And we were going to put my mother in it.

"Why'd we have to come here? Couldn't they have delivered it?"

Luke gestured toward the ambulance. "Go get it."

"What?"

"The ambulance. Go get it."

"Go fuck yourself."

"What?"

"Don't tell me what to do." I said. "I don't like being ordered around."

"I'm not walking out there and getting into that ambulance, Billy. That's not going to happen." Luke's eyes glittered with rage and panic, as if I were putting his life in danger.

"I'm not on your payroll, Dad."

"Dad? Dad? Look at me, man. Do you really think I'm your father?"

"Really? Once and for all?"

"Yes. Really."

"There is no doubt in my mind—"

"Your mind?"

"—or in anyone else's, for that matter."

"What do you know about your fucking mind, man? Do you know what a thought is? Do you know a synapse from a dendrite? You don't know the first thing about your mind. You can't touch it. You can't smell it. You can't even control it. It's a monkey swinging from branch to branch. You don't even know how half the things got there—what you read in a magazine, what you heard through the bedroom wall." He waved his fingers in my direction, as if batting away an insect. "And I don't even know why you'd want such a thing, for me to be your father. Don't you have enough troubles?"

I don't know exactly why or how I had the insane and hopeless courage to do it—but I hit him. It was completely unplanned, though it was not exactly the last thing I expected. I had dreamed of it, often. I had dreamed of grabbing him by the neck and running him into a wall. I dreamed of crushing his face with my fist. I dreamed of slapping his face over and over. But as it happened, I smacked him, an almost parental, grazing blow, a kind of openhanded swat across the forehead, something between the rousing camaraderie of the Three Musketeers and the feverish, comic impatience of the Three Stooges. Yet Luke was stunned, to say the least. Grandpa might have been the last man who had raised a hand in anger to him. He was too rich to take a poke at, and it was that shield of cash I wanted to penetrate.

He touched his forehead and then checked his fingers for blood. Nothing there. Then he opened the car door and got out, and I got out, too. We walked around to the back of the car. We were getting ready. It was time. I felt it in me, a living presence, that luminous cluster of possibilities and yearnings. That heart within a heart within a heart within a heart, that thing I called my soul, was rapturously, outrageously alive: had been waiting forever for this moment.

The art class on the porch was watching us carefully. Did they recognize Luke? It did not seem so.

Squinting, snake-eyed, his chin trembling, Luke made no immediate move to retaliate. The air felt suddenly warmer, heavy with heat and steam. Mist rose from the unmowed field behind the Van Fleet Lodge. A single crow, its wings oily and black, swerved from the topmost gable of the old house, passed directly over us, and then veered suddenly toward the open field, flying low. It skimmed the seedy heads of the wild grasses, heading toward the horizon, where it suddenly disappeared, as if through a seam separating the here from the there, the present from the past.

"Do you really think you can stop me?" he said, his voice so low I felt it in my bones, like the growl of a guard dog.

"I can try," I said.

"Yeah? Well, people have been trying to stop me my whole life. They've tried to tell me to stay home. They've tried to tell me what to sing, and what to believe, and where I gotta lead them, and be an example, and who to pray to, and what side of the street I gotta walk on. People been throwing their arms around me, but they're ghosts. I can't even feel them. So you want to stop me? Fine. Do it."

And so our ancient ceremony began. Unduly encouraged by my father's initial passivity, I stepped toward him, baring my teeth. He made no move away from me, nor did he put up his hands to defend himself. I reared my arm back to hit him, and then kept it poised for a long moment, wondering where the blow ought to land. I hit his shoulder. I hit it hard. I felt the bone of it, its knob, groove, and tendon, the complex, mortal machinery. The force of the blow turned him thirty degrees. And then, looking back at me, his eyes were full of astonishment.

"What the fuck are you doing?" he said.

But he didn't wait for an answer, and I wasn't going to answer him, anyhow. He grabbed for my shirt front, grasped it for a moment, and then ripped down on it—or was that me, pulling back? The sound of the fabric tearing incensed me, as if that shirt (my mother's, after all) were a flag I was pledged to defend. I swung wildly, hit nothing but the air between us; yet there was a violence even in that, because for the moment everything was connected—the father, the son, the air, the crow carving enigmatic black circles in the sky, the steam rising from the field, the people on the porch who were standing now, gathered at the railing.

I lunged for him, and the force of my leap brought us both down into the dirt. I was on top of him, if anyone was on top of anyone. We ceased our grappling for a moment, to get our bearings. The deep and aboriginal taste of the dirt was in my mouth. A wind, like a presence, rustled through the treetops; the leaves shuddered silver green. The sun was directly over-head, peering down curiously, like an eighteenth-century doctor on a balcony overlooking Bedlam.

"Billy," Luke said, softly. He pressed his hand against my chest with a curious gentleness, not to push me off of him, but as if to feel my heart.

At last the drying-out drunks on the porch got up, and moving in an oddly congealed mass, as if bound to each other by invisible shackles, they surrounded us. Two of the more adventurous patients—a skinny woman with chestnut hair down to her waist, and a burly, olive-skinned Sergei type, his massive, hirsute thighs straining the slits of his purple velour shorts—put themselves between us, the woman's hands on my chest, the man's on Luke.

"Hey hey hey hey hey," said the weightlifter. "You guys want to kill each other? Find somewhere else to do it. Okay? This is a violence-free zone."

The guy who'd been washing the ambulance stood next to it, jiggling his leg and tossing the keys up and catching them, over and over. He looked miserable as a whipped dog.

"You guys gonna behave?" the skinny woman said to me, in the drawl of the poor South. "There's people here working their bee-hinds off tryin' to get well, and ain't none of us needin' two punkinheads goin' after each other like that. Now you guys gonna cool down? Or do you want us to call the cops?" Her pale stick-figure arms were darkly freckled; she had the furious but hopeless determination of someone whose strong opinions are rarely heeded.

"We're all right," Luke said.

"Now you say it," the woman demanded of me. She was starting to smile, shocked to be getting results.

"We're fine," I said. "Just a little family dispute." I looked around. The others from the art class nervously stared at us, filled with that bystander ambivalence—wanting peace and curious what it would be like if there were a little more violence.

"Family!" she cried. "Don't you ever get me started about family."

There was a murmur among the others; they all seemed to agree that getting her started about family wouldn't be a wise move.

"Let's give these folks a chance to start remembering us," said Luke, gesturing toward the ambulance.

I followed behind him, deliberately placing my shoes in the footprints he left in the packed dirt and then rubbing out his tracks.

Luke took the ambulance keys from the boy, whose former apprehension had by now turned to outright misery.

"George is supposed to drive," he said.

"George?" said Luke, his voice rising, incredulous. "*George* is supposed to drive?"

"I'm sorry, sir, I was told—"

"You were told? No. You are *being* told," said Luke. He may have thought he was acting masterfully, but there was a petulant bullying in it, too, a moneyed abuse of power, like scolding the maid.

"What are you doing?" I asked Luke. I half expected him to turn on me, as if my questioning him meant I had struck some spontaneous alliance with his enemies. But he simply looked in my direction, shrugged.

"I guess you're right," he said.

"He's just doing his job," I said, moving past the fact that Luke had already conceded the point.

He smiled at me, my father. What did it feel like to him, to have me there, contradicting him?

Just then, a short, thick man of about forty came bounding off the porch. Except for a carefully tended fringe of straw-colored hair, he was bald. The sunlight ricocheted off his glasses like gunshots. He wore a blue zipper jacket with "Van Fleet" stitched over his left breast, and matching trousers. His uniform fit him as tightly as a diving suit. George.

I could tell by the way George avoided looking directly at Luke that he had already recognized him, and perhaps the jauntiness of his stride—he looked like he was walking across the parking lot of a bowling alley after having rolled a perfect game—was his subterfuge, like a guilty kid who starts whistling. And sure enough, as he neared us, the subterfuge exhausted itself and George was suddenly hesitant, even frightened, like an actor who has entered stage left only to realize that someone has changed everything and tonight instead of *Henry V* they are to perform *The Hairy Ape*. George looked imploringly at me, as if to beg me to rescue him and tell him what to say.

"Are we all set?" I asked.

He nodded emphatically, while risking a quick sideways glance at Luke. He consulted a slip of paper, pink as a tropical dawn. He cleared his throat. "E. Rothschild. Leyden Hospital. Right? Transfer to Roosevelt Hospital, New York City."

"Let's go," said Luke.

It was all George could do to stop from looking at my father; the effort sapped his strength like a raging fever and undermined his sense of himself like a hazing. He licked his parched and peeling lips. His eyelids fluttered. The work-order slip writhed and crackled like something burning between his two small, freckled, trembling hands.

In the meanwhile, the boy who had been washing the ambulance opened the back door and found there a blue zipper jacket exactly like the one George wore. He zipped it all the way up and then, for some reason, tried to zip it up even higher.

"Ready, David?" asked George.

David rode in the back, where there were two stretchers, oxygen cylinders, a tin cabinet with a peeling red cross on the door. George, Luke, and I rode up front. The seat was high and hard; there were a lot of unfamiliar, vaguely obsolete-looking controls on the dashboard. The ceiling was covered in fraying gray velvet; the leather seat had as many cracks as an Etruscan vase. The engine came on with an expensive purr, and George put it in reverse and slowly backed out of the driveway. The art class had gone back to the porch but not back to drawing: they were all of them watching every move we made. In a kind of reflexive gesture of noblesse oblige, Luke raised his hand and waved once.

I was seated in the middle, between George and Luke, with my feet uncomfortably perched on the carpeted hillock encasing the drive train.

As soon as we were off the Van Fleet grounds, I said to Luke, "I've been talking to a lot of people about you, you know. Not just Eliot Shore. Really a lot of people."

"You told me you were a schoolteacher."

"I am."

"That's an important job. Isn't it enough? What are you? Some kind of loner?" He pronounced the word as if it had some subdefinitions, such as "creep," "voyeur," "assassin."

"You know what I'm going to do?" I said to him. "I'm going to write a book about you."

If he knew that this was my confession, and that I just told him something I, a moment before, would have wagered my life I would never reveal, he gave no indication. He shrugged and said, "Great."

"I have to," I said.

"Why?"

"To get rid of you, or at least get past you. I have to put my hands on your shoulders and push you aside."

He smiled at me; like mine, his teeth were dirty from rolling around on the ground.

"It's not that easy."

"I don't have a choice. There's no other way. I want my real life to begin."

"You and me both."

"Okay. Then maybe it'll work for both of us."

"Listen, kid. I never laid eyes on my mother. She was dead when I was three minutes old. Boom. You've got a mother—you've got a great mother. Your mother is maybe the sweetest woman in the world."

"Strange coming from you."

"Is it? Why?"

"You didn't exactly treat her very well, now, did you."

He gave me an appraising look, as if trying to figure out if I actually meant it.

"That's what you're going to say in your book?" He shook his head, as if to give me the impression that he pitied me.

"I don't need to say it. Your actions speak for themselves."

"Do you know how many love songs I wrote to your mother?"

"Yes, I do."

He was silent. In the back, the long-haired kid was making an inventory of what was in the tin chest, concentration registering on his face as a kind of sharp pain. George had twisted the rearview mirror at an extreme angle so he could look at Luke without turning his head.

"You know when people part, Billy, there's more than one side to it. Love is the sharpest knife there is, sharper than hate, and it cuts both ways."

"So you were her victim?"

"No. And she wasn't mine. It's hard to know. Here's what Paul Celan said: '*I know / I know and you know, we know / we did not know, we / were there, after all, and not there.*' "

"How convenient."

"You think so?" He pressed his hands together, and then closed them and squeezed. Such a small and mundane movement, an unconscious firing of a well-worn pathway of nerves, but it filled me with incoherent agitation. It was a gesture I often made, and I felt like a monkey seeing himself in a mirror for the first time.

"I loved your mother with everything I had and when it wasn't enough I learned something about myself that's been pretty hard to live with."

"Revisionism. You moved on, that was all."

"You don't know the first thing about the truth."

"Oh, the truth. I didn't realize we were talking about the truth. Like in your songs, right?"

"No. My songs turn into lies as soon as people start calling out their requests, or cheering when they hear the first chords, and by the time everyone's singing along they're worse than lies. Much, much worse. Sometimes you can bounce off a lie and get to the truth—there's a chance, you've got a shot. You reach for something to kill the lie and sometimes if you're lucky you pick up the truth. But what kills you is the consensus, what you read in the papers and hear on the television, it's an invisible fence of received wisdom, and government-inspected ideas, it's the conspiracy of common knowledge. Common knowledge is worse than lies. Common knowledge eats the truth and then shits it out and buries it."

We were packed close together in the front seat. On one side of me, George, his body pumping out waves of heat like an Arizona highway. And on the other, the object of George's feverish passion. My hipbone touched Luke's and when he spoke he jiggled his leg and his knee hit mine over and over.

"How come you never admitted you were my father?" I asked him, as if for the first time. I think I really did imagine he would finally answer.

"What makes you think you needed a father?" said Luke. "You had Esther, you had Irv. That's a pretty nice launch."

"That's not an answer."

"I was thinking about my own father, a while back," Luke said. "I don't even have a snapshot of him. I can't remember his voice, or the color of his eyes. I sort of remember him being big, but that's because I was so small. The only memories I have of him are some sleepless Jewish raccoon shuffling around the house in a dirty bathrobe and torn slippers. I remember his tears—strangled, pathetic, lonely tears. I remember the garbage on the floor. The smell of beer—I think it was Pabst Blue Ribbon. I don't think they even make it anymore. He was so out of it he couldn't keep his cigarette lit. He'd take it out of his mouth and look at the tip and shake his head, like it was some great inscrutable mystery why it wasn't burning. When he fired the gun into his mouth he was resting his head against the bedroom wall. He blew his brains out, but they didn't have anywhere to go. Some of them slipped down the back of his shirt."

"I'm sorry."

"But I lived my life. I went on."

"I know you did."

"Then why don't you?"

"I am. I'm trying. This is how I'm doing it. I'm not like Felix or Tess."

Suddenly, I couldn't tolerate George's obvious obsession with Luke and his hanging on to every word the great man said. I turned sharply toward him and said, "Would you mind giving us a little privacy?" And with that, I straightened the rearview mirror. "My father and I are having a private conversation."

"I'm right here," said George. "What am I supposed to do?"

"Then be less overt about it. Have the decency to be ashamed and sneak it."

"I didn't know you were such a hard-ass, Billy," Luke said, smiling with what certainly looked like pleasure. He cupped my knee, and then left his hand there for a few moments, without moving it at all, without the slightest cover or justification; he wasn't warning me, he wasn't making a point, or trying to be funny, he was just leaving it there for no particular reason.

I had a thought to take his hand and press it to my lips, but I didn't have anywhere near the courage that would have taken. And then, a few moments later, he removed his hand, folded it into his lap, and closed his eyes. He let out a long, breathy sigh, permitting the second half of it to puff out his cheeks and then letting the rest of the air out in little, rhythmic bursts—it sounded like "When Johnny Comes Marching Home"—until his lungs were empty. It was what a man does when he is completely alone.

11

A S S O O N as we entered the hospital, a sense of urgency overtook us. Luke and I hurried down the hall, our footsteps clacking in unison against the white vinyl floors. We passed an orderly dragging two empty gurneys behind him. We pushed through a set of swinging double doors so quickly that they crashed into the walls.

When we were some fifty feet from Mother's room we saw Little Joe Washington sprawled out in a chair, sobbing into his enormous hands. I stopped; I knew she was dead, that she had slipped away in the time it had taken us to organize the ambulance. I was paralyzed with loss; my grief seethed at the very bottom of me. Luke touched my elbow, by way of telling me to wait. He strode over to Little Joe, with that rolling cowboy gait.

"Joe," he said, blunt but merciful, like a pulled punch.

It was the first these two had seen of each other since Joe's day in court, and then it had only been briefly, as Dad, dressed in shameless psychedelia (blue silk pants, a silver shirt, wrap-around glasses with silvered lenses), testified and destroyed his own case. Sitting with his legs crossed, his pointed right toe lodged behind his left heel, his skinny arms wrapped around his chest as if for warmth, Luke faced the judge and spoke to him directly. "Justice is a beautiful thing, Your Honor, and a judge like Solomon—that's King Solomon, Your Honor, not Solomon Burke—he leads his people to righteousness, just like Jesus Christ or Che Guevara. But let's face it. We aren't here to talk about justice. We're here to talk about money. Little Joe wants money. I got money. So let's pick a number and get it over with." By now, Luke's lawyer was pulling out his own wavy white hair, and Joe's lawyer was tugging at Joe's salmon-colored sports jacket, trying to prevent his client from rushing the witness stand and crushing Luke's head between his massive hands.

And now Joe was standing again, but this time he threw his arms around Luke and pulled him close, the way people will when death makes our squabbles so small, when it suddenly seems that our grievances and competition make as much sense as cattle vying for position in the slaughterhouse. Joe embraced Luke with the passionate magnetism of life itself, was as full of power as a box of lightning. Luke hedged his emotional bet by patting Joe's back with a certain aloof heartiness, but then that gesture spent itself and he just held on. "Oh man, oh man," they both murmured, so you couldn't tell Joe's voice from Luke's.

"What's going on, Joe?" he asked. "What's happening with Esther?"

"She's awake, Luke. Her eyes are open and she asked for Billy."

I staggered forward, almost falling. It was not as if a great weight had suddenly been pressed upon me, but that it had suddenly been removed. The lack of burden, this magical removal of the freight of feeling that since Esther's accident had become as much myself as my smell or my shadow, disoriented me. I was, for a moment, insubstantial, Mayakovsky's *Cloud in Trousers*.

I made my way past the two of them. I grazed against them both, deliberately, as I passed, and I felt their fingers on my back. She was alive! As the fear of having lost her subsided, I began to sob.

When I entered her room, Irv was seated next to the bed, and he, too, was weeping. For a moment, I thought a hideous error had been made and that my mother had died, but then I saw her eyes were open and looked at me through her bandages. It was as if she had come back from the dead. The dead had awakened—but with what body? Though she did not, could not, move her hand, her fingers stretched toward me.

"Mom," I said, touching Irv's shoulder as I passed his chair, and falling to my knees at her bedside. I was afraid to touch her, afraid to hurt her, and still a little fearful that she might not be real. I placed my open hand on the sheet. She was looking directly at me—her eyes at once saintly and bewildered, as if all of her worldliness had disappeared during her long sleep, and she had awakened innocent, a holy fool, a messenger from the eternity she had just eluded.

"Oh, Billy," she whispered, "you're here."

"Oh, Mama, Mama, I'm so happy."

"I lost control of the car, Billy."

"I know. It's okay. You're going to be fine."

"I don't feel like myself. I know everything I know, but I know it inside someone else's body."

"We're going to take you to the city, Mom."

She nodded. Her eyes were starting to close.

"Luke's here, too, Mom," I said. I immediately wanted to take it back. It wasn't what I meant to say. I don't know what I meant to say. But it wasn't that. I think I just wanted to keep her attention. I didn't want those eyes to close, ever. But this talk of Luke was where we'd left off. Perhaps she hadn't heard me. I glanced guiltily back at Grandpa, to see if he had heard me mention Luke, but now he had his handkerchief out and was drying his face.

A few minutes later, Mother drifted back to sleep and I went to the waiting room to find Luke and Little Joe. They were facing each other, seated in bright orange molded plastic chairs, practically knee to knee. Luke was speaking, with nervous, emphatic gestures, and at first I thought they were fighting, but when I got closer I realized they were debating prophecies.

"The thing is," Luke was saying, "the Bible is real specific about dates, and the whole thing goes in progressions of five hundred years. All right, we can leave Adam and Eve and the Flood of Noah out of it."

"I don't see why we would do that," said Joe.

"We'll just concentrate on redemption. Without redemption the Bible's just a history book. Redemption. That starts with Abraham, the human father of the Jews."

"And the Arabs," added Joe, shaking a finger at Luke, in a more or less good-natured way. "What is that? Genesis or Galatians? 'Know ye therefore that they which are of faith, the same are the children of Abraham.'"

"But listen, listen," said Luke. "The next big thing was the Exodus—and guess what? Five hundred years after Abraham. The first Passover, the parting of the Red Sea, the Law of Moses—"

"Luke? Joe? I think we better get the show on the road."

"I'll tell the doctors," said Joe, slapping his big knees and mightily exhaling as he stood. "It's up to them to get some people to put her in the truck."

"How is she?" asked Luke.

"She's okay. She's sleeping now. But I talked to her."

"Is she in pain?"

"I don't know. I don't think so."

"Does she know I'm here?" asked Luke.

"Yes."

"Do you think it's okay for me to go in and see her for a minute?"

"Yes. I do."

He stood up, but made no move toward her room. He was afraid to go in.

"Luke," I said. "She loves you. She always has, and I guess always will. I don't know what it means to her, or what it means at all. But I do know that."

He nodded and kept his gaze on me an extra moment. By way of thanks. The directness of the gesture, and how natural it seemed, the manly understanding it implied, its secret cargo of history and missed opportunities, accusations and evasions, and the single thing that pulled it all together, the love of Esther we both shared—all of it went through me like a quiverful of arrows, and I was dying, dying of happiness. For that moment, I was getting what I had always so blindly and ceaselessly desired; yet I was not so besotted to fail to note that I was getting it at a price dearer than any I had ever dreamed of paying.

LUKE and I sat up front with George, and Grandpa stayed with my mother and David in the back. It had taken *hours* to finally get her out. Esther had been silent, more or less unconscious, since I'd spoken to her in the hospital. Her eyes had remained shut, the lids motionless, while Joe and two nurses loaded her into the ambulance, under the edgy, disapproving supervision of some young doctor who was a stranger to all of us. The nurses unhooked her IV, wrapped the tubing around the chrome pole, for no better reason, it seemed, than that it was the hospital's property and it wasn't to leave the building.

Luckily, there was equipment in the ambulance—IV bags, rubber tubes, needles, oxygen, antibiotics—and Irv and David had her hooked up long before we were on the thruway.

When we'd first gotten back into the ambulance, George had the radio on. Luke and Wendy Crabtree singing "Shiva the Destroyer," recorded at the Martha's Vineyard concert, was just ending. As Luke slid into the front seat, he glared at George, and George reached to turn off the radio. But before he touched the knob, the disc jockey's voice came on.

"He's here, folks, right here in the beautiful Hudson Valley."

"Wait," said Luke, and George slowly moved his hand away.

"Luke has left the Leyden Hospital," the radio voice was saying, "and our informants tell us he is in a Van Fleet Lodge ambulance heading down to New York City."

"Oh Jesus," said Luke.

"It wasn't me, Mr. Fairchild," said George, his voice quaking.

"What difference does it make now?" said Luke.

"It wasn't me," George said again, and I was pretty sure he was lying.

We drove in silence. It was the end of the afternoon, nearly evening. The blood-orange sun hovered above the river. The orchards were in bloom. The black shadows of old barns lurched across the green fields.

I looked back at Irv. "How is she doing?"

Grandpa waggled his bony white hand back and forth.

George sat bolt upright as he commandeered the ambulance around a traffic circle. He seemed unused to driving, unsure of himself. His hands gripped the steering wheel with lunatic force.

"See that?" Luke said. "Goddamnit."

I looked out the window. An open field. A Ford dealership. Traffic signs.

"See what?" But as soon as I said it I realized what he meant.

A few cars, pickup trucks, and vans were idling along the road's rocky shoulder. As soon as we passed them, they fell into line behind us. I looked out of the sideview mirror—and saw myself: lined, haggard. I adjusted the mirror and then it clicked into view, the sight of a procession of cars.

"That was quick," I said.

Luke pressed his lips together, a picture of grim, pessimistic acceptance. George sped up, but what good did it do? The closer we came to the thruway, the more cars there were following behind us. How many were there? There were perhaps no more than a couple dozen, but it seemed like hundreds.

As we approached the toll booth, Grandpa noticed we were surrounded. "What's going on here?"

"They know it's me, Irv," said Luke. "Cocksuckers."

George stopped at the toll gate, cranked down the window, stuck out his hand to receive the light-blue perforated toll ticket. But as soon as he reached for it, the attendant, a stocky woman in a denim shirt, pulled the ticket back.

"Can I get your autograph, Mr. Fairchild?" she called out, in a harsh, slightly accusatory tone, as if she were a cop asking to see his license and registration. Behind us, voices were calling Luke's name. Whistles. Whoops. Honking.

"God almighty," Luke growled. "Let's go! Now."

George didn't give the matter a moment's consideration. He stepped hard on the accelerator and sped through without the ticket. I watched through the mirror: every car raced through after us; none of them stopped for their toll cards, none of them gave a rat's ass about the law—like starving hunters, like hit men.

With Luke urging him on, George sped onto the approach to the southbound thruway, going over eighty, as if there were any chance at all of outrunning the fans behind us. They felt like a forest fire gaining on us, implacable, without intelligence, at once chaotic and monolithic. When we were on the thruway itself, we passed still others who had been lying in wait for Luke. People sunning themselves on the roofs of their cars and vans. Who knew how long they'd been parked along the side of the six-lane highway? A guy standing in the bed of a red pickup held up the *Cash Machine* CD and when we drove past him—the cars full of fans were already slowing us down—he side-armed it at us. The plastic case opened midair; the sun glinted on the silvery disk before it hit the pavement and was crushed beneath the tread of God knows how many tires.

"Luke?" Grandpa's voice was tired, fearful. He was straightening himself in his fold-down seat, after having just put his ear next to Esther's lips to hear what she was trying to say. "Esther wants me to tell you that it's good to see you."

"Yeah?" His face colored. He bit down hard and breathed through his nose, in manly sublimation of emotion, but not without its own lone-wolf nobility. Like a tethered dog, my heart lunged toward him, pulling its choke collar ever tighter. "Tell her it's good to see her, too," he said. "Tell her it's real good."

Grandpa whispered into my mother's ear, stroking her forehead as he repeated Luke's words.

"Mom?" I said, turning in my seat. Grandpa and David were adjusting the oxygen flow. They looked worried, they looked grim; some silent communication of a crisis brewing seemed to pass between them. Had Death wandered back into her hospital room, found the empty bed, and then rode the wind to find us here?

Either from exuberance or with the hunting instinct of a pack of dingoes, many of the cars that had been chasing after us had by now passed in front, and we were surrounded. I could not tell how many of them there were, but I felt a sudden and hideous kinship with each of them. They were pursuing Luke, just as I had, and still was, and if it was so clear to me that they wanted him to fill some terrible emptiness in their own lives, then what would it take for me to understand that my own reasons for tracking him down were not altogether dissimilar?

We were just a couple miles from the next thruway entrance, where there would undoubtedly be more cars waiting for Luke. We were going to be absorbed in the pack.

"What station were you listening to?" Luke asked George. "We have to call them and make them tell everyone to get off the roads."

"I don't know," said George. "Like ninety-four point something." He blinked rapidly, licked his lips. "I'm sorry."

Was he apologizing for having called the radio station himself? I still don't know the answer to that one.

Luke switched on the radio; it came on loud, and his voice from twenty-two years in the past filled the ambulance. He turned the volume down. The station was giving Luke's arrival the full treatment. Nothing was beneath them. They were playing "Esther."

> I came to the city
> With my poverty complete
> With flies on my forehead and sores on my feet
> You were the red maiden
> In a castle so cold
> No one could buy you with silver or gold
> Esther, oh Esther
> You dazzled my eyes
> You were the sword in the stone
> The Pulitzer Prize.

"Oh Jesus," Luke said to himself. Then, to George, "Hit the siren. Let them know we have to get through."

George activated the ambulance's flashing red light and the hoarse, pitifully weak siren, which seemed at first to come from beneath the chassis, or from out of the seats. The strobe light, the imploring wail—none of it did any good. The drivers that surrounded us might have been too high on their own excitement to even notice. Maybe they didn't believe there was anyone injured in our ambulance, or maybe there was nothing to do about it even if they did believe. There was no shoulder for them to pull onto, because the shoulders had long before become traffic lanes.

> *Your daddy a doctor*
> *Your maw just a maw*
> *How they hated the kid from old Wichita*
> *His hair was unruly*
> *His manners were rough*
> *However I loved you it wasn't enough.*
> *Esther, oh Esther*
> *The things that you told me still haunt my life*
> *Esther, oh Esther*
> *You were my mother, my sister, my wife.*

"Billy?" Grandpa said. "Your mother says don't be afraid."
"Tell her I'm all right," I said.

> *I loved you for your beauty*
> *And your wisdom and such*
> *I loved you most of all for your sweet healing touch*
> *To be with such an angel*
> *It hardly seemed real*
> *And it hurt me so badly when your heart turned to steel*

Esther, oh Esther
Mystical daylight
Breaks in your eyes
Esther, oh Esther
I worship your soul, so eternal, so wise.

"Are you okay, Luke?" Grandpa asked. "She wants to know if you're okay." If Irv objected to carrying messages between his beloved, broken daughter and Luke, he betrayed nothing of the sort. His voice was soft, affectionate, as if he wanted to convey the feelings behind Mother's words.

"I'm okay," said Luke.

"She wants you to tell Billy you're his father."

Did she really? Or was Irv putting this in for his own reasons?

"Tell her . . ." Luke went silent. Then: "Tell her I already did."

I didn't dare look at him.

I've held the world
In the palm of one hand
I've sung for the king, I've played with the band
I've bought twenty yachts
Then I sunk the fleet
And I still miss the cafe on Sullivan Street
Esther, oh Esther
Try to stop time from slipping away
Esther, my Esther
Where will you be on Judgment Day?

Remember Hotel Paris
Room Nine Thirty Three
Remember the words you whispered to me

Remember the sheets
Croissants in the bed
Rue de Jacob is still stuck in my head
Esther, oh Esther
You squeezed my fingers as the plane took off
Esther, oh Esther
You finally let go when we were safely aloft.

Now the tents are all folded
The circus shrinks in the rain
The kid's disappeared on a southbound train
Where is the anger
Gone is the lust
My scheme for breaking even has turned into dust
Esther, oh Esther
Like Lucifer I've fallen from heaven above
Esther, oh Esther
Take this cursed gift I give you, this goddamned love.

"Hurry," said Grandpa.

"What? What does she mean, Irv?"

"No, no, she's sleeping," said Grandpa. "It's me telling you to hurry."

"Esther" was finished and another song started in. Luke glanced at me, lifted his chin, and I switched the radio off.

I prayed for my mother. I did not think it would mean anything, but there was nothing else for me. I had not been on the docket pleading my case before God since I was a very young boy, begging for my father to come into my life and rescue me from my loneliness and isolation and otherness and fear with his rough and gentle love, love that I had once imagined to be as firm and as fair as a handshake, and it seemed to me now that if I prayed and the prayer was unanswered then I would forever live outside of God, all faith, all solace: denied.

We drove the middle lane, our revolving emergency lights strobing red, our siren like the dying howl of a wounded animal. On one side of us was a rusted-out Subaru station wagon driven by some guy who looked as if he were on the lam for operating a home distillery. He was one of those country people who look to be sixty and turn out to be nineteen. He had a starving horse face, skinny bare arms, milk-white chest, and a leather vest. On the other side of us cruised a black Saab, driven by a fleshy middle-aged guy with rosy puckered lips and loads of black-and-silver curls, the sort of lovable schlemiel whose every gesture carries the message: I mean you no harm. Next to him was a gaunt, ponytailed woman, pie-eyed with wonder as she stared at Luke. In the back seat were a sleeping baby in a carseat and a hyperventilating yellow Lab.

I looked at Luke to see how he was taking it, and to my surprise he seemed not only worried, but embarrassed, as if this mob of followers proved there was something cheap and unworthy in him, something too accessible, and that he was for all his airs a kind of junk food. Was he seeing himself through Irv's eyes for the moment? Was the configuration of Esther and Irv pushing Dad back through time and awakening those feelings of awe and intellectual inferiority he experienced when Stuart Kramer first came to New York, raw from the Midwest? It was hard for me to hold on to the thought, because he was the source of so much of my own sense of banishment, but maybe all Luke ever wanted was a home. Maybe it was as simple as that; maybe that's all it ever turns out to be. Irv and Mom had gotten it wrong. Luke wasn't sitting at their Brooklyn dinner table pawing through their ideas like a shopper looking for bargains; he was memorizing the words they said and the books they had learned them in and adopting their opinions as a kind of plea for their acceptance, believing with his orphan's abject and storm-tossed heart that the right analysis, the right opinions, the right political line might lead him to the safe harbor of their steady regard. Like any homeless boy, and like a criminal, too, he wanted to be admired.

"It never ends, does it," I said to Luke. He squeezed his hands, again and again.

"I'm frightened," he said.

I looked at the speedometer. We were going twenty-eight miles an hour. Twenty-seven. Twenty-six. Our distance from the bumper before us was shrinking, the margin for safety disappearing. And the cars behind us were also squeezing close. What was supposed to have been a two-hour trip was going to take us four or five—if matters didn't get worse.

The sun slipped away and darkness rolled like a carpet over the fields. The evening light was doing something to all of us, I could feel it happening. It was making us a little more afraid, and in some way I don't know how to explain it was making the moment feel holy.

Yet it was not the holiness of life everlasting, or of resurrection, or of answered prayers; I felt something immense holding all of us in its implacable neutrality.

"Daddy?" It was my mother's voice, coming from the back.

"I'm here, baby, I'm right here," said Irv.

We turned to see her. Grandpa loomed over her, his hands humbly folded, and then he leaned back, and we knew she had fallen back to sleep.

Color flooded Luke's face. His eyes shined as if he'd been slapped. Just then a sign appeared announcing that a service area was coming up on our right. There was really no way for us to move over the two lanes and make the turn.

"Go into the right lane," Luke said to George.

"No room," he said. George's body temperature was by now so high I wondered if it was he whom Death pursued.

"Just turn," said Luke.

"I can't do that," said George.

"You want that woman back there to die because we're stuck in this?"

"No."

"Then do what I fucking tell you." Luke turned in his seat. "Hold on to her tight, Irv," he called out.

And a moment later, our front bumper collided with the rusted-out Subaru. Like most of us, I had been witness to thousands of car crashes, in the movies and on TV. In those, the aggressor car can plow through cars like a bowling ball scattering tenpins; but here, our first contact, with a car clearly our inferior, resulted in an animal-screeching howl of twisted metal and a hysterical pounding noise from beneath our hood. And George, seized by the idea that he was no longer responsible for anything that was happening, maybe even feeling a kind of madness, continued to steer us toward the service area. We bumped into someone else. Someone else and someone else and then someone else slid into us. I looked back at Grandpa. He and David steadied Esther's stretcher; they didn't seem overly disturbed by our having suddenly been plunged into this demolition derby. They knew better than the rest of us how little time we had to waste. As we made our way onto the access road to the rest area, the other cars began following us in.

"What good can this possibly do?" I asked.

"I'm going to talk to them," said Luke. Then, calling back to Grandpa: "Is she okay?"

"Resting."

The service stop was a dozen gas pumps and a large iron-and-glass box of a building where they sold the usual—Burger King, Roy Rogers, Dunkin' Donuts, etc. Surrounding the restaurant complex was a vast parking area, where enormous trucks, wheeled behemoths, seemed to be standing in some state of abandonment. Parked among the trucks were four or five vans, small, battered, with Yiddish letters hand-painted onto their doors. And near the vans were thirty or so Orthodox Jewish men, pale, bearded, dressed in black overcoats, fedoras, yarmulkes. Several of them held prayer books in their hands. They were making the run from their jobs in the city to their hardscrabble bungalow communities in the western Catskills, little mountain villages where the shop signs were in Yiddish, and the way of life was as close as they could make it to the life of the religious Jews in the Eastern European eighteenth century, lives of prayer and disputations of doctrine, rituals, songs, births and marriages. It was the beginning of the Sabbath. At home, their wives were preparing the Sabbath dinner and lighting the candles, and a multitude of children looked up from their books and begged to turn on the TV because as soon as the sun went down and the Sabbath began nothing mechanical or electrical could be touched, not a blender, not a vacuum cleaner, not a car, let alone a TV. But the men, husbands all, even the youngest of them, hadn't made it home in time, and so they were chanting their Friday sunset prayers right here.

A long streak of red, thick as a paint brush, ran along the horizon.

As we drove into the rest area, Luke watched the Jews pray. They swayed back and forth. Luke was staring at them so intently it was as if he could hear and understand their devotions. He was perfectly still, frozen; and then he said to George, "Stop here." He started to leave the ambulance.

"Don't," I called after him. "They're going to mob you."

"They already have," he said. He slid gracefully out, closed the door behind him.

"Be careful," I said.

"Come with me," he called back.

"Shhh . . . shhh," Grandpa was saying, patting his daughter

with one hand and adjusting something on the IV with the other.

As soon as Luke was out, his fans began pouring out of their cars and rushing toward him. Luke jumped onto the hood of the ambulance. His priest shoes, with their slippery soles, lost contact for a moment and he stumbled forward, falling toward the windshield and stopping himself with outstretched hands. He left his handprints on the glass as he righted himself. A moment later, he scrambled onto the ambulance roof. I got out to keep an eye on him. He stood there, with one foot resting on the top-light and his arms stretched high over his head, pointing straight up, so he looked like a capital I, and then from side to side, so he looked like a T, up and down, back and forth, in an impromptu semaphore language that for some reason stopped his fans from engulfing him.

The minion of commuting Jews turned their faces toward him. Did they think Luke was a priest who'd gone completely mad? Did any of them recognize him?

"Listen to me, everyone, listen," Luke shouted. "Come on in close, I wanna tell you all something."

With surprising orderliness, the crowd surrounded him. For the first time, I could see they were really not quite a mob. They seemed calm. They were smiling, genuinely pleased to be in Luke's presence.

"I got a badly hurt woman in here," Luke said. He was speaking in his most public voice, a kind of Appalachian twang, his heart-of-America voice, the one that conjured Daniel Boone, Pretty Boy Floyd, Will Rogers, Joe Hill, banjos, steel guitars, fishing boats, houses of the rising sun, men on strike for a decent wage, boys in overalls and girls in gingham, and the stoic, decent heart of the common people. In front of his public, he channeled this great strain of Americana; Cisco Houston, Woody Guthrie, Leadbelly, Hank Williams, and ten thousand nameless troubadours lived within him, and they would continue to live as long as Luke drew breath. "We're takin' her to this hospital where we think the folks'll be able to help her out."

"Who's in there?" a man called out.

Luke turned toward the sound of the voice, though the crowd was so tightly packed it was impossible to know who had said it.

"Who's in there?" Luke repeated the question. He took his foot off the top-light and paced the small platform of the ambulance roof. He was full of angularity, exhaustion, and power; he looked down at his followers like Lenin at the Finland Station. "You want to know who it is? Okay. I'll tell you. It's Esther."

My mother's name dropped like a net over the crowd. They seemed not only stunned, but captured by the fact that Luke was here with his legendary lover. In the deep, dying blue light of evening, I saw something very much like wonder in their faces. There were even cheers, though none of them seemed to realize that just by being there, and being in the way, they were destroying the reunion they wished to celebrate.

"So you guys just clear a path and let us through," Luke said. "We can't make this trip goin' no twenty miles per hour."

The cheering only got louder. But for what did they make all this wild and hungry noise? For the love he had once given so freely, with the winged, boundless passion of youth, a love that reminded them of their own dreams of happiness? They were in awe of Luke, in awe of his life, and they thought that if only they could know him they could know themselves. They were like me. Luke was our tiny, holy kernel of hunger for heaven, sealed in a package with a hundred layers of gaudy paper. He was wrapped in money, and he was wrapped in fame, in sex, drugs, politics, nostalgia, privilege; but when all of that was torn away, what was left? A soul, just a soul, a tiny, frail human soul, racing blindly and in terror through the dark woods.

Yet to see him there, and to hear his voice trying to reason with the zealots, brought blood to my face. I had been chasing after him for so long, I had somehow neglected to listen to him, I had never heard him, never heard him try to tell the truth, find what was decent in himself, and what was decent in America, never heard the love or the confusion, never quite believed the pain: all those songs. I had been so consumed by the certainty that if those who worshiped him knew how badly he had treated my mother and me, then they would turn on him, they would realize they loved a mirage. I had managed to overlook what everyone else seemed to know: there was magic in him, he made something happen in the air, he changed you, he made you, for a moment at least, willing to risk everything for speed, or music, or love.

"One song!!" a woman's voice shouted out from the back. "Oh, *pleeeeease.*"

"Folks," Luke said, "we need you to make a way for us. You gotta hang back and let us through." He looked out at them and shook his head. "It wasn't supposed to be like this," he said.

Luke looked down and saw a familiar face, or what was left of it. Eliot Shore had fought his way to the front. He had gone to fat, but extravagantly so: he had reached and passed the point of no return. He bulged out of his overalls. He had sliced open the sides of his sneakers to accommodate his poor swollen feet. His face was spread out like an anvil, his stringy black hair hung limply down to his shoulders. He looked like a gangster's slow-witted brother, the one who gets to work as a bouncer in a mobbed-up dance club. But Luke seemed happy to see him. Eliot sucked in a bit of his gut and stood straight up, as if at attention, his eyes doglike with love and uncertainty, his face streaked with tears, and Luke saluted him, as if they had once flown together in the RAF.

"Eliot," Luke said.

"Hey, man," said Eliot. "Is there anything I can do?"

"Get us out of here."

"You got it. No one's gonna get in your way."

Luke jumped from the roof to the hood of the ambulance. I was at the bumper, with my hand outstretched to help him down, I wasn't sure why, he probably didn't need it, but there I was, feeling servile and awed.

"Are those your mother's clothes?" he asked, rejecting my aid and leaping to the ground.

The crowd kept their distance.

However, one of the Jews—a wraith with a wispy beard, and delicate fingers that nervously worried the buttons of his once white shirt—called out to Luke.

"Luke, don't forget who you are. You go running around like a chicken with its head cut off looking for what we could have given you all along."

Luke turned toward the young man and then answered him in Yiddish. I had no idea what he was saying, but all the Jews were nodding, and all but the graybeards were smiling. Then Luke unbuttoned his shirt. His chest was white and slack and in the deep hollow between his breasts grew a dozen or so gray wiry hairs. Resting in this meager nest was a mezuzah, and he pulled it off over his head and handed it to the young man, who held it for a moment in his cupped hands, as if it were a flame or a tiny creature, and then lifted it to his lips to kiss it, and then handed it back to Luke, who said "Thank you" in English and bowed his head deeply.

"Let's get out of here while we still can," Luke said to me.

We backed up toward the ambulance doors. George had gotten out and Luke slipped in from the driver's side. How much time had we spent? Tick tick tick. The earth continued on its stiff compulsory rounds. The sun was gone, sunk for good, headed for the Far East, but I think there is a moment, a moment of universal darkness, when it shines on no one. Luke's followers had not made a move toward their vehicles but stood there watching us, a human forest. The ambulance's interior light went on and then was gone when George closed the door. I remember doing a few quick calculations of how long it would take us—going fifty-five, sixty-five—to get Esther to the hospital. I remember noting my hunger, and I remember wondering where Luke would eat that night, where he would sleep. I remember wondering if I should go back to my substitute-teaching job tomorrow and then remembering it would be Saturday. My day off, and Joan's day off, too. I remember thinking of Joan. An impulse to stretch out next to her, to hold her body one more time. And I also remember thinking it was too late for that, too late. I hurried to the passenger side to let myself in. I remember most of all how unusually cold the door handle was as I yanked it open.

12

AFTERWORD

CLEARLY it would not have been possible for me to compose this admittedly incomplete memoir of my father (and me) without the help of a great many people. Some I need not acknowledge here because I have done so personally, but there are others whose assistance I would like to formally appreciate.

First of all, I would like to acknowledge Neil Schwartz, who not only has written extensively about Luke but who also made me privy to his notes and the transcripts of literally hundreds of interviews and who, after the bulk of this book was completed (and I, frankly, had no heart to go back through it) gave me a telephone number in Puerto Vallarta, Mexico, where none other than Sergei Karpanov was waiting for my call. Sergei, who I am not acknowledging here, since he had no intention of helping me in any way, and who was only interested in somehow finding a way in which my book might exonerate him and gain him entrance back into the States, sounded winded, exhausted, and small. It was hard to reconcile that unctuous and anxious-to-please voice with the photos I'd seen of the ferocious knucklehead who palled around with my father.

"To me, the story that I killed little Katarina is the greatest lie of the twentieth century," Sergei said to me, in the weary voice of a man who does not expect to be believed. His breath traveled through the edifice of his words like wind through a ruined city. "Why would I harm her? I was living a good life— thanks to your father. Girls, celebrities, anything I wanted. It would take a madman to throw it away. And if I was a madman I belonged in a hospital, not a stinking jail." Even here, making the familiar, despairing little point, he seemed hopeless and put upon. He was a magician who had plunged his hand into the top hat a hundred times and each time come up rabbitless, but who was condemned by his own inflexible nature to try it over and over again.

I need to thank Neil for more than his extensive storehouse of Lukology. Not only did he create the occasion on which my mother finally told me that Luke was my father but, after Esther and I returned from Italy, Neil gently and gallantly courted her. It was a courtship that might have begun out of a certain morbid careerism on Neil's part—what biographer could finally resist romancing the love of his subject's life?— but soon it developed into one of the very best relationships my mother ever had. Neil was respectful, attentive, adoring, and, while he never presumed to be a stepfather or even a father figure to me, he treated me incredibly well in my earliest teenage years. He took me to ball games, we skated in Washington Square Park, and he even taught me twenty or so chords on the guitar during that phase when I felt genetically destined to be a singer. Once, when I was about fifteen, in a paroxysm of hungry-hearted need, I threw my arms around Neil and kissed his soft, freshly shaved face. Neil, who was sitting on our sofa and writing (undoubtedly about Luke) in his spiral notebook, gathered me in his arms and held me. But the real pinnacle of his kindness was that he said nothing while we sat there, and never mentioned the incident, and never looked questioningly at me, and never expected it to happen again—which it didn't.

Best here, then, to also thank Neil's friend Marty Drizdo, who, while appearing nowhere in the preceding pages, shared with me his many valuable insights into l'affaire Karpanov. It was Marty who, after abandoning his own book, bitterly entitled *Luke Fairchild: Guru to the Lemmings*, provided me with a fairly complete picture of where Sergei got his forged Finnish passport (information I could not use because of legal constraints) and the various cities throughout the world where Sergei hid from justice, or, if one were to accept Karpanov's story, where he kept himself a jump ahead of another false arrest. It was also from Drizdo that I was able to ascertain that the various post-Katarina violent felonies attributed to Sergei were—and here legal constraints dictate my diction—not necessarily baseless rumors.

Drizdo arrived with Neil for Esther's funeral at the Riverside Chapel. They must have walked over from the subway stop at Seventy-ninth and Broadway, because they looked chilled and windblown, the backs of their black suits were wet from the rain the wind blew beneath their umbrellas. I was standing under the overhang beneath the massive funeral hall, that auditorium of the dead, watching as a few Riverside employees, six security men (courtesy of Luke) built like brick shithouses, and ten city cops coped with the surge of reporters, camera crews, freelancers, autograph hounds, and faithful Fairchildians who had learned of Esther's funeral, despite all our attempts to keep it off the radio and television and out of the papers, to keep it from being sucked into the swirl of publicity and gossip. Special passes had been delivered by courier to anyone who belonged there that day, but already we'd run into a few forgeries, and now I was posted to double-check the people whom security let through. An *Entertainment Tonight* helicopter had been hovering over Amsterdam Avenue, but a sudden soaking gale had blown it toward Central Park and now it was gone.

Marty Drizdo hadn't been sent a pass to my mother's funeral and he had mistakenly assumed he could come in on Neil's ticket. One of the cops, who was sick of standing in the rain and who, it turned out, had all of Dad's Christian records, was getting a little carried away with his responsibilities, and he pushed Marty forcefully back, causing the poor man to slip on the wet pavement. I quickly intervened, said it was fine for Marty to be admitted, and took Drizdo by one hand while Neil grabbed the other and we pulled him to his feet. A few of the photographers recognized me and fired their power-drive Nikons at us. The domino principle might not have been applicable in Southeast Asia, but it sure did hold at Riverside Chapel. The paparazzi's attentions engendered a small riot of interest—not only in the media but among all the hangers-on who were willing to loiter in the filthy rain on the chance they might catch a glimpse of some grieving celebrity.

Neil, Marty, and I took shelter in Riverside's lobby. Now that he was safe and on his feet again, Drizdo was furious, letting forth a stream of invective that strongly suggested a morbid preoccupation with anal sadism. Neil tried to shut him up with a glance and then turned to me. Neil looked much as he had when I first met him, well over twenty years before. Now his whiskers and hair were white as linen, making his face and body seem incongruously youthful. He looked like a summer-stock actor hastily powdered to look old.

"Are you okay, Billy?" he said. His teeth were worn, nicotine-stained; his breath was a mixture of mortality and mouthwash, like lamb with mint jelly. He put his hand on my shoulder and I realized that Neil had not touched me since that evening on Sullivan Street so many years ago, when I had kissed his cheek.

I nodded, and then shrugged. It would have been insane

to say "Yes, I'm all right, I'm fine," and it would have been melodramatic to say "No, I'm terrible, my life has been radically diminished," he didn't need to hear that, he could just assume it.

And Neil—if you are reading this—thank you for nodding and then saying, "Yeah, me too." And thank you for embracing me and thank you, as well, for whispering to me as we embraced, "She had the biggest heart of anyone who ever lived." I acknowledge you for feeling that way, and I acknowledge you for saying it to me when I really needed to hear it, and I also acknowledge you for helping me finally shed tears from eyes that had been sirocco dry since an hour or two after my mother died of an embolism in the back of an ambulance on the New York State Thruway.

I must also acknowledge the various musicians who played with my father over the course of four decades, many of whom drifted in and out of my mother's life when I was a child, as the Seven Dwarfs might have, had things not worked out with Snow White and the Prince, and Snow White had taken a little walk-up apartment a stone's throw from the forest. In those prefeminist days of Luke's early career, when rock and roll was a boys' club and girls were prizes in a sexual scavenger hunt, Esther, being unattainable, became a sort of den mother to the boys in the band—she sewed buttons on their shirts before gigs and pressed cool wash cloths on feverish heads in drunken hotels after, she even taught wild-man drummer Milan Tomjanovick how to read—and the guys never forgot her. They came for dinners, played chess with me, looked over my homework, while frowning and scratching their heads; they kept in touch. Nearly all of them knew I was Luke's son and knew that he denied me, but they never mentioned it. Like all good players, they knew what to leave out. The music, the past, the memories made us a family. They were avuncular with me: I had ersatz uncles with earrings, I had ersatz uncles in velour pants and pirate shirts, and I had more than one or two ersatz uncles with monkeys on their backs. I could have done worse.

They all came to Riverside Chapel, and when they saw me they tried to be cheerful. They hated funerals, and by now they had attended dozens upon dozens. They had buried colleagues who died of overdoses, or from AIDS, or from car wrecks, or who had blown their brains out, or otherwise violently ended life. They had buried parents and brothers and sisters and wives and lovers and children. The earth was fertile with the remains of their dead. They shook my hand, they clasped my shoulder, they did not quite look me in the eyes. They looked as if they would have rather been on the road, or in a studio. No hard feelings. I would have rather been somewhere else, too. They made a semicircle around me and then they all said something that they apparently said often: "Hurrah for the next one that goes!"

Mike Silverman, Dutch Conners, Ken Yoshiba, Graham Ross, Skeeter Thomas, and Harley Caswell, all were as helpful as could be in my search for Luke, though my father, after taking the cure for heroin addiction, and once again coming to the mistaken notion that he had been given a clean slate upon which to begin life anew, had his new law firm get all the old sidemen to sign statements promising they would never write about Luke. A check for ten grand was given to each who signed, and they all signed. They would have done it for less. They would have done it for nothing. They still loved him and they still treasured the time they had spent with him. Even getting them to talk to me about Luke was difficult, especially when they learned I was writing this book. And when they did open up, it was impossible to get them to say anything that put Luke in a bad light. That was okay; there were plenty of others who would.

Which brings me to Loren Nelson, who deserves acknowledgment here, though most of what he told me did not find its way into these pages. Had I been writing a book about why Luke Fairchild does not deserve to be thought of as a legitimate folk singer, however, Loren's insights into Luke's early Greenwich Village folk-club career would have doubtlessly proven valuable. Had I been writing a book about why the young Esther Rothschild was so alluring and so magnetic, and how living with her was as close to heaven as a young man could get in New York City, then Loren's torrent of late-night remarks would also have come in handy. When Loren arrived at Riverside Chapel for my mother's funeral, I made no move toward him; I was fine with him being there—in fact, I myself had put him on the list—but I was wary of his bitterness and the wide swath of permission to express it that he had somehow managed to cut for himself over the years. Loren had dropped out of my mother's life more than thirty years ago, and had left the Village not long after, and he seemed lost and isolated in the lobby. If anyone remembered or recognized him from the old, old days, they pretended otherwise. I was talking to Little Joe and Felix and Tess when I noticed Loren reaching into the pocket of his black silk jacket and taking out a white satin skullcap and placing it carefully on his head. Low-grade anti-Semite that he was, it surprised me that Loren had come with his own yarmulke—but perhaps it was just his idea of traveling wisely in alien territory, like bringing quinine tablets to the Amazon. I didn't see him again until Luke and I, along with Little Joe, Neil Schwartz, and a man named Ezra Rudy, a cabinet maker and poet who had been Esther's lover intermittently over the past six years, carried my mother's coffin out to the hearse. Loren was standing next to Joan Odiak, holding his canary-yellow umbrella over her, and though nearly everyone was silent as we trudged past them holding our tragic cargo,

Joan was up on her toes whispering something into Loren's ear, and he was nodding, not yet allowing himself to smile, but it didn't seem like he'd be able to hold out long.

I learned later that Loren and Joan went to dinner that evening. I'm not assuming they spent that night together; I'm not in a position to know, since I never again slept in my old apartment after Esther's death. (It was all I could bear to have lost my best friend in the world. To spend the night with a woman who did not love me would have been, on top of that, intolerable.) However, I do know that Joan and Loren began seeing each other with some regularity after that and that Joan eventually moved into the cottage Loren bought for himself with the proceeds of the sale of his Southampton house, and that the two of them developed a mail-order business selling expensive boating equipment imported from England, caps and compasses and twenty-thousand-dollar sails. The whole enterprise surprised me, but as Luke once put it: "*Known a lot of people / Their lives pass like shadows on the walls . . .*"

As for Joan herself, I would like to thank her for abiding with me while I prepared to write this book. Joan has perhaps been ill treated in some of my remarks and descriptions. Sorry about that, Joan.

I would also like to thank Father Richard Parker, not only for his memories of Luke's Christian period, but for his putting me in contact with Alice Burns and members of her Bible study group, who also were generous with their stories and recollections. There was neither time nor room for Father Parker to speak during the long service at Riverside Chapel. Between the music and the many, many personal reminiscences—which I listened to with Luke on one side of me and my grandfather on the other—the funeral took over two hours. Though inexpressibly moved by the service, I admit to feeling that the time was dragging on. (Luke and I were planning to sneak off as soon as the ceremonies were finished. We were going to drive up to Leyden and lock up Esther's house—though we ended up getting sloppy drunk on a bottle of gin she had hidden away, and we slept in her house, with Luke in her bed and me on the sofa. The next morning, Luke wanted to drive further north, with no particular destination. We ended up in Montreal, until he was recognized in the lobby of the Ritz-Carlton, and then we went to Quebec City for another day and a half, and then we drove hours and hours to Toronto, where we stayed in a mansion owned by a Chinese banker friend of Luke's, where we drank many liters of red wine out of the dusty old bottles and tried to sober up in our host's spacious cedar sauna. When we first entered Brian Lu's home, Luke introduced me as his son, though when I confronted him with this later that evening he refused to admit to it. All right, fine, all in good time, is what I thought. The next day, we abandoned the car, probably forever, at the Toronto airport (*"We drove that car through the northern tier / Then ditched it in a lot. / The boy asked me who I was / I said ask me who I'm not"*—"After," 1997, unrecorded), and flew to New York, where Luke's private jet was awaiting us, and from there we flew elsewhere, to a place I am not at liberty to mention because we didn't have proper documentation and had to get in on a visa made of Luke's celebrity and cash (*"Just me and the kid / A couple of Yids / Looking for a quiet spot"*—Ibid.).

After the caravan of cars made the long, rainy journey across the East River, Father Parker was given a chance to say a few words at the cemetery in Queens, where my mother was placed in a grave next to her mother, a site purchased by Irv many years before, with two extra places left, one for him and one for me. Judging by the names on the gravestones in this part of the necropolis—Berger, Spitzer, Lenhoff—Parker might well have been the first cleric in a turned collar to ever pray over a body here. Standing between Louis Provanzano, who in the late forties had been a socialist city councilman from the Upper West Side, and a rabbi named Steven Medoff, Father Parker intoned "Yea, though I walk through the valley of the shadow of death . . ." while the cemetery crew, in their yellow slickers and black knee-high boots, waited to lower my mother into the earth. When Parker was finished and it was Rabbi Medoff's turn to speak—and suddenly the secular, anecdotal man who had orated at Riverside Chapel was speaking Hebrew and swaying back and forth—Father Parker folded his small, reddened hands over his full Friar Tuck belly and never took his eyes off of Luke. And when the graveside service was over and the coffin was lowered into the narrow, precise hole that had been dug for it—even if she were to come to life down there she would never escape; the box was flush against the stony soil, with its weave of severed roots—Father Parker walked straight to Luke and offered his cold, eczema-ravaged hand in greeting. I had been so absorbed in looking after Irv, who, after seeming so sharp and attentive during the memorial at Riverside, was now suddenly a very old and feeble man, tearful, trembling, and confused, that until Luke took Parker's hand I had failed to notice that my father had dissolved into tears. His face was twisted into a grimace of nearly unbearable pain, with that kind of grief that looks almost like madness.

"I miss our little talks, Luke," Parker said.

"Still fishing for souls?" Luke asked. He pulled himself together. And even though his face was stricken, his voice was level, even a little teasing.

"Naturally."

"Then I guess I'm the one that got away."

"Not really, Luke. I haven't given up hope."

"I took the bait but I broke free of the hook."

"Maybe. But why do I still feel the tug on the line?"

Luke tried to smile. He put his hand on Parker's shoulder, and then Parker put both of his arms around my father and seized him in a mighty embrace. Luke closed his eyes, and for a moment, I think, he might have imagined that he had found his match in that ovoid man of God.

The casket was in the ground now, and some of us lined up to throw thundering handfuls of cold, damp dirt onto the box. It was like a twenty-one-gunshot salute, with the rifles fired one at a time. Then there were goodbyes, murmured expressions of regret, delivered and received with a certain uneasiness, as if we were all suddenly embarrassed to still be living while one so beautiful and blameless was dead. Irv held on to my arm, his fingers like talons. The burial was draining the life out of him, and as soon as I could I walked him back to one of the waiting cars, which in turn would drive him back to Little Neck, where he would again be warehoused with the other old men and women whose bodies had outlived their lives, and where he would stay until, with Luke's financial assistance, I was able to move into an apartment large enough to have my grandfather live with me.

A wrenching, somehow hurtful sob burst like a glass bubble in my throat as I watched the long black limousine pull away with Irv. I stood there at the curbside, trying to collect myself. The roadway through the cemetery was gray and winding, like those little streets built in suburban housing developments. We were in Deathdale. A low-flying jet roared overhead, on its final approach to Kennedy Airport, the red lights on the wings flashing in the heavy rainy air. By the time I got back to my mother's grave, all the mourners had gone back to the rushing waters of their own private lives and the cemetery crew was just leaving, probably off to gouge out another casket-sized wedge of earth. For a moment, I felt a surge of panic; I didn't see Luke and I thought he might have somehow contrived a way of leaving there without me.

But then I saw him, leaning on a tall headstone a few feet away from our family plot. He was talking to two women. It wasn't until I was within ten paces of them that I saw it was Rosa and her mother, Maya.

"There you are," I said to Luke.

"Hi, Billy," said Rosa. She took my hand and I kissed her on the cheek. Her skin was scalding.

"These two have come down from upstate," Luke said. "And the people they came with left without them."

"We told them to," said Maya. "We just weren't ready to leave."

"You were such a good friend to my mother," I said. "Both of you."

"Your mother was a beautiful woman and you're her beautiful, beautiful son," said Maya.

Maybe I cast my eyes down, or maybe I did nothing to acknowledge her kind words. But I felt Rosa's eyes on me, and when I looked at her, she smiled and said, "It's true, you know. You are. And you made her very proud and happy."

And for that glance and those words I wish to acknowledge Rosa Trotman. It was a moment, just a moment, and in the deluge of all the moments that preceded it and all the moments that came after, it could not attain any real centrality in my life. I could not, as I would have liked to, hold on to it firmly and lift it above the torrent of time and all its contradictory lessons and say: This. Now. Here. Forever. This is my truth.

Luke suggested Rosa and Maya ride with us on our way up to my mother's house. We had the last limo take us back to Manhattan, where Luke had a car waiting for him at his hotel. Maya, raised poor in the Bronx, and Rosa, raised in Woodstock, seemed fascinated by the limo, and by Luke's posh hotel, and the liveried footmen who scurried around when we arrived. We drove Luke's car north, with me at the wheel, and Rosa sitting up front with me. Luke stretched out in the back and soon fell asleep with his feet on Maya's lap. By the time we were on the Taconic Parkway, Maya, too, was sleeping, and Rosa's eyes were closed. Her hands were folded in her lap and a tiny, childlike snore buzzed through her parted lips. I felt awfully happy, not because my life was good, but because it was my life and I was in it. It was like the one time I'd gone trout fishing and I stood in the middle of a rushing stream and I felt the powerful, unstoppable water humming on every side of me, from my feet to my knees, and my thighs and belly, and all the way up to my chest, and it didn't matter in the least whether I caught a fish or not, it just felt so good to be there. I reached over and touched Rosa's hair, softly, so as not to awaken her. We were by now thirty or forty miles into the journey, and the sun, as it set, struggled to make its first appearance of the day. There were too many clouds for it to burn through, but it sent its dying light down anyway, and for a few moments the car sped along with the fleet trembling shadow of itself.

AUTHOR'S ACKNOWLEDGMENTS

WHILE writing a novel is a solitary experience, there were, nevertheless, several hands to help me set *The Rich Man's Table*.

First of all, I want to thank my editor, Victoria Wilson, with whom I have had the great pleasure of working since 1976. In a business in which stability has become almost as antiquated as carbon paper, I am extraordinarily fortunate to have been able to work for twenty-two continuous years with an editor of such truthfulness, patience, sympathy, and skill.

I want to thank Dana Reinhardt, with whom one stormy evening I took refuge in a church near Times Square, where I was given the title of this novel; upon reading my first draft, she was kind enough to mention that the sequence of events was nearly impossible to follow. I also want to express my appreciation to Anne Lamott for her indispensable encouragement and insight. My great friend John Eskow's extensive library of American music histories and his instinctive feel for what I was trying to create were crucial to my gathering some important information.

Finally, thank you to Bob Dylan, whose records kept me company through the thousands of hours I worked on this book.

THE
RICH MAN'S
TABLE
Scott Spencer

Berkley Signature

QUESTIONS AND TOPICS FOR DISCUSSION:

1. The novel's title is taken from a passage from the Gospel according to Luke (see the book's introductory quotation). Did familiarity with this passage and the phrase "the rich man's table" affect your approach to and reading of this novel, in particular your feelings about the book's opening? In what ways does Billy's life parallel that of Lazarus, including Lazarus's being raised from the dead? Do you find any significance in the author's choosing "Luke" as the name Billy's father assumes upon casting off his given name, Stuart Kramer? Why?

2. What does the description of the "Is That Your Dad?" game reveal about Billy's character and motivations? How does this game capture the desperation Billy feels as a fatherless child? What is his attraction to the "death-defying . . . even death-wishing" aspect to the game (p. 7)? In what ways does he continue this recklessness in adulthood, even after outgrowing this dangerous childhood activity? What does the reader learn about young Billy upon discovering that he has named his absent, fictitious father "Zero?"

3. Billy's love for Esther is palpable and intense throughout the novel. How is the book enhanced by Billy's describing first Esther's voice, then her beauty, and finally her history—much as any child experiences his mother in the course of matura- tion? What does the non-linear progression of the plot contribute to your experience of the novel? Did you find the flashbacks to be a distraction? Why, or why not?

4. Luke is a complicated character who is viewed by others in widely disparate ways. Billy refers to him as "the monster" (p. 34); Esther believes that "Luke made people brave" (p. 23); Father Parker sees him as a man who "struggled for his serenity . . . [and] longed to be good" (p. 40); and Irv calls him the "sonofabitch who left all of us" (p. 131). Which viewpoint is, in your estimation, closest to the truth? Why?

5. What accounts for the "Lukologists'" passion for all things having to do with Luke Fairchild? How does their relentless pursuit of him reflect the cult of celebrity that some social analysts feel has overwhelmed and distorted contemporary culture? In what ways is Billy's obsession with Luke different from that of the Lukologists? How is it similar? What disturbs Billy most about these fanatics?

6. Loren Nelson brings the evening with Billy and Joan to an end by musing, "Maybe not being raised by Luke Fairchild was the luckiest thing that ever happened to you" (p. 96). What motivates Loren to say this? Do you agree or disagree with his remark? What aspects of parenthood do you feel would have been most difficult for Luke, the "avatar of the Age of Self-Expression" (p. 96)?

7. Why are women attracted to Billy? Do you find any similarities among the women with whom he has had relationships? What does Billy mean when he tells Esther, "I'm stuck. I'm spinning my wheels" (p. 23)? Does Billy's relationship with Rosa show signs of being different? Do you feel they have a chance for a fulfilling future together?

8. Why does Esther attempt to increase Luke's isolation from Billy, starting immediately after Billy's birth? Is Irv an accomplice in shutting Luke out of Billy's life? What does Billy mean by writing that Esther tried "to stanch the bleeding of my wounded heart with a tourniquet of relatives" (p. 13)? Do you fault Esther for initially hiding the truth of Billy's paternity from him and for raising him the way she did? In what ways does her alcoholism exacerbate his fears and pain?

9. Do you feel sympathy for Luke when he complains, "Everybody's got advice for Fairchild" (p. 151)? What is the advice you would have given Luke as a young man to help him avoid the painful experiences of his middle age? Do you think he would have been able to follow this advice? Why, or why not?

10. What is the importance of Luke's wearing a mezuzah around his neck? Why is Billy moved when he discovers this? Why does Luke hand the mezuzah to the young Jewish man in the crowd blocking Esther's ambulance (p. 258)? How does Luke's struggle with his identity as a Jew contribute to his other battles for self-acceptance? How has Luke changed as the novel concludes?

11. The moment in which Billy understands "maybe all Luke ever wanted was a home" (p. 251) can be viewed as the turning point in Billy's life. How does seeing Luke as an orphan release Billy from the forces that have prevented him from "getting past" Luke's abandonment? How do Luke's feelings for Esther and Irv finally allow him to acknowledge that he is Billy's father?